SHADOWCRAFT ACADEMY
HEXED

SHADOWCRAFT ACADEMY SERIES
BOOK ONE

YVE VALE

SHADOWCRAFT ACADEMY: HEXED

A DARK ACADEMY PARANORMAL ROMANCE

SHADOWCRAFT ACADEMY
BOOK ONE

YVE VALE

Published by Entraverse Publishing

Sedona, AZ 86339, USA

YveVale.com

To my hubby, Mr. Vale,
thank you for being my Alpha... reader,
my sounding board, my cheerleader,
and my inspiration for many aspects
of my fictional guys.

AUTHOR'S NOTE

*T*he Shadowcraft Academy Series is a steamy dark paranormal academy why choose romance.

The female main character will end up with more than one of the love interests. Group scenes are on the agenda.

This series also has male/male romance within the group that will occur with and without the female present. *Swords* will cross.

But there's no cheating.

If you believe love is love and of course, some very spicy times, then please charge forward!

This series contains several dark elements that some readers may be sensitive to. For more information, visit: ValeRomances.com

AN ORDINARY LIFE

SHAYLA

*L*iving in a town full of supernatural beings, my vague gut-feeling that something weird is about to happen doesn't rile me up as much as it should. It's par for the course. So I go about my day. I'm alert. But hell, I'm always alert. I've had to be.

"Please tell me you're going," my best friend, Myra, says as we pass through the swinging kitchen doors, both of us balancing plates of greasy diner food.

Yum.

The rough-rider trucker at table three gives me the stink eye because his food has taken so long to arrive.

I ignore Myra's persistent attempt at peer pressure and head over to deliver the heart attack on a plate. "Anything else I can get you?" I ask pleasantly.

"How about an apology for taking your sweet ass time?" He cocks his head, expecting me to grovel. Then his eyes slide down my body as if he were licking it along the way.

No, thank you.

I resist the urge to vomit. Whatever energy this guy has, it does *not* jive with mine.

In times like these, I wish I had magic instead of being a null. I could hex this damned fool for being such a jerk, and he wouldn't even know it. Or, if I had my mother's gift, set his ass on fire.

We're right on the town's border between supernaturals and normals, but even with my non-existent magical ability, I know this guy is just a regular jerk, not an extra special, magical asshat.

"The kitchen is a bit backed up today," I explain, "but I'm sure Big C would love to come out and apologize to you personally."

Just the mention of the ex-con owner/cook, and this guy backs down. "Whatever. I need a refill." The jerk drains his coffee and shoves the empty mug across the table at me.

Fortunately, I'm fast enough to catch the cup before it flies off the table and crashes to the floor.

"Sure thing!" I plaster an obvious and obnoxious fake smile on my face and spin away, mentally daring the guy to smack my ass so Big C will kick him out.

This is the type of customer who comes in to throw his tiny dick around and harass the servers.

Despite my ass being the perfect target, he doesn't touch me. Clearly, the reminder that Big C owns the joint was enough to make him back off. He doesn't even know that the owner is half-ogre, and he's already afraid of him. If this customer only knew the damage my boss could do without even trying.

Fortunately, the big lug likes me as an employee. He says it's because I'm not stuck-up like a lot of supernaturals. Of course, I'm not a snob, but I'm not really a supe either.

As I approach the counter to get a coffee refill, Myra raises her perfect eyebrow and flicks her chin in the customer's direction. "Charmer, huh? Maybe you can invite him to the party," she says with a wicked grin.

"Oh. Great minds think alike! Since you're so insistent on going, I already asked him to be your date instead of me." I smirk.

Myra rolls her eyes. "Come on, *please*." She grabs my arm, lightly tugging on it like a toddler about to throw a tantrum. "Shay, I won't get to see you after I leave for school."

And here it comes, the pouty lip. Dang, she has it down to an art form. But I guess that's what happens when your parents actually care if you're unhappy.

I sigh outwardly, already giving in. But inside, I bristle at the reminder of her leaving. Myra has magic, and from all indications, she'll develop into a powerful mage once she learns to harness her gift at school. As a null-born mage, I'll never be accepted. Soon, I will lose her to the magic world.

Myra would have gone after high school, but she goofed around too much, and her grades weren't high enough, even though she had the money to attend. She's been going to community college to demonstrate her newfound academic dedication and taking magical tutoring lessons in the meantime. Although I'll miss her, I'm happy Myra finally gets her wish to attend the fancy magic academy.

Personally, I never wanted magic. I want freedom from the magical world altogether. Fortunately, I've never shown any magical promise. Sure, I have an occasional premonition, but plenty of humans have that ability.

However, I wouldn't mind if Myra could run away with me, but she has magic, so that's not a possibility. She must master the powers that are coming to the surface. Mages can lose their minds if they don't learn to control their magic. Or that's what the authorities *tell* us happens to supernaturals. However, I've always been skeptical of authority.

"Whatever," I grumble. "I'll go to your silly party. But why do you want to go to a normal's party, anyway? Soon you'll be tossing back butterbeer and making out with wolves."

"*Stars*, Shay, you make it sound like a perverted Hogwarts. They wouldn't be in wolf form when I make out with them. That would be too kinky... even for me."

I chuckle at how kinky I know she is, at least in her fantasies. Unfortunately, I'm still a virgin—I just haven't met the right person to give that moment to.

"Be ready by nine. I'll swing by and pick you up with a car share," she says with a glare like she knows I might flake out on her.

I won't, but I'm tempted.

Huffing my irritation at giving in, I head back to deliver a fresh cup of coffee to Mr. Sunshine. I remind myself that I'll soon have a whole new life when I escape this town.

After my morning shift at Connor's Diner, I walk the few blocks home. My sluggish steps are a sign of how much I don't want to return to the hell that is my home life. It takes twice as long as it should to arrive.

My mom's beat-up Corolla is parked cattywampus in the driveway. Weeds grow in every crack in the concrete, further destroying the decaying visage.

I used to care, pull the weeds and tidy up, but I've long since lost interest in what people think about my mother or me.

I only have to make it to my twentieth birthday, prove that I have no magic hidden in me, and I can leave this stupid town and my mother behind. I've saved up as much as possible to fly the coop. Well, except for the money I've had to spend to keep myself in the finest cheap clothes I can find on the sales racks or in thrift stores.

I've already set up a deal to buy a used car from Myra's cousin when I'm ready to leave. I'll live in it if I have to. I'd get the car now, but my mother would force me to sell it off and give her the money.

It hasn't been easy hiding my nest egg from my mother. I let her think I make crappy tips and I have a drinking problem, just like she does. She only tolerates the idea of my supposed partying because she believes I'm at supe parties potentially entrapping a rich and powerful supernatural guy.

What she doesn't know is that I'm not actually partying when I disappear in the evenings. I'm down at the diner, pulling extra shifts to get the hell out of her house. She's often passed out by the time I get home, so I usually don't have to feign drunkenness.

I suck in a deep breath and enter through the kitchen door, hoping to evade contact with the enemy.

"Spawn's home," Bruce, my mother's current boyfriend, mutters as he pops the cap off a beer. Not the first of the day—I can smell it. Delightful as always.

"Hey!" my mother shouts from the living room. "Get your ass in here."

I drag myself into the disheveled living room, cross my arms, and cock my hip, conveying a defiant attitude. "What now, Leeann?"

"Don't sass me." My mother sniffs and looks me up and down.

"I haven't sassed you... yet," I sass.

"I can knock some sense into this girl if you'd like," Bruce offers. Such a giver, this one.

My mother pauses as if she were considering it.

I remain standing, waiting for whatever bullshit she's about to throw at me. Finally, she says, "Magic Social Services called. They want to meet with you and me to review your null status."

"When?" I study my nails, trying to appear nonchalant.

This is it.

I'll be free. But I can't let her in on the fact that I have the means to bolt. She'd hate to lose her punching bag, after all. Besides, it will only get worse for me once my use as a potential cash cow is officially over.

"Next month. Day after your birthday. Nine in the morning." Leeann glowers at me as if I've let her down. I suppose I have.

She hoped I would have magic and trick some rich asshole into a mate bond, just like she tried and failed to do. When she was younger, she was pretty enough to catch any guy's attention. But the guy who knocked her up with me must have figured her out and decided not to stick around. Now, she's just a ghost of the beauty I've seen in pictures.

"If I'm lucky, they'll cart you off to the asylum, experiment on you, cut you open, and see why you're a fucking no good null." Leeann waves her hand dismissively.

My mother has been threatening the asylum thing as my personal boogeyman for as long as I can remember. I know now that it isn't somewhere I want to go, but I won't end up there if I don't have magic.

"Whatever. I'll make sure I don't have anything booked that day." I shrug and escape to my room, acting flippant about the drastic change just around the corner.

My anxiety spikes as I shuffle down the threadbare carpet hallway to my room.

Please, don't let anything go wrong.

But the Fates have never been my friend.

Once inside my room, I close the door, lock it, then press my ear against the door and wait. I need to make sure that Bruce or my mother haven't followed me down the hall. On the other side of my twin bed, hidden from the door, I kneel down to check on my nest egg. I pop open the air duct grate to ensure that my roll of cash is still safely inside the duct. My arm reaches down into the dark. A darkness that reminds me of the tortures that I've endured. I wrap my hand around the cloth bag containing my hopes and take a deep breath.

All I have to do is make it through another month in this hellhole.

Goddess, please get me out of here.

2

THE PARTY

SHAYLA

*a*s I leave for the party, I yell, "I'm going out!" Not waiting for a response from Leeann, I slam the front door shut. Along the poorly lit street, I walk a few houses down from mine to wait for Myra. I don't need my mother seeing me in the front yard and coming out to harass me.

Sitting on the curb, I scan my neighborhood. It isn't a horrible area—just tired. It's the poorest in the magical half of town, the houses are shabby and the sidewalks riddled with weeds. Ours is by far the most dilapidated house on the block. A third of the roof tiles have blown off. The paint isn't just peeling, it's down to exposed, rotting wood in several places. My mother doesn't take care of anything, and it's almost past livable.

I don't have many good memories of this block, except for a few with my childhood friend. Ten years ago, he lived in the house sitting across from me only for a short while. I still think about him whenever I pass by. The grandmother he lived with has moved away. So now, there's officially no reason to want to stay in this area infested with supernaturals.

Half of this town is made up of *supes*, and the other half are humans or 'norms' as they are commonly known by the magical half. Some norms know about magic and other realms, but most don't. Not far from my place, where I'm headed tonight, is the norms' side of town.

When a car turns onto my street, I get up and brush off my butt, squinting into the headlight and hoping it's my best friend, Myra.

The car slows to a stop. The light reflects off the dark glass so I can't see into it. The backseat window rolls down. A voice from within asks with a sugary tone, "How much, baby?"

"Honey, you can't afford all this." I wave my hands over my full breasts and wide hips. I'm not model skinny, by any means, but I don't give a damn.

The driver snaps, "No solicitation, even as a joke. *Please!*"

Shaking my head in amusement, I slide into the back seat with Myra.

She immediately fusses with my hair. "Brushing your hair isn't the same thing as doing it. You're lucky it's a pretty color… and thick and wavy."

"Get off me. You're lucky you're my best friend." I swat her hands away. "Besides, I'm not going for a hookup. I'm your wingwoman, remember? I can't get involved with anyone. I'm leaving this town soon." I bounce happily, telling her the news. "I have my MSS meeting the day after my birthday. Then I vanish."

"But I don't want you to disappear," Myra whines.

"You'll be at school anyway. And I can't let anyone know where I am. Who knows how my mom will react. She's crazy enough to come after me just so she has a punching bag."

"All right. I'll drop it… for now." She tosses me a lip gloss to use. "I can't have my wingwoman looking plain as hell."

"Thanks," I mutter.

"Seriously, you need to just *do it*. Get it over with. There will only be norms at this party, so you might as well just have a one-night stand and punch that v-card."

In the rearview mirror, I catch the driver's eyes widening with her statement. "Will you drop it? *If* I find a nice, cute guy, I'll screw his brains out. Happy?"

"Yep!" Myra hands me a little vial of green liquid—magic birth control. "Just in case."

Begrudgingly, I uncork the bottle and down the contents. She's right, of course. I don't need any complications. My life is complicated enough.

The music is thumping so loudly that I'm already developing a migraine as we walk through the tiny front yard toward a rundown, suburban house. I can see bodies dancing and milling about through the window. This place is packed.

Myra looks at me excitedly. I attempt a smile. A house party. With norms. *Ugh*.

Then I remind myself that I'll officially be a norm soon. The real problem for me is that I just don't like socializing.

Soon, I'll have to learn to socialize with norms in every aspect of life. This will be great practice. Or so I tell myself to give my legs some reason to move toward the blasting wall of sound. I swear I can see the vibrations and distortions in the air. If I had magic, I might believe that I *actually could*.

Myra drags me along by the hand. Why do I feel like I'm being led to the gallows, to be left hanging?

Because Myra always finds someone to hook up with on these excursions. I'm the tag-along whose sole purpose is to get her back home at the end of the night.

As we enter, I watch sweaty, hot bodies undulating and

grinding to the beat. The warm summer night air isn't doing anything to cool off the house. With this amount of body heat, there's no chance for it to get any more comfortable inside. We head back to the kitchen and grab a couple of cold beers.

Myra cracks hers open and chugs half of it. She eyes me until I open mine and pretend to take a sip, the liquid barely touching my tongue.

She tilts her head toward the large living-dining room area to indicate that it's time to join the dancing.

Dancing—well, I can handle that for a bit. Myra loves to do the whole we-are-sexy-girls dance, hanging all over me like I'm the one she wants to take home.

As per usual, she quickly catches the eye of a couple of guys, and they move in to become her new stripper pole.

Immediately, I extricate myself from the Myra sandwich and dance alone, a few feet to her left. I'll wait long enough to ensure that Myra approves of her new dance partners.

Then I let myself get lost in the beat. It's a rare thing for me to let go, but it's why I allow my friend to drag me along. I sway and wiggle, and I don't give a damn if I look good doing it.

I probably look possessed.

A tingling sensation crawls up my spine, and I know someone's eyes are on me. Probably wondering if I'm having a seizure.

Glancing up, I instantly lock eyes with a golden-haired god across the room who has just entered the party. His muscular arms are crossed over his broad chest, and it looks like he's staring... at *me*.

I turn to see if there's anyone else near me he could be watching. For some inexplicable reason, it takes everything in me to look away from him.

Nope. It's just me in this corner.

A second guy moves up to him and begins talking. His friend is as devastatingly handsome but with jet black hair, dark eyes, and cheekbones so sharp they look like they could cut glass.

The golden-haired voyeur turns to reply to his friend, and I use this distraction to head through a slider door to the back patio and sit by the pool unnoticed.

The way Goldie was looking at me was a bit unnerving. Maybe it's how my body responded to his gaze that leaves me uneasy. I don't usually react to hot guys like that. And even with how gorgeous most supernaturals are, I've never had a response like that.

I breathe in the fresh air to clear my head and calm my pulse. I finally feel less overwhelmed.

My ringing ears thank me for the reprieve from the pounding bass. I recline on a chaise lounge lawn chair, happy that only a handful of people are using the quieter backyard.

I close my eyes, enjoying the reprieve and relative silence of the midnight air and nearly empty yard, and think about Goldie.

I must have drifted off because suddenly, it feels like someone is standing next to me.

My eyes pop open.

A shadowy male form hovers right over me.

I yelp in alarm and lurch forward, almost smacking my head into his. Fortunately, he's fast and springs backward.

"What the hell are you doing?" I yell and throw out my hands to prevent an attack.

"Shit. Sorry. I thought you were sick—alcohol poisoning or something. I was just checking on you."

"Oh." I slow my breathing, realizing that he wasn't trying to scare me to death. "I'm good." Embarrassed, I wave him off without looking at him. I can't believe that I zoned out at a party. Where are my wits?

"You sure you're okay?" he asks, not taking the hint at my brush-off.

I finally look up at him. It's the guy who was staring at me.

Goldie. The light from the patio is illuminating his face. *Holy mac and cheese*, this guy is *stupid* handsome. He has to be an idiot because anything else would be unfair to the hot-smart median curve.

I realize I've been checking out his light brown hair with golden highlights and his chiseled jawline. His eyes are so deep blue they could be black, like the night sky. My brain catches up to the moment, and I say, "I'm fine, just tired and bored."

"Of me… *already*? That has to be a record." He grins at his own joke.

"Yep. I mean, seriously, do you always go on about yourself this much?" I quip back.

"How about we talk about you instead?" Without waiting for my reply, he pulls another lounge chair closer and sits on the edge. His nearness makes me appreciate how broad his shoulders are and the mass of his muscular build.

I wonder how long he's been watching me while I dozed. "Did you follow me out here?"

"You disappeared."

"Why would you care?" I ask because guys don't usually hunt me down at parties. Myra says it's because I have a fuck-off vibe. Maybe I do. This guy must not get those signals—which, to be honest, is a bit of a red flag. "Do I know you from somewhere?" I ask, but I already know I don't recognize this guy. I would have never been able to forget his magnetic energy that seems to take up an entire room.

"I would have remembered meeting you," he says, echoing my own thoughts.

I blush and gesture back toward the party. "I'm sure you can find more interesting company than some random party napper."

Goldie shakes his head and looks back over his shoulder at the thriving party. Then his gaze lands on me, and I squirm with the intensity. He grins, making me suck in a breath. I believe he knows *exactly* how attractive he is, so why is he flirting with me?

I have literally no game. But weirdly, he makes me feel like I'm the most interesting person in the world. I should be wary of his charm, and I am. But just like the sun, I want to bask in the warmth and light, but I know eventually I have to retreat or I'll get burned.

So, I'm of two minds right now. One half is urging me to shove my tongue down his throat. The other half worries that a one-night stand with this hunk will only break my heart and ruin me for all males in my future.

"Nah. I'm good right here." He thumbs toward the noise. "Besides, have you seen this crowd?"

"Then why did you come to this party?"

"My friend dragged me along. He likes to party before we go away to school."

"Yeah, same. My friend is probably hooking up with your friend." I glance back at the house. "*Someone* should be having fun at this thing."

"*Again*, I'm hurt." He clutches his very defined pectoral, which I can see clearly under his tight cobalt-colored tee, matching his unusual eye color.

His body is too perfect not to admire. I swallow down my drool.

I remind myself that this guy is just bored. There's no way he's interested in me. He looks like he kicks supermodels out of bed. I can't deny that I'm drawn to him, but that could just be his dazzling smile. Right?

"Come on," I scoff. "I'm sure you'd rather be doing a million other things than chatting up some narcoleptic girl at a house party."

"Maybe." He shrugs. "But maybe I don't mind hanging out here a while longer."

"It's the ambiance." I wave my hand around the unkept yard, with its broken lawn chairs and half-burnt out Christmas lights left over from several seasons past.

"Won't your girlfriend be upset that you're talking to a *strange* stranger?" I prompt because I'm slick like that.

"No girlfriend. Nice question, by the way." He smirks at my obvious tactic to obtain his dating status. "What about you?" he asks and cocks an eyebrow.

"No girlfriend," I answer succinctly with a blank face.

"Any significant other of *any* persuasion?" he asks casually, as if he couldn't care less.

I shake my head. I don't elaborate, but honestly, I doubt I'll ever find someone who could put up with my weirdness… and my damage.

He leans back in his lounge chair. "Tell me something interesting about yourself."

"Interesting? About me?" My mind scrambles with the challenge. This is a norms party, so I can't exactly dive into the fact that I'm a null from a long line of mages who were supposed to be descendants of the first known human mage. When I see how weak our line has become, I doubt the claims for my lineage. No, not just weak, I'm magicless.

"How about two truths and a lie?" I counter.

"A game?" He laughs and nods approvingly. "I like it."

I hum while I think of a good set of fun facts. "I've never had more than a sip of a beer in a night. I love jogging. I plan to move to the other end of the country next month."

"Hmm." He scratches the little scruff on his chin, thinking it over. "The beer is the lie."

"What? No." I laugh, and he grins at me like he finds the sound delightful. As if. My laugh is more akin to honking geese than tinkling bells. "That was an easy one. The lie is that I enjoy jogging. It hurts the girls."

"Girls?" He looks confused until I point to my large breasts. "Oh," he says. "Never thought about that being an issue."

"For me or women in general?"

He chuckles but doesn't answer. "So, why are you moving across the country?"

"To escape."

His brow arches, studying me for a long moment. "From what? An asshole ex-boyfriend? Loan sharks? My insistent questions?"

"Definitely your questions." I cover my face and groan. "My mother, if you must know."

"I must." He turns his head to face me properly, eager to hear about my stupid life. "How bad is it?" His voice isn't one of pity, but is one of someone who gets it.

Even Myra doesn't really understand, since her family is TV-sitcom level nice. I've told her stories of my abuse, but people just don't get it unless they have experienced something similar.

"Bad," I answer and change the subject. "Now give me your truths and a lie."

He sucks in a breath and thinks. "I love house parties." I chuckle at his lie, and he continues, "I enjoy getting what I want. And I wouldn't mind joining you on your escape."

Yeah, right, this guy wants to run away with me. But I'll play along and tease him a bit with my answer.

I tap my mouth thoughtfully, and it seems he can't look away from the action. "Hmm... I think you secretly love house parties, so you can bother girls who are taking naps. As for number three... well, *of course*, you would want to immediately run away across the country with these weirdo girls. As for number two... you don't strike me as someone who likes to have things *handed* to him. I go with getting what you want as the lie."

"While you are correct that I don't like things 'handed to me,' I do enjoy claiming what catches my attention."

"Join the club." I roll my eyes in response. "That's what one-click purchases are for."

"House party was the lie," he states.

His gaze falls into the distance, as if thinking about the third option. Running away... not necessarily with me, but I see the same desperation to be free. His expression flickers, then he quickly wipes it away, as if he's had practice hiding in plain sight. He needs to escape something too.

Is he hurting like I am?

"So why do you want to run off?"

"Parents. Pressure to be the best. You know, whiny white male problems."

"Problems are problems," I say, knowing we all have our troubles. And when we're in them, we often can't see a way out. "I'm leaving in a month." I grin. "So make sure you pack your bags lightly."

"Don't tempt me," he sighs. "But alas... I cannot join you."

"I get it. We can't always get out of our obligations. I would have left a long time ago if it weren't for... *reasons*," I cover, almost blurting out about the magic world to a norm. It's just so easy to talk to him that I forgot where I am. "However, I finally have enough money to bolt, so now I'm taking off and never coming back."

"I envy you." He rests his head on his arm like a pillow while turning entirely onto his side to better observe me. Damn, his arm is so thick with muscles that he's looking down at me from just a couple of feet away.

I turn to match him. We stare into each other's eyes for what feels like an eternity.

The longer this goes on, the more I want to crawl the small distance between us and kiss him. But as fun as this banter has been, I don't assume he would want that from me. And with my inexperience, I'd likely make any attempt awkward and unsexy.

My eyes slide down to his luscious lips. I catch myself leering and look back at his eyes, which are now fixated on my mouth.

I bite my lip nervously. Is it my imagination, or does he have the same attraction for me as I do for him?

"I meant it when I said I enjoy claiming treasures." His hand slowly reaches across the distance, which feels like a million miles away and far too close all at the same time. His fingers graze my hairline behind my ear, and his thumb glides over my bottom lip.

My eyes widen at his brazenness. Surprisingly, I don't flinch at his touch.

My mouth parts slightly, wishing it were his lips on mine instead. It takes everything in me to resist the strange urge to draw this stranger's thumb into my mouth and bite.

My heart races with his electric caress. Never has someone's touch made me feel anything at all—except for fear.

Then he leans over to kiss me. Some deep part of me panics that there may be no coming back from this moment. Why does it feel as if I will lose myself in his kiss... be forever changed? But isn't that what I wanted—to escape to a different life?

Then the thought of never seeing him again makes my heart ache. This irrational feeling is so confusing because I don't even know his name. Should I pull away now and save myself from the inevitable heartache?

I should. But I don't. I'm not sure I can. I'm not sure I want to.

The intense draw to him truly makes no sense to me. It's like we were meant to have this crazy brief moment in time. I know I shouldn't feel this way with a stranger, but I do.

His full lips descend upon mine, gently at first. His tongue slips inside my mouth. Our tongues tangle. His hand slides around to cup my head and grip my hair. His grasp is not hard but firm—as if he were claiming me.

Suddenly, the rickety lounge chairs turn over, and we crash to the ground. Somehow, he's now on top of me. His muscular thigh wedges itself between mine, pressing against my center in the most delicious way.

"Are you okay?" he asks, his hands roaming over my body for signs of injury.

"Yeah," I say, and a laugh bubbles up out of me.

He joins me in my amusement, seeing the absurdity of the moment. But then, once again, his eyes darken with lust and his mouth crashes down onto mine.

The lounge chairs turned on their sides give us a strange sense of privacy as we kiss again.

His hand slides up my shirt slowly, giving me time to protest, but I don't. His strong hand is so large that it palms my entire ample breast, and he squeezes, eliciting a moan from me. He pulls down the cup of my bra, and lightly pinches my nipple.

My hands clasp his head. I return his kisses with a passion I've never experienced before.

We break for a breath, and he pulls back to look at me. Both of us are panting and breathless, like we are starved for oxygen when we aren't connected. His light and beauty are so intense that it feels like I'm staring directly into the sun. I avert my gaze. The feeling of being trapped underneath him, his beautiful, hard body above me, and his excitement pressed against my upper thigh is all just too much. And yet, it's not enough.

My straying gaze catches a glimpse of the stars above. I believe this is the most beautiful sight I have ever seen—the most handsome man I've met and the Milky Way slashing across the sky behind him. The ground below me is still warm from the day's sun. For some reason, it feels right to be connected to nature while I have this moment. It's the fae way—a distant part of my lineage, one that feels alive right now. A connection to the magic in the world that I rarely experience.

He nods toward the rickety chairs and asks, "Do you want to go somewhere else?"

I hear what he's really asking… *Are we going to finish what we've started?*

"We don't even know each other's names." I brush a wayward lock of golden hair away from his face.

His eyes close briefly, luxuriating in the sensation of my soft touch that lingers on his temple. "Maybe we shouldn't know," he whispers.

"Because we're both going our separate ways in life after tonight? Never to see each other again?" Why do the words taste like ash on my tongue?

He frowns, as if the idea of going our separate ways upsets him more than it should.

"Then maybe we shouldn't go further with this?" I suggest.

"No," he says quickly. After another kiss, his voice becomes sultry. "I want you."

"Right here? In the grass?" I ask, not sure what answer I'm looking for.

"Wherever. I just *need* you." He kisses me along my jawline and it's like electricity dancing over my skin.

I grind myself against his thigh. "I need you too."

3

ONLY THE FATED

SHAYLA

*M*y mystery man kisses me one more time, and I feel a bit dizzy from his passion.

"Come on," his voice rasps with desire. He lifts his body off mine and helps me to my feet.

I already miss the weight of him pinning me to the ground.

"Where are we going?" I ask, brushing the grass from my jeans. I pull a face at the house. "I don't think I want to use some rando's bed."

"I have a better idea." He takes my hand in his. "It'll be private. Not in this roach motel." He leads me back through the house.

As we enter the living room, I see Myra. I wave to her and point at my future devirginizer.

She takes a good look at his face, and her eyebrows rise.

Yeah, I know… stupid hot, I communicate with my expression.

"Give me a second to tell my friend that I'm leaving with you," I say to him.

He nods and heads toward his mysterious and brooding friend, who is hovering by the kitchen. The dark-haired male eyes me with an intensity that makes me shiver.

Myra breaks away from the guy she's dancing with. "What. Is. Happening?" she asks excitedly—like she's about to hook up with him herself.

"I don't know, but we're going somewhere to do it."

"Should you be leaving with him? You don't know him," Myra asks cautiously.

It's an odd statement coming from her. She's run off with strange guys before. Then I realize she's trying to be protective of me. "I don't... but it weirdly feels like I do."

"Text me where you're at when you get there."

I nod, but we both know that technology and electronics aren't reliable for supernaturals. Her cellphone rarely works. And my cheap burner phone doesn't work any better, even with my lack of magic. She might never get my text.

"And when you're... done," she says with a sly grin.

Pretending she's taking a selfie, she snaps a pic of him talking to his dark-haired friend. "Just in case." Myra checks to ensure that the camera actually worked and the photo was saved. Then she bites her lip and eyes my guy's friend. "I might have to bag his buddy."

She studies the pic on her phone. The image is a bit blurry, but it's dark, so that makes sense. There aren't any telltale flares to suggest they're using a glamour.

"If this weren't a norms' party, I'd say they were too hot to be norms."

"Right?" I say in agreement. "Wish me luck."

"With him, I don't think you'll need it."

"From your lips to the Goddess' ears!" I smirk.

My golden mystery man says goodbye to his friend and waves at me from across the room to meet him at the front door.

I tell Myra, "I'll catch up with you afterward." I rush to join him.

Once outside, he leads me down the street lined with parked cars. Half a block away, we come to a blood-red vintage car with thick black stripes.

My eyes widen when I recognize it. "Is this really a 1972 Cutlass Supreme 4-4-2 Super Sport?"

His eyes go round with surprise. "How do you know what kind of car this is?"

I roll my eyes. Guys never think a female would know anything about sports or cars. I barely do, but that isn't the point. Other women might.

"I'm not a vintage car expert or anything, but one of my mom's ex-boyfriends—one who actually treated me like a person—was obsessed with this car." I frown as I look at the classic beauty. "That boyfriend didn't last long. He was too nice."

Goldie nods his understanding and then at the car. "Well, sorry to disappoint, but this isn't my car. It's my friend's." Seeing my sadness as I think about my past, he teases, "Do you wish you were out here with my friend instead?"

"No," I say quietly. "I don't care about cars. Besides, your friend seems a bit... intense." I cock my head and look at him. "Unless you're suggesting that I would be better off hooking up with your buddy?"

He pulls me against to him, circling his muscular arms around my waist. I look up and note he's over a full head taller than me. "Not a chance." His hard bulge in his pants grinds into my stomach. "I want you all for myself."

He leans down and captures my lips. After a dizzying kiss, he breaks away.

The trunk pops open with a click of a key fob. Nice upgrade. Suddenly, a disturbing thought crawls through me. He could throw me in the trunk, and no one would see it happen. I don't come closer.

He doesn't appear to notice my apprehension, probably because he never had to worry about what women worry about. He grabs a sleeping bag and foam roll used for camping and shuts the trunk.

"You have camping gear in the car?" I ask with an arched eyebrow. "Is this just a regular thing for you? Luring women into the woods with your seductive eyes and muscular body?"

He grins. "Seductive eyes?"

"You're avoiding my question."

"Nah, this's my friend's stuff. He... likes to be prepared for anything."

"Like screwing random chicks from house parties."

"Like, if he has to sleep somewhere other than his own home," he says with a bit of gloom.

"Oh." I glance back at the house, thinking about the friend he left behind.

"Don't worry. He's fine. He's... like one of those apocalypse preppers." His easy smile returns, and he holds open his hand for me to take.

I sigh with the relief of contact. I've never felt that before—craving someone's touch. This sense of connection to him is perplexing, but I want to explore this, even if it's only for this one night.

Remembering we are in the middle of a suburban street, I glance around. "Um? Where are we going?"

"There's a green belt of undeveloped land hidden back behind these houses. It feels like we should enjoy this beautiful night sky."

"I do like seeing the stars and being in nature." An hour ago, I wouldn't have said that, but now... "There was something hot about making out with you in the grass," I add shyly.

He chuckles softly as we walk down the empty street. "I feel the same way." When we reach a narrow trail leading away into the trees, we turn off the road.

Logically, I know this could be a dangerous mistake. Emotionally, it feels like a beautifully romantic moment. I tap into my only *extra* ability—my 'spidey' sense. Checking in with my intuition, I don't get the impression that he intends to harm me.

We walk for several minutes until we come to a bit of a clearing in the trees. The ground looks smoother here and is covered in wild, green grass. He inclines his head to the spot, and I nod. With proficient moves, he sets up the foam base and unfurls the sleeping bag.

Raising his head, his gaze pierces me.

I stand frozen, hypnotized by his intensity.

He closes the distance with two strides, and one hand slides around my waist, pulling me tight against his broad, muscular chest. The other hand palms my head, fingers tangling into my long, brown locks.

He kisses me with an urgency that sucks all the oxygen from my lungs. My heart thumps wildly.

My arms remember that they can get involved in the action, and I wrap them around his shoulders. I slide them upward slowly and lace my fingers behind his neck.

His strong hand cradles my back, thumb pressing on my side. I feel cherished in this moment as he takes his time exploring my mouth and learning how I like to be kissed.

The soft scruff of his stubble tickles my chin, and I'm so giddy I smile.

I pull back to take another look at this man. I pant as I catch my breath.

He uses this moment to pull off his shirt. *Stars!* His body is even more impressive than I had pictured in my mind. His muscles have muscles. His skin is flawless and golden, like his hair.

Hesitantly, as if I were in a museum and he's a work of art, I reach out to touch the masterpiece. The hard planes and ridges of his chest and abs mesmerize me. I feel a tug on the hem of my shirt. I glance up and meet his eyes, black depths from which I may never return. I squeeze my thighs together. This is happening… with a guy who is so sexy that I might just climax from his hungry gaze alone.

Suddenly, I feel self-conscious—like a mere mortal displaying my meager offerings to a god.

He slowly pulls my shirt over my head and tosses it on top of his discarded shirt.

I curl my shoulders in a weak attempt to hide myself, but he places his hands gently on them, nudging me to stand tall. He stares directly into my soul. "Are you still okay with this?"

I nod. "Just nervous."

"I won't do anything you don't want to do." He catches my chin with his finger, making me look into his eyes. "We can stop—"

"No. I want to do this."

"Good." He smiles, trails his hands down my back, and unclasps my bra. His fingers pull the straps forward, and my full breasts tumble free. As he takes in the sight of my exposed tits, he licks his lips. He skims his thumbs over my hardened nipples. "Damn, you are more beautiful than I imagined." He dips down and drags his lips slowly over my skin from my clavicle until he reaches my left breast. He sucks the sensitive nub into his mouth and rolls it with his tongue.

I moan, lean back, and stand on my tiptoes to give him easier access.

He sucks hard on one nipple while pinching the other.

"Fuck me," I hiss.

"Oh, I plan to, sweetness," he promises in a raspy voice that sends goosebumps down my body.

His hands move down to the button of my jeans. My breathing hitches with his intent. Holding my breath for a moment, I do the same with his jeans.

He kicks off his shoes. No socks, and even his feet are perfect.

With a break in our kisses, he pulls down his jeans. His boxer briefs quickly join the pile of discarded clothes.

My eyes go wide at the sight of his cock. Never having seen one in person, it's *larger* than I thought it should be. I'm a bit intimidated that this one will be the first I will take. I wonder if I should have opted for the beginner size.

He drops to his knees to help me slip out of my sneakers, then pulls down my skinny jeans at a pace so slow that it feels glacial, taking my panties down with them. When the jeans are tight around my knees, he leans forward and kisses the spot between my hip bone and my mound. He follows that with a lick closer to my center, hinting at what's coming.

My legs are immobilized, but that only heightens my arousal.

Did I just discover a kink?

Finally, he helps me slip my jeans off my feet and tosses them onto our pile of clothes. I take a deep breath as he kisses me higher and higher from my knees to my pussy, his hands skimming along the back of my thighs, holding me to his talented lips.

"I need to taste you," he whispers as he hovers over my center. Both hands cup my ass, and I lean toward him. His tongue flicks out and grazes my seam. "On the ground," he orders.

Before I can move, he stands, picks me up by my thighs, and lays me down on the sleeping bag, one hand cradling my ass, one behind my head. Kissing me one more time, I feel his cock brush my inner thigh. I tilt my hips, hoping to get some relief for my throbbing sex.

He chuckles darkly at my neediness and then retreats down my body until his face is level with my spread legs. Staring at my wet center, he bites his lip.

I think that I might die from spontaneous combustion.

Dipping his head down, his eyes lock with mine as he swipes his tongue over my exposed pussy.

I gasp and buck into his face. I've never had someone down there before, and I think it might be my new favorite thing. But the event has just begun. I'll wait until the final act before I put in my vote.

He takes another long lick and hums. His eyes fall closed as if he were savoring the first bit of his favorite dessert. Without warning, he begins feasting on me like a starving man. His hands reach up and knead my breasts. I undulate, working myself onto his tongue, which feels impossibly long. However, I'm far too gone to question the sensation.

Within moments, I cry out as an orgasm grips my body, turning me into a moaning mess of pleasure.

"You're so damn hot when you come," he says. "I need to be inside you."

He reaches over, grabs his pants, and begins digging into the pockets. His hands come up empty, and he curses.

"What happened?" I ask.

"I dropped the condom somewhere."

"I'm on birth control," I assure him.

"I'm clear of STDs."

Even without magic, my fae blood doesn't allow me to contract a disease. I've never come down with a virus in my life. And then there is the other reason. "Well, I *definitely* am," I say.

"What do you mean?" he asks, hearing the conviction in my voice.

"Uh," I should probably admit my experience level. "This is my first time."

"Seriously?" He rubs his face and sits back on his heels. "Shit. How old are you?"

"Twenty… almost twenty," I amend.

"How has no one had your sweet ass before?"

"I'm not really a hot commodity." I shrug, feeling shy now and closing my legs. "We don't have to do this if you don't—"

"No. I want you very, *very* much," he growls. Crawling

forward and opening my legs back up to him, he kisses me fiercely. "I'm going to make you come *so* many times to make up for all the losers who passed you by."

His fingers are at my center, and he circles my clit. I moan as I find my arousal again.

"I need you," he whispers over my mouth.

"Then give us what we need," I demand.

He takes hold of his cock and lines it up with my opening. I suck in a breath, and he coaches me, "Relax. I'll take it slow until you get used to my size."

"Okay." I breathe out, and he claims my mouth while his cock claims my innocence.

Holy macadamia nuts. He's *too* big.

He breaks the kiss to suck and lick at my tits while he works his way inside me. There are pinches of pain as he does, but then it gives way to pleasure.

"Oh, shit… yes," I say as I begin to meet his thrusts.

He takes the cue and finally slams home, filling me up with his entire length.

"*Stars!*" he cries out. "You feel *fucking* amazing."

The weirdness that he used a supe's curse word falls away as he thrusts into me. He's hitting spots that I didn't know existed, taking me further into the abyss. Staring up at the stars, I feel like I might fall into the night sky. His face comes back into my focus, and he gazes down at me with adoration, like I'm a treasure he can't let go of.

My mind wanders to us walking away from each other after tonight. It makes my heart sting with pain. I mentally slap myself. I'm just going through a rite of passage. I didn't find the love of my life. At least, I hope not. If he is, and this is all it will be, then that sucks. I realize that I'm overthinking everything. I just need to be in this moment. Enjoy it for what it is.

So I get lost in his touch again.

Then I feel it—like fire under my skin. He's reaching the

moment, too. His thrusts become frenzied, and his eyes go wild. I'm sweating like the air is on fire.

"*Fuck*. I don't think I can last much longer. You're too fucking perfect." He grunts, his head dropping down to my throat.

His teeth scrape along my flesh.

I come undone and clench around his girth, screaming out to the Goddess.

His fingers dig into my skin. Beneath his touch, my skin feels like it's burning.

Shit. Am I burning?

I panic. I've been burned before. I don't want that.

Could he be a supe after all?

A strange glow ignites between us… over our hearts.

"*Shit!*" I cry out. "What's that?"

But just as I ask, he finds his bliss and releases inside me. His teeth nick at my throat.

After his spasms subside, he collapses on top of me for a brief moment.

The glow is still there. It's as if my heart were being pulled toward him—into him.

Then I feel his cock expanding inside me.

How could he be getting *bigger*?

"What the fuck?" he gasps. He opens his eyes at my squirming and sees the glow.

He yanks back, but he doesn't budge from between my legs.

"What's happening?" I try to scramble away from him, but he's locked inside me.

Fucking hell.

"Are you a supe?" he demands.

"Are *you*?" I fire back.

"Yes." He glares at me. "What *are* you?"

"Nothing!" I yell. "I'm a null."

"The hell you are." He growls in my face. "You're a damned mage?"

"I should've been a mage," I whisper. "But I'm not."

"This isn't possible! I *reject* you!" he shouts.

"Reject me?" Now, it dawns on me. *Fated mates.* I feel the thread connecting us. And I can feel him trying to rip the magic cord from my heart. "No. I reject you first!"

"Yeah, right!" he shouts. "I bet you planned this whole thing! You lied to me!"

"*You* were the one who didn't even want to know my damned name!"

"You tricked me!"

"I can't *plan* a mate bond!" I shove at his shoulders, hoping that he will get off me. "How do we make this go away?"

"I don't know." He wraps his large hand around my throat. It's a clear threat, but he doesn't squeeze. "But you won't tell a soul! Understand?"

Not to be outdone, I grab his throat too. "Same for you."

"Really?" he sneers. "I'm the one who should be ashamed of *you.*"

"Well, you obviously don't recognize your own lack of appeal right now," I snarl. "If anyone lied, it was you. I don't have any magic. You do!"

He just glowers at me.

The intense pressure in my pussy draws my attention. "Get out of me!"

"Quiet," he hisses and presses his hand over my mouth. "Do you want someone to find us like this?"

I shake my head under his hold. I certainly don't want to be caught in this... position.

He pulls on his cock, but it won't break free. "I think...," he sighs. "I have to come again."

"*What?*" I mumble under his hold.

I close my eyes, and a tear travels down my cheek. Apparently, I have found my mate, and he rejected me just seconds later... still inside me, no less.

"Hey," his voice softens, and he removes his hand. "I don't

33

want to do this. I don't force myself on anyone. But it seems our bodies and our magic have something else in mind."

I nod. "But we don't want each other anymore, so what do we do now?"

"We hate-fuck."

Oh... *This* is something I can do.

4

HATE SEX

SHAYLA

Sure… we can have hate sex. Because right now, I hate him. I hate that he has rejected me, even if I never wanted him for more than tonight.

But… I feel how much my body wants him, and my soul does, too. However, my mind is pretty solidly against this whole situation.

"Wait. How do you *not know* if it will work to separate us?" I ask.

"This is my first knot. It happens when… my kind finds his mate."

Mating. Goddess, this sucks. "Okay. Fine. Let's get this over with."

"Yeah. *Let's!*" He snarls and grunts as he rocks into me. The magical mate cord pulls between us, trying to solidify our forming bond.

"It… hurts," I admit, as I glance down where we are joined.

He sighs. "How the fuck did Fate pick *you*?"

"You really are an asshole," I snarl. "I should have known your nice guy charm was all an act."

"Back at ya." He glares. "And calling me an asshole isn't going to make me come any faster."

"I thought you wanted to have hate-sex. This *is* me hating you." Once again, I try to wiggle loose, but we're stuck together.

"*Fuck*," he hisses with my wiggling. "I can't believe I'm saying this, but try to remember when you thought you wanted me."

"But… I can't think straight!"

"Don't think." His mouth slams down on mine, his tongue probing my mouth, dominating me.

Taking his advice, I give it right back.

His hand squeezes my breast. He angles his hips just right, and his groin grinds against my clit. *Damn.*

The glow over our hearts brightens as I feel the arousal hitting me again.

I bite down on his lip. He grunts and thrusts harder.

My nails rake across his back, pulling him closer. My body wants this. Wants him. I'm so screwed. I dig my nails into his skin. He jerks with the sting. But I find that I don't like hurting him, so I release my hold.

With some burst of strength, and maybe because he allows it, I roll him until I'm on top. Sitting up, I can put some distance between us. But looking down at his perfect face, his hungry expression despite the claimed rejection, I'm drawn in.

I see the thin magical cord linking us from heart to heart.

Closing my eyes, I rock and grind on his inflated dick. I'm setting the pace now. And I can work the perfect angle to stimulate myself. My body has taken over. Primal instinct is in action. I realize our bodies were meant to dance this dance together.

His hands grip my hips, dimpling them with the pressure of

his fingertips. He doesn't try to control my pace, which is good, or I would slap him.

After a moment, his hands inch over my waist and my ribs until he cups my swaying breasts.

"At least you have perfect tits." He pinches both nipples while massaging an entire breast in each of his large hands.

"That's all I was to you, huh?" I ask with a snap of my hips.

"Like you didn't just want me for my money and power."

"I don't even fucking know who you are!" I shout.

He shoves his thumb into my mouth and demands, "Shut up and suck."

I close my mouth around his thumb and contemplate biting it off, even as I grind on his fat cock.

He reads the look in my eye. "You need to be quiet. And since it isn't my dick in your mouth, you can suck on my thumb."

He's right. We *don't* need to be caught like this. I need to be quieter. If the MSS finds out about my matebond, I might be forced to stay here. I give his thumb an experimental suck.

"Good girl." He grins wickedly. "Too bad I'll never know how that mouth feels wrapped around my cock."

Holy slip'n slide. All my body wants to do now is taste him.

Stupid traitorous body!

The sensation of his inflatable dick locked inside satisfies some deep carnal need. My body feels like it just now knows what it has been missing for all its existence.

And I let go… of everything but that feeling.

An earth-shattering orgasm rocks me. I arch and tremble, flailing with pleasure. I lose consciousness for a moment as I feel my cunt milking him. I collapse onto his chest.

Without warning, he flips us around so that he pins me to the ground, working himself to completion.

I'm so blissed out that I don't want him to stop.

If it wasn't for the insane circumstances, this would be hot, satisfying sex.

With several more thrusts, we both climax again. I can feel him filling me with his cum. He softens just enough to break free and yanks himself out of me.

It's painful, but it's worth it for this to be over.

He launches himself to his feet and hurriedly puts his clothes back on.

As I gather up my own clothes, the hurt of rejection slams into me.

Not bothering to roll up the sleeping bag, he grabs it and storms off toward the road without so much as a backward glance.

Logically, I know this is what needs to happen. I don't need him in my life.

However, my heart cracks, fracturing into shards.

Through the mate bond, I *feel* his rejection in my very soul. And of all the horrid torture I've ever endured, this might be the worst feeling yet.

I found my mate, and he doesn't want a damned thing to do with me.

But why do I sense that this isn't the last I will see of him?

5

MAGICAL SOCIAL SERVICES

SHAYLA

*T*hree days after discovering my fated mate, Myra and I clock out of our morning shift at the diner. A chill runs up my spine as we stand outside in the parking lot.

A warning from my intuition signals that something isn't quite right—although nothing has felt quite right since my encounter with my fated mate. My skin always itches now, craving his touch. There's a aching pain in my heart, perhaps even in my soul, that never goes away.

I rub my arms to rid myself of the odd feeling that someone is watching me. I scan our surroundings, but I don't see anyone looking my way. It must be my nerves.

"What's up?" Myra asks and glances over her shoulder. "You get one of your vibes?"

"Just jumpy, I guess. Probably from the big change around the corner." I haven't told her about my mate situation. I plan to take that horrible news to my death bed. Not only is a mate bond a threat to my escape plan, but what happened is embarrassing as hell. My fated thinks that I'm a conniving loser. I flush with anger, thinking about how he rejected me while still locked inside me.

Not cool, Fate.

"Yeah." Myra nods. "I suppose it's kind of like how I feel. I have all this bubbling anxiety. I'm worried I'll be a crappy mage, or no one at the academy will accept me."

I wave her off. "Please! You walk into a room, and people fall at your feet. Your big mistake was taking me in as a stray." I chuckle when she frowns at me. But we both know it's true. Everyone in my neighborhood knew my mother was a bit crazy and I hadn't shown any small signs that I would eventually have magic. Myra didn't turn her back on me when the other supe kids shunned me at school.

"I'll see you tomorrow." I give her a nod goodbye and head down the road.

The prickly feeling returns. I spot two huge bruiser, hanging out on the corner just ahead. They're likely supes by the look of them. Part of me wonders if my mate has hired someone to get rid of me. If he's as rich and powerful as he implied, then it's possible. But I'm probably being paranoid since we are on the geographical border between supernaturals and normals. Maybe they're just hanging out. However, they're glowering at me. So this isn't *all* in my head.

I cross the street to avoid them. I keep walking and pass them. As I do, they cross the road and follow me. They leave a twenty-foot distance between us. Okay, no need to panic... Yet. They could be just walking home, too.

I hear one mutter. "Nah. I got nothing. You?"

"No. Let's go."

When I turn back to see if they are closing in, I find they've disappeared. Completely. Too fast to be human. So they were definitely supes. But it appears they weren't there to attack me.

Was the whole drama all in my head? Have the years with my mother made me insane? I'm sure they have.

It's almost a week after meeting my fated, and my heart still feels as if it's burning and being shredded to pieces at the same time. I hope this suffering eases with time or distance. I just have to make it a few weeks more to my null verification. If I don't show any magic potential by my twentieth birthday, then I can escape this whole town and magic.

I had the morning shift at the diner again. When I return to the house, I find a shiny car in my driveway. It isn't my mate's friend's red Cutlass, but my mind still reels, wondering if I want to see my mystery mate again or if I would rather he vanish into another realm. Would that ease the ache in my soul?

As I enter the house through the kitchen door, hoping to avoid whatever is happening, I hear the sophisticated, resonant tone of an upper-class supernatural speaking to my mother. Great.

"Shayla?" my mother calls me sweetly from our janky-ass living room. Goddess, that sickly-sweet fake voice she uses in public makes my skin crawl.

I stand in the doorway to the living room, praying that this has nothing to do with me but intuiting that it does.

"This is Ms. Dixon, a representative of Magical Social Services. And this is Mr. Holt, a lawyer for the Lewellyn House."

My forehead crinkles in confusion. "I thought my null confirmation wasn't for another few weeks."

Ms. Dixon clears her throat. "That is why we are here. It appears that you have magic, after all."

I fold my arms over my chest. "No, I don't." This *cannot* be happening.

Mr. Holt cuts in. "It appears you are my client's fated mate."

Shit. I still haven't told anyone, not even Myra. She thinks I screwed his brains out, and we went our separate ways. I conveniently skipped over the fated mate bit.

My wretched mother grins. "The good news is, we're going to be rich."

Mr. Holt glares at my mother, and I join him.

"I don't know what you're talking about," I state. Maybe I can talk my way out of this.

"A magical matchmaker sensed a fated bond was revealed recently. And that you are fated to Rourke Lewellyn," Mr. Holt explains, looking as irritable as I feel.

"I don't know anyone named Rourke." The words ring true because I *didn't* know his name.

"Well, whether you know his name or not, you have a bond or the initiation of one," Ms. Dixon says. "And that means you must have magic. It has just been... suppressed." Her eyes dart to my mother, as if she suspects my home life is to blame for it.

"Or the little magic you have is extremely weak," Mr. Holt adds unhelpfully.

"I don't want him!" I say in a panicked tone. My body tenses, as if I could run from this. But they probably could find me anywhere I went. That's why I haven't run before now.

"Doesn't matter what either of you wants," Mr. Holt explains. "This is a fated mate bond. And in our current circumstances, the only way out of this magical contract is if you can confirm you have no signs of magic—which is doubtful considering you were able to create the bond."

"But I *don't* have magic!" I raise my voice, hoping they will understand.

Ms. Dixon shakes her head. "We must wait until your twentieth birthday, when you come of age, to see if that's true. If your magic doesn't manifest by then, as it should, Rourke will be able to petition to officially dissolve of the bond—which will be extremely unpleasant for both of you. And likely dangerous."

It was devastating when Rourke rejected me and walked away… like my heart was ripped out. How much worse can *officially* dissolving a bond be? I shiver with the thought.

Mother glares at me. "You better show some damned magic. I'm tired of supporting your lazy ass."

"Lovely," Mr. Holt says with pure disgust.

I'm feeling the same about her.

The pair show themselves out.

As they back out of the driveway, Leeann says, mocking me, "You may be a dumb whore, but at least you're smart enough to spread your legs for someone with money and status."

Who the hell did I bond with?

Anger bubbles up inside me.

I'm tired of my mother's abuse. "Yeah, but you're *just* a dumb whore, huh?"

My mother slaps me. It was worth it.

As far as pain goes, it doesn't even register compared to what she has done to me in my life.

I thought I was mostly done with her torture, but no, my mother is the gift that keeps on giving.

For the last several days, my mother and Bruce, her jerk of a boyfriend, have done everything in their power to activate my magic—to prove that I'm magical, to no avail.

I've been staying with Myra as much as possible, but my mother demands that I come home tonight. *Fuck me.*

When I walk in the door, Bruce grabs me by my collar and throws me to the floor. Such a lovely welcome.

"Come on, whore," he taunts. "What are you going to do?"

I scramble to my hands and knees to get away from him. He pulls his leg back and kicks me hard in the ribs, knocking the wind out of me.

My mother appears in the kitchen doorway, blocking my path of escape. Her look of disgust tells me everything I need to know about our relationship.

I'm nothing. Less than nothing.

I'm a shit stain on her entire existence. And I better start making up for her disappointment in how her own life unfolded. So yeah… classic loving mother-daughter bond.

Leeann snaps her fingers, and fire appears at her fingertips, like living matchsticks. My insides feel like they turn to ice, trying to shut down my pain receptors before the torture begins. This won't be the first time she has burned me. I doubt that it will be the last. My burn marks have yet to heal from her previous attack, when I dared to come home to get some of my things. At this point, she isn't even bothering with salve to cover up her abuse. She is allowing my wounds to fester.

I haven't asked Myra's parents to supply me with the costly ointment. Maybe they would help, but I've been dealing with the burns my whole life. I'll deal with it now. Besides, I need my cash to escape.

I fall back against the kitchen cabinets, all my fears from childhood resurfacing. I cover my face with my arms and curl up into a ball. The only thing it does is protect my face from the worst of her burns.

I swallow down the sob bubbling up within me. She will *not* hear me cry out.

Never again.

I feel Bruce's boot pressing me against the worn, broken cabinets and the shabby linoleum flooring. His heel digs into the side of neck.

Stars, if I *did* have powers, I would use them to fend off the coming searing pain that I can almost feel on my skin.

My mother's evil fire claws pierce my flesh at my waist, and I feel the burn that eradicates my resolve. I might be crying out in agony, but what do I know? My mind is lost to the consuming fire.

Burns are strange things, especially magical burns. It's so hot that after a few seconds, my brain believes that it's burning cold. Then the magic slips into the wound, electrifying every nerve ending in my body.

A true out-of-body experience would be a blessed thing right now. But I've never been that fortunate. I can only hope to pass out.

I can't take this any longer. I'm tired of being her toy to mutilate, to control, and to torture.

A strange swirling energy stirs. This is new. How is my mother doing this? It gathers momentum like a tornado ready to wipe out the entire house. I feel pulled inward, retreating, *and* like I'm about to burst—as if there were a bomb about to blow.

"You are such a fucking disappointment!" my mother shouts.

I bellow a curse. "Stop!"

There's an explosion.

I'm not sure what happened exactly, but when I open my eyes and pry my arms from my face, the entire kitchen is decimated. The glass from the window is all around me, and the floor is charred. My mother and Bruce are holding their hands over their eyes. I blink, wondering what happened.

It couldn't have been me.

It *can't* be.

Shit. It sure looks like it was me.

Ms. Dixon from Magical Services arrives at our house not even an hour after Leeann's excited call.

One look at the kitchen, and Ms. Dixon demands to know what happened.

"My mother tortures me and has since I was a baby," I confess. Damn, that feels good to finally tell the truth. So many times, the authorities checked on me because of complaints from the neighbors or when my teachers suspected something. But I was afraid to tell on her, believing my mother's promise that she would do something even more heinous... and kill me.

Ms. Dixon doesn't look the least bit surprised—like she already knew. "I think it's best if Shayla stays with Magical Services until she can be enrolled at Shadowcraft Academy."

"What?" I blurt, stepping back.

"Shadowcraft Academy." The woman looks at me, perplexed. "You're a supernatural being—perhaps a powerful mage, or perhaps just an unstable one. Either way, you must have the proper training to control your abilities. The Lewellyns will expect nothing less of a future member of their clan."

I gesture to the demolition around us. "But this whole thing might not be me." I argue, "It's probably my mother's power. She's trying to make it look like I'm a supe."

Ms. Dixon cocks a brow at me, clearly not believing that theory. "If there's a *chance* it was you, you need to be trained."

Dammit. I was so close to getting everything I wanted—freedom. I was weeks away from being declared a null, and I had to have a disastrous fling with a supernatural asshole.

I groan and rub my temples. I'm sure Rourke will be at the school. I don't think I can face him after what happened. "Do I have to go to the academy?"

"You do." Ms. Dixon glances around the house, repulsion clear on her face. "Do you really want to stay *here*?"

"No." I sigh and lean against the wall. "But can't I stay at a friend's house? Get tutor lessons?"

Ms. Dixon shakes her head. "Go collect your things. Only one suitcase. I'll wait here."

"I'm already packed," I say and shuffle to retrieve my oversized backpack from where I dropped it when Bruce attacked. I see that my cheap phone has melted. *Crap*. Covertly, I check that my escape money and the fake IDs I had planned on using to create my new life are still hidden at the bottom.

I might need them to get out of this.

6

ENTRANCE EXAMS

SHAYLA

*T*he last two days staying at the Magical Services halfway house have been blissfully uneventful. At least I'm out of my mother's house. It's just not in the way I had expected to leave.

I call Myra to tell her why I quit the diner... and everything else. I know that she'll be pissed that I didn't tell her about the whole fated mate crap with Rourke.

I explain what's happened so far in a rush of words over the phone, and silence follows.

Finally, Myra yips. "You're joining me at the Academy!"

That's her takeaway?

Sure, that's the saving grace about this whole ordeal—I'll have one friend there. Myra never judged me for being a null. And now, she'll have my back as I face the unknown.

"You aren't upset about me keeping the whole fated mate thing from you?" I ask with surprise. She's forgiving, but not usually when it comes to withholding gossip.

"Yeah. I'm totally pissed about that, but I get it. You wanted to run. But now, you're one of us!"

She's thrilled that I'm a supe like her, now. Well, I'm *close* to being like her. I still have a lot of catching up to do. I know absolutely freaking nothing about magic. My mother has never taught me anything. Although, she doesn't know a lot about magic either. She was trained at a cheap school and only in basic control.

However, my fated mate's family has sprung for the tab at the fancy school that's located, conveniently enough, just outside our run-of-the-mill town.

"What's your guy's name?"

"He's not *mine*," I grumble. "He rejected me, remember?"

"Whatever. Just tell me."

"Some asshole named Rourke Lewellyn."

"Crap. His family pretty much runs the Magic Council. Snobby dragon shifters mostly."

"That would explain his freakout when he realized I was a trashy null."

"Don't talk about yourself like that. First of all, you aren't a null anymore," Myra lectures with a mix of irritation and love. "Second, your mom might be a walking dumpster fire, but that doesn't mean you are."

"Thanks."

Silence falls between us, and Myra tries to lighten the mood with her unfaltering enthusiasm for life. "I hear it's amazing there. The magic—you can truly feel it, not like in this realm where it's so washed out."

"Oh." I worry my lip, realizing I didn't even hit me yet that I'd be going to another realm.

Everton is only one of several entrances to the fae realm. Apparently, the fae world has slowly been shrinking. The once vast countrysides are now the size of cities. Shadowcraft Academy is located in one of these alternate dimensional cities.

"What if I'm not really magical? Will I be able to enter?" I ask, hoping that the answer is no.

"Sillyhead, even humans can travel through the portals. Some have enough magic to open the door." Myra huffs. "And the blast you created at your mom's proves you have magic. Why are you still doubting this?"

"Because I might be expected to spend the rest of my hexed life with an asshole."

"A fucking gorgeous asshole."

"Still an asshole," I mutter. If I'm forced to stay with him, I'd be trading one wretched home life for another.

"Well, I'll see you on the other side!" Myra says cheerily.

Ms. Dixon drives me out to a remote location bordering the forest preserve. She pulls up to the main gates of what I assume is the Shadowcraft Academy portal.

"Here are your instructions." She hands me a parchment envelope and nods in the direction of the dirt road ahead of us. "That's the entrance exam."

I look dumbly at the sealed envelope and then back at her. "What if I don't pass the entrance exam?" My stomach flops. Dread washes over me. I intuit that I won't like the answer.

"Don't fail," she warns. "Failing means you will be incarcerated and tested to see if you need to be institutionalized at Ravenhollow Asylum."

The asylum... maybe my mother's threat will come true. "For *one* failure?"

"Magic is no joke. I saw what you did at your mother's house. What if you were to lose your temper with mortals and hurt someone? You'd be considered a threat to the magical community—potentially exposing us to the world. And if you can't learn to control your magic while under supervision at the school, then drastic measures must be taken—measures which I suspect that the Lewellyns would be perfectly willing to take."

Drastic? A shiver runs down my spine as I imagine what Ms. Dixon considers extreme. I'm likely to find out very soon.

I don't respond. Instead, I clamp my hand around the fancy-looking envelope. I hate to admit it, but I can feel the energy radiating off it.

Magic.

Screw magic.

It's ruined my childhood, and now it appears to be demolishing my adulthood—if I live that long.

I drag my cheap, oversized backpack onto my shoulder with a grunt. All my crappy worldly possessions now amount to what one could fit in a small trash bag.

With a nod goodbye to Ms. Dixon, I head down the rough dirt road—alone. I glance up and down the lane. I don't see any other students. Am I the last to arrive because of my late and chaotic enrollment?

Or is this some sick joke?

My life feels like some sick joke right now.

I walk for five minutes and come to a wide locked gate. The walls on either side are covered in flowering yet thorny vines.

As per Ms. Dixon's instructions, I open the envelope. I crack the wax seal open and wonder if they got the idea from Rowling or the other way around.

She isn't a supe. *Is she?* Then my mind reels with the question of how many famous people *are* supernatural.

Shaking my head to remind myself that my whole freaking life is on the line, I pull the card from the envelope and focus on its contents.

Which is… nonsense. Great.

I can't read a word of it. I recognize the letters, but that is about it.

It's not Latin or any *modern* language that I can discern. Then I recognize it… It's Elven.

I don't understand Elven!

I've barely even heard it spoken. Sometimes my mother mumbles words of it when she is being particularly creative with her attacks. But I doubt my mother knows more than a few phrases.

I sound out the words, attempting to emulate the slithering, rolling vowels my mother used.

After a couple of attempts, I feel a buzzing sensation in the surrounding air. I'm close to getting it right. Then I intuit I need to do something else. Letting my eyes fall shut, I focus on only what is *now*. My hand reaches out and swirls in the air as if I were suddenly blind and needed to know what was just ahead of me.

The air is thicker, and I wonder if this is the portal's anchor. I set my intention to open the gateway, and a breeze hitting my face. Opening my eyes, there's now a circular opening wide enough for someone to drive through. Brighter colors than I'm used to jar my senses. Blue is somehow bluer. Greens are more vibrant. Things feel… *alive.*

I take a tentative step forward, then another, until I'm standing in another realm. My heart pounds so hard that I just might have a heart attack.

The portal door seals shut. Startled, I jump and look around at where I'm now trapped.

Even though I'm in another realm, the time of day seems the same.

A dense forest completely surrounds me. Nothing else.

Where is the damned school?

I hope to walk around a tree and see the school in all its freaking glory. Although, I'm not sure I want to find it since the school will surely suck all the joy from my life like a giant magical vacuum.

Adjusting my pack, I pick a direction and begin to walk. It

isn't easy. I have to trailblaze over rocks and through thick brush, but what else can I do?

No GPS. No map. No damned clue how to get to the school that I must attend or die.

This is why I hate supernaturals.

I only make it a hundred strides before a root pops up out of the ground and ensnares my ankle.

What the flipping hell?

My head swivels, scanning my surroundings. Is there a mage conjuring this tripping hazard? Or is nature itself a heck of a lot more aggressive in the fae realm?

I tug on my leg in an attempt to break free, but the root only tightens itself around my foot.

A cackle emanates from behind the foliage.

Kill me now—cackles are so cliché.

"Looks like some trash blew in," someone says.

A young woman around my age emerges, followed by her posse of five other college-age students. They all have a look that I've seen before. Hate, disgust, and a dose of *I'm-gonna-kick-your-ass*.

I recognize one of the girls in her gang from my high school days, which taught a mix of supernaturals and norms. Big surprise, she was a bitch to me there, too. I was poor and powerless null and, therefore, open season... *every* season.

With a flick of the leader's finger, another pair of roots shoot out of the ground, wrapping around my wrists and pulling me to the ground. *Fuck.*

"So *this* is the worthless null trying to take my rightful place by Rourke's side?" Millie, the leader glares at me with her nose crinkled, as if I smelled like garbage.

"Have him. I don't want him." I keep my voice calm, as if I weren't freaking out that I'm pinned to the ground with people threatening me and cracking their magical knuckles. "He didn't tell me he had a girlfriend when we met."

"Stay away from him," she snarls.

"I plan to!" I snap back. "Now, let me go."

"Not until we show you just how much I mean what I say."

Here it comes...

I close my eyes and shut myself down. I've done this a thousand times with my mother. Endure by dissociation, then come back and deal with the injuries.

My consciousness hovers over the group as they slam boots and pound fists into my semi-unconscious body.

"Is she dead?" someone asks.

"Nah. I think she passed out," Millie says.

I get another kick in the side. Then they scurry off, leaving me trapped on the hard rocky ground, bound by magical roots. None of them cares that I'm likely dying from internal injuries.

As I register the pain in my broken body, I switch over to the part of me that can suppress the pain. I wish I could just let go and reincarnate as a house cat or something. But some deep hope keeps me moving forward, hoping I might escape all of this. I'm determined to find a way to release the magical contract with Rourke, appease the authorities that I'm not a danger, and hide where no asshole supernatural can find me.

7

OLD FRIEND

SHAYLA

a deep voice rouses me from my nearly unconscious state.

A chant. Magic glides over my skin. The roots loosen, and blood rushes back into my feet and hands.

When I feel myself being jostled and nestled into someone's arms, I groan and crack open an eye.

"I got you," a man says.

"Leave me alone!" I yell. I squirm to escape, but that only makes me cry out from the bruises on my beaten body.

"You're going to hurt yourself more." He tightens his hold on me.

"And what do *you* plan on doing to me?" I ask suspiciously. He could be a new threat.

"Help you." He stops walking and stares down at me. His deep-emerald green eyes are powerful yet gentle. And they seem *very* familiar. "I'm taking you to the academy, and I plan to have you healed immediately. Is that alright with you?"

His firm tone and commanding gaze shut me up. Not to mention that he's freaking stunning.

Holy hellions… he makes me ache in another way.

His long, wavy golden brown hair is pulled back in a messy bun. He has a full beard with a hint of red. Celtic-looking tattoos peek out from the collar of his tight t-shirt. But I'm drawn in most by his eyes—the color of the forest after a rain—vibrant and alive.

"Are you a Viking?" I ask stupidly.

He chuckles. "Druid."

"Is that how you got me out of the roots?"

He nods.

I study him as he carries me toward the hell that awaits me. I feel tiny in his massive arms. He's a giant god of a man, and I blush just being near him. But there's also a solid, grounded quality about him that somehow settles me.

"You seem familiar," I say. "You remind me of a boy who used to live in my neighborhood with his grandma. I was nine years old then, and he was a couple of years older than me."

"You remember a kid from years ago?"

"He was my… he was special. Way too cool for me to hang out with, but he was always so kind, even though I was a null."

"But you aren't a null if you passed the entrance exam to get into Shadowcraft."

"Was the beating part of the exam?" I mutter.

He crinkles his forehead in confusion. "No. You opened the portal."

"Couldn't the portal just be reacting to my fae blood?"

He shakes his head, not even straining to carry me. "You aren't a null."

"I'm not convinced." I almost shrug and think better of it. I'm still holding on to the hope that only my blood triggered the portal, not any magic. But I can tell that this male is set in his opinion. "Well, anyway, I cried the day he moved away. I never heard from him again."

A strange uncomfortableness washes over this man. I guess he doesn't like hearing about feelings.

To change the subject, I ask, "Are you a teacher at the Academy?"

He chuffs his amusement at my guess. "A student."

As soon as he answers, he crests a hill, still carrying me. The school comes into view, and I suck in a breath. From our vantage point, I can see that the campus is enormous. Large gothic-style buildings form a square with an open quad in the middle. Outdoor recreation and sports fields surround the buildings and make up the rest of the campus. A high wall, which looks like it was left over from the days of castles and moats, surrounds the entire campus and keeps it separate from a dense forest. In the distance, I see a town.

With his long gait, we're at the entrance in minutes.

The gate guards eye us with concern.

An obviously hardened male guard, with scars marring his handsome face, winces at my appearance. I must look bad.

"What the hell happened to you?" he asks.

"Someone attacked her. I came across her after the fact."

The guards look to me for confirmation.

"He helped me."

He waves us through the gates, and an odd sensation tingles down my spine. It must be a magical ward to protect the school. Why does it need protection?

My rescuer takes me inside the main building and down a side hall that immediately opens to a reception area. Seeing us, a woman behind a desk hurries over to me, surveying my body and tallying my injuries. "Bring her in here," she orders as she leads the way.

He sets me down on a gurney in a semi-private healing cubicle nearby.

"Thanks, Arden," she says and notes my bruised wrists.

"Arden?" I yelp. "*You… you're… him.*"

"What's she talking about?" the healer asks Arden with a worried glance.

Arden looks at me with a bit of shame coloring his cheeks pink. "Yeah, I'm the kid from your neighborhood."

"Why didn't you say anything?" I blush, thinking about how I practically confessed my crush on him.

"I guess I was in shock you remembered me."

He removes both of our bags from his broad shoulders and sets them down. I can't believe that he carried me and our two heavy bags, without breaking a sweat. My little friend has grown to be over six-four and two hundred fifty pounds of muscle. He's a damn beast, but so far, a gentle one.

I decide to let go of the whole *not-telling-me-who-he-is* thing since it will only make me look more pathetic. He must have figured out how ridiculous I am for crushing on a boy who I barely knew. Thankfully, he doesn't know that in the past decade, I thought about him every time I walked by his grandma's old house, which was almost daily.

"Thanks for bringing my bag," I say. "I kind of forgot about it."

"Probably because you were knocked in the head a few times," the healer says, reminding me that we have an audience for our awkward reunion. "You can go, Arden."

He looks at me once more and then back at the healer. "Shouldn't I help her check in?"

"You need to check in yourself." She huffs. "Don't start the year on a bad note… again."

"Thank you for finding me," I say to break the rising tension.

"I just wish I came across you sooner so you wouldn't have gotten hurt at all," Arden says, pulling his pack onto his shoulder. "See you around, Sparkles."

I grimace. He actually remembered his silly nickname for me? Some weird nervous energy twists in my gut. Is that what they call *butterflies*? I swear, I hit twenty, and my hormones are out of control. Wasn't that supposed to happen during my teen years? Apparently, I'm a late bloomer—in magic and libido.

The healer waits until Arden leaves and then introduces herself. "I'm Ms. Boyd, the school's primary healer." She brings attention to my ripped shirt with a nod, her hands hovering over its hem. "I should probably see the extent of your damage before proceeding."

"*Boyd?*" My gaze darts to where Arden disappeared through the door. "Are you related to Arden?"

"You remember him *that* well?" She raises her eyebrows and looks impressed. "And yes, I'm his aunt. I helped raise him once I was able to. I was a lot younger than his father."

She pulls the t-shirt over my head, and I whimper with the sharp pains zipping through me. Her kind eyes darken when she sees the mess of cuts and bruises and... barely healed burns. She demands, "Who or what did this to you?"

"I don't know."

"Students?"

I shrug. "Maybe. They didn't seem to be keen on my existence. But they need to take a number and get in line."

Her eyes snap up to read mine. "Where did you get the older bruises and burns?"

I try to make light of my growing list of enemies. "Well, the bad times all began when I was born... And then the fun just never stopped."

"Seriously, what pointless excuse did the students have to attack you? You didn't do anything to them."

I sigh. I don't want to start off my first day in hell as a rat. I'm not going to tell her that I know at least one of my attackers. I deflect instead—a tried-and-true tactic. "You don't know that I didn't do something to deserve this."

"I read auras, so I kind of *do* know. Or at least, I know your core being. And I can see that you're not someone who wishes to do harm."

She presses on what feels like multiple bruised ribs. I close my eyes and suck in a breath.

"I guess you aren't going to tell me anything, so let's move on," she grumbles. "You have to check with Registration soon."

"Looking like *this*?" I gesture at my battered appearance.

"I'm giving you a healing potion. You should be functional within the hour, and you will feel better after a solid night's rest." She hands me a familiar-looking bottle. I've taken this bitter brew before.

"But rapid healing will drain you," she warns.

"I'm very familiar," I mumble.

She stares at me, probably reading my aura again. "I suppose you are. Fortunately, you're stable. But it also means I can't use my healing magic on you. I have to reserve it in case I need it for an emergency. The good news is that I don't sense any internal bleeding—which is a miracle."

"I get it. No worries. I've been through worse." I drain the bottle of healing potion, flinching at the bitter sting on my tongue, and wave her off. "I'm just going to rest for a bit if that's okay."

8

ORIENTATION

SHAYLA

*G*ingerly, I leave the healer's wing on my own two feet an hour later. Ms. Boyd gives me a wheeled cart, so I don't have to carry my oversized backpack.

I'm dressed in the damaged and bloodied clothes I wore earlier. I couldn't change into another outfit because my attackers had clawed up my clothes. They also sliced open my shampoo and body wash bottles, making a mess all over my things.

Fortunately, they hadn't gotten far enough into my bag to find my cash and fake IDs.

With a heavy sigh, I follow Ms. Boyd's directions and easily find the large tables set up by the academy entrance. I stand in the queue, waiting my turn and eyeing the other students. I recognize most of the supe types by their mannerisms and/or looks, but there are a few who leave me curious.

I scan the dwindling crowd for Myra to no avail. She's

probably already inside with almost everyone else. Only about thirty or so late arrivals are waiting to check-in.

A pair of almost full-blooded high elves stand in line, appearing completely bored and irritable. I call it *resting-elf face*. They are immediately recognizable by their tall, lean bodies, which emanate a beauty that seems to glow. Usually, they're arrogant snobs.

I note wolf-shifters and perhaps some other animal shifters. By the looks of them, I'm sure a few are bears and maybe a mountain lion or other large cats.

A couple of vampires leer at other students around them, running their tongues over their descended fangs. Posturing idiots.

If the academy's roster is anything like the town I'm from, there'll be all varieties of part-fae hybrids: every kind of animal shifter, vampires, minotaurs, incubi, succubi, non-shifting fae mages, druids, and maybe even some with demon blood. The majority of supes will have mage powers, such as fire or water magic, along with their species form.

My mother is a basic part-fae—a weak excuse for a fire mage. That means I'm probably a simple mage or mage hybrid, depending on what's in my father's lineage.

The student in front of me walks away from the table, and a squatty little man calls to me, waving me forward. "Name?"

"Shayla Willows."

The brownie fae hums while he looks up my name, and I move closer to the table. "I see you're a late addition. There's quite a lot of information missing from your file."

"I only found out a couple of days ago that *apparently*, I'm not a null."

"And…" He peers up at me and frowns. "*What* are you?"

Rationally, I know that he doesn't mean it to sound the way it came out, but I bristle nonetheless. "I don't know *what* I am." I take a deep breath and shrug. "But my mother is a mage. Her affinity is fire."

"And your father?"

My mouth is instantly dry. "I don't know anything about him."

A condescending chuckle comes from some girl behind me. "She doesn't even know who her daddy is. Her mommy must be as big a whore just like *she* is."

I close my eyes and count to ten. The academy probably frowns upon murder on the first day. Besides, I'm not exactly in fighting form at the moment.

The tiny administrator in front of me glares at whoever is behind me with the nasty insults. "Five points will be docked from your total. Already starting out the year on a deficit. Hmm." He shakes his head in disappointment at the student.

Great. I'm sure I'll be blamed for that. I glance out the massive double doors at the view outside. Maybe I can run. Escape back to the mortal realm and hide forever.

"Miss Willows?" the brownie calls. When I turn back to him, he continues, "We'll get the whole thing settled. I'll assign Mr. Hollis as a mentor and advisor. He will be able to detect your precise species and affinity." He hands me a stack of sheets. "This is your dorm room assignment, your schedule, and Mr. Hollis' contact information. You should drop by his office tomorrow after classes finish and introduce yourself."

I nod dumbly.

Then he adds, "You don't have enough time to locate and settle into your room. I suggest heading to the meeting hall and waiting for the welcoming ceremony to begin. It will start in a few minutes."

Trying my best to smile, I thank the brownie and limp in the direction he pointed.

I make it about twenty feet before someone grabs the handle of my carry cart out of my hand.

Great. More fun times.

I whip around, ready to throw a punch, and the guy lets go of my cart, allowing it to topple onto the floor, bag and all.

His hands are up in surrender. "Hey, I was just trying to help!"

My fists are still poised to strike. When I sense no nefarious intent, I drop them to my sides.

"Rough day," he says without question.

I suppose it doesn't take a psychic to figure out that I've been through the wringer today. Anyone could see that by my torn and bloodied clothes.

I glance at my bag, not looking forward to bending down and picking it up since my body still aches. My gaze travels back up this guy's long, leanly muscled body—a dancer's physique. Then I meet a pair of mesmerizing gray eyes. They remind me of a sky over a stormy sea. Tousled dark auburn hair falls roguishly over his forehead. His eyes are lined with dark lashes. He has a strong jaw but not chiseled like a supermodel's. He's strikingly handsome yet somehow approachable. He smiles at me with an ease that I could never master.

My mouth drops open in awe of his beauty. My core heats in response. I guess my body is feeling better than I realized.

"I'm Landis," he offers. Still flustered, I don't say anything, and he prompts, "And you are?"

I blink, remembering my name, and answer, "Uh, Shayla Willows."

His eyebrows raise as if he recognizes the name. I'm sure he does. The bullies are probably running around announcing how horrible I am for having Rourke as my stupid, rejected mate.

Whatever. I don't need anyone's help. I don't need any friends besides Myra. I'll find her, and we'll have each other's back. Hopefully, we'll be rooming together.

I squat down to pick up my fallen bag, and Landis beats me to it.

"You don't have to help me," I say with a tense jaw.

"I knocked it over." He shrugs and my attention is drawn to his broad shoulders.

What is up with me lately?

"You've probably heard the stories about me," I say. "So either you think I'm easy, which I'm not. Or you plan on messing with me, just like everyone else."

"There's always another possibility." He smirks playfully. "I could want to help out someone in pain."

I glare at him. Dammit, he's right. I'm assuming a lot. He didn't seem to know my name *before* he helped me. "You don't want to get caught up in whatever shit pile I landed in."

"I don't know." He pulls my cart to his other side so I can't snatch it back. "I wouldn't mind being caught in some kind of pile with you."

I shake my head and huff out a laugh. "Oh, I get it... an incubus?" I accuse.

"Guilty." He raises an eyebrow. "So, are you going to snub me now?"

"No," I huff and look around to see only a few stragglers entering the meeting hall. "Let's hurry. We're going to miss the ceremony."

We fall in step toward the hall, and I wonder if I just made a friend out of an incubus. Out of the corner of my eye, I watch his graceful walk and feel his magnetic pull. I don't know if I'll be able to keep my attraction to him in check. But there's no way a romantic relationship with an incubus cannot end in heartbreak.

I scan the crowded meeting hall for Myra but don't see her. I do see Arden several rows deeper, closer to the front of the room. He towers over most of the other supes.

As if he feels my eyes on him, he turns, gives me a nod, and then glares at Landis standing next to me with my bag cart still in his hand.

There are at least six hundred students packed into the large hall. It's already stuffy from all the bodies and the late summer heat.

"Attention!" an older man on the stage calls out. The room

instantly falls silent. Yeah, this guy is a powerhouse. Even I can feel his magic at the back of the room.

"Welcome to Shadowcraft Academy. I'm your Dean, Mr. Cranish. As you know, our school was founded to give young adults a place to develop and learn to control their magic. It also serves as an accredited college so that you can integrate into the human world once you graduate... if you so choose. We even have graduate and doctorate programs in various fields. For those first years who haven't chosen a concentrated field of study, please use this year to explore our workshops and audit classes you may want to specialize in."

He clears his throat. My intuition tells me that something is irritating him.

Mr. Cranish continues, "This year, you are prohibited from going beyond the academy's walls unless supervised and escorted by one of the faculty. Any violation of this rule will lead to immediate expulsion. Do I make myself clear? There will be *no* exceptions. Each student now has one hundred points. If you misbehave, act disrespectful toward the staff, are caught fighting, misuse your magic against others, or are late for classes, you will be docked points. If you lose all your points, you will be expelled. However, you will be awarded if you behave properly, volunteer for community service, or complete extra credit assignments. Classes start early tomorrow morning. Don't be late, or you'll be docked."

The Dean blathers on about being an upstanding supernatural in the school and then the community at large, but all I can worry about now is that I might be kicked out of the school. What would happen to me if I were? Would that mean an automatic trip to the asylum?

My attention is brought back to the moment when Mr. Cranish chants in a low voice and throws out his hands. A sparkling burst of confetti shoots out of his palms and rains down on the students. As it lands on my skin, I feel a strange magic wash over me.

"What *was* that?" I ask Landis.

"I assume he's marking students with some kind of tracking spell to detect if we leave the grounds," Landis grumbles.

The Dean smiles at the sea of faces, trying for a welcoming grin and missing the mark. "Good luck to all of you! Now go settle into your room assignments and remember, no roaming the halls after curfew."

9

ROOM ASSIGNMENT

SHAYLA

*a*s the Dean dismisses the assembly, Landis snatches the stack of school papers from my hand.

"Hey!" I try to grab them back, but he's quick and has much longer arms to keep them out of my reach. Besides, I don't have the energy or strength to make a genuine attempt.

He nods appreciatively at my room assignment and then hands the papers back. "I'll help you find your room."

"You don't have to do that." I reach for my cart handle, but Landis already has it and is moving toward the exit.

I look back to see where Arden is, but with all the tall students pressing closer to the exit around me, I can't see him. Giving up, I follow Landis into the halls, through a breezeway, and into another huge building.

Inside and off to one side is a modern yet quaint café with the snobby name of Heritage Café. It has a dragon logo with a crown. Wonderful. Rourke's family probably owns it. Along with the wide selection of meals and beverages on the menu, it also has a small selection of convenience store items near the ordering bar. Cute bistro tables dot the vast open space, where students can hang out and chat. To the right are wide stairs spanning twenty feet.

Landis points to our left, "Heritage is this dorm's private café. If you need a quick bite or coffee, it's the best on campus."

"How many dorms are there?" I ask.

"Two dorms. This is the snobby one. On the other side of the quad, another dorm houses the school staff and the students with less... disposable income."

"Then what the hell am I doing on this side?" I ask.

Landis looks at me as if he doesn't understand what I'm talking about. Shaking his head, his long legs carry him away.

I groan when I see he's heading toward the stairs. I don't know if I can make it up the damned things with how badly my body still aches. The healing tonic has wiped me out.

A huge presence looms behind me. "I can carry you up," Arden says quietly into my ear as he leans down.

My body shivers when his rich voice rumbles through me. I look over my shoulder at him and shake my head. "I've already been a spectacle today. I don't need to draw more attention... but thanks."

Halfway up the stairs, Landis realizes that I'm not right behind him. He turns to find Arden sliding his arm around my waist. Then the giant druid lifts and carries me as if I were walking alongside him. My feet dangle, barely touching the steps.

"Show off," Landis grumbles as Arden sets me down on the second-floor landing.

Before I tell them I can handle it from here, Landis races ahead, pulling my cart down the dark, wood-paneled corridor.

My cheap, trashed sneakers shuffle on the lush carpet. I feel completely out of my element. This place has to be one of the nicest buildings I've ever been in. My hand runs along the wainscoting down the wide hallway.

Arden's intense attention is on my weird behavior, although he isn't looking directly at me. Maybe that's just how he operates—his senses taking in his surroundings. And right now, it feels like I'm the center of his perception. But maybe that's just how it feels to be around him. What do I know? I've never hung out with a full-powered adult druid before.

Landis is merrily traipsing ahead with my cart. Then he pauses and waits for us to catch up. With a flourish, he opens the first door to the left in the hallway.

"What—" Arden begins to ask something, but Landis hushes him.

I freeze. I eye them both suspiciously. "Is this a trap?"

Landis' eyes twinkle, but I don't read malicious intentions. I glance inside beyond the door and see no one lying in wait to attack.

There's a vast, open space roughly twenty-five feet wide and forty feet deep. Two huge, plush sofas face each other in the center of the main common room. Behind the sitting area is a long, wooden table with six chairs. A kitchen runs along the back wall, complete with a full-sized fridge and stove. Along the sides of the great room, four doors are on the left and four on the right. The first two doors on both sides are closed.

"Let me see your paperwork," Arden demands.

I peek at the room number printed on the sheet and check the outer room plate. Oakes Hall, Suite 201. So, I'm in the right place.

Confirming that this is the correct dorm suite I'm supposed to be in, I tentatively step inside the shared space and walk to the first open door on the far right. The bedroom is small. A twin bed is pushed against the wall in the far corner. There's an open closet to the right with dresser drawers built in. A tiny antique-looking desk sits just inside the door. Simple, but it's all nicer than what I came from.

I can't bring myself to step inside the bedroom, as if that act makes this all too real. Instead, I peek in the other open doorway just beyond this room. I discover a large bathing suite flanked by a long vanity with three sinks and three shower stalls with privacy doors. There's a separate toilet room. Thank goodness.

When I turn back toward the common space, I see that Landis has already deposited my bag in the room I checked out. I walk in after him and see that he's studying my class schedule.

"Thanks for your help, but you can leave me to it now," I say with more bite than I mean to. I'm just not used to trusting strangers. And essentially, he's a stranger, snooping through my stuff.

His eyes dart up to consider me. I shoo him out of the room, and he concedes, "Fine. But if you need me, I won't be far."

I roll my eyes.

I limp out behind him as we both exit my new room.

At the same moment, across the dorm's common space, the first bedroom door opens, and Rourke walks out, closely followed by his dark-haired, mysterious friend from that fateful night at the party.

Before I fully register it's Rourke in front of me, he launches himself across the room and pins Landis against the wall.

Rourke's forearm crushes Landis' windpipe. He growls, "What the fuck did you do with my mate, *Shadow-cock*?"

Landis pulls at Rourke's arm on his throat with no luck.

Worried that he might hurt Landis, I grab Rourke's elbow and pull on him with all my weight. "Stop this!"

A zap of energy rockets through me where our skin connects.

I recoil with the sensation.

His skin ripples with dragon scales—an iridescent golden-red. His fingernails turn into dark claws.

He turns to look at me. His eyes flash with a fiery glow. "Don't touch me!" He loosens his hold on Landis and shifts fully back to his human form.

The incubus drops to the floor and rubs his neck, coughing.

"What the hell?" I snap. "You rejected me! And there's no law that says I can't have friends even if you didn't."

"He's an incubus!" Rourke growls, glaring at Landis.

"And you don't want me, so what's the problem?" I cross my arms, so I don't reach out for him again, feeling the call of the mate bond. Why does it have to hurt so much?

"Until we sever this contract... *you are mine.*" Rourke huffs out a few harsh breaths.

He's trying to control his fire, but I can smell the smoke emanating from his throat.

I should back down, but I've hit my limit of bullshit. I resist flinching away from the threat of fire. I've lived my whole life with burns and abuse. I will *not* let my fated mate intimidate me as well. If we can't break the contract, I need to set the rules now.

I take a challenging step toward him. "No. *I am mine.*"

"You're here at this school only because of *my* family's responsibility to the sacred magical contract. Since we're technically betrothed, you'll be housed with me. But make no mistake, as soon as you screw up in any way or fail to master your pathetic magic, you'll be thrown into Ravenhollow, and our contract will be void. But until then, we must continue this joke of a bond."

"If you hate me so much, why not just toss me in the asylum now?" I counter, my hands landing on my hips defiantly.

His face flickers with what suggestion. For a moment, looks like hurt, but I must have imagined it. "Don't tempt me," he warns.

Rourke spins on his heel and storms toward the exit. As he moves past Landis, he threatens, "Don't go near her."

"Going to be hard since I'm rooming here, too," Landis says with a cocky smirk.

Rourke freezes. "What?"

"You know how campus magic is. It likes to mix up the

species to keep us all nice and friendly-like. This year, it wants you to have a sweet taste of incubus."

"And a druid," Arden adds.

Rourke groans, dragging his palm over his face.

I suck in a breath. *"What?"* It's my turn to be surprised. "You're *both* in here?" When they nod, I glance at Rourke's friend. And I look at the rooms across from mine. "You too?"

His friend's stoic face has given nothing away during this whole encounter. His onyx eyes match his jet black hair, dark and unforgiving. And now, he only responds to my question with a curt nod. Then a flash of red in his eyes startles me. If I wasn't now certain he's a vamp, I'd say he was a dragon as well. Fire rages behind those eyes. I suppose he hates me as much as Rourke does.

The tension in the room is driving me insane. I was pretty good at avoiding my mother over the years, but avoiding all *this* in such close quarters will be challenging.

"Fine. We're stuck together this year, but you better remember who's in charge," Rourke announces to the room.

"Do you have to be such a jerk?" I ask.

"I do." He looks me up and down for the first time since entering the suite. He notices my ripped, dirty, and blood-stained shirt and jeans. "It's bad enough that you're little more than a null. Could you not look like a hellcat dragged you into the school and embarrass me even more?"

"Hey!" Arden snaps. "She was beaten to an inch of her life when she arrived in this realm. Back off."

Rourke's eyes widen slightly in surprise, but it doesn't stop him from sneering at my cheap shoes. "I can't believe the Fates thought *we* belonged together." He turns his back to me and heads out of the dorm, followed closely by his vamp friend.

Once again, despite my logical mind telling me otherwise, my heart feels like it's being twisted and mangled, insisting I go after him. Damn this fated thing! Proximity will make the incessant pain of rejecting the bond that much harder to handle.

"Lovely mate you have there," Landis says, finally feeling safe enough to get to his feet with Rourke gone.

"Seriously, Arden's right," I warn my new incubus roommate. "I was almost beaten to death when I arrived here. You don't want to get caught up in all this." I point at Rourke's room. "And don't provoke him."

Another glint of mischief twinkles in his eyes. "I'm not the type that backs down from a challenge."

Wonderful. He's only going to make things worse.

HEALER'S TOUCH

ARDEN

Shayla glances down at her shaking hands. This whole situation has her more rattled than she lets on.

"Why don't you get cleaned up?" I suggest. "It might make you feel better."

Her shoulders sag. "I would, but all my things were trashed. My shampoo and body wash are gone. I don't even have spare clothes that I can wear. My stuff was ruined."

"Hold on." I pop into my room, which is the first on the right. I open my drawer and pull out a t-shirt and drawstring shorts. They will be huge on her much smaller frame, but it's better than nothing. As I imagine her *in* nothing, my cock wakes up, but I slam down that line of thinking. I can't let myself feel that way about her.

When I return from my room, she's leaning against the wall, barely able to stand.

"The rapid healing is hitting you hard, huh?" I ask.

Shayla nods, and I offer, "I could give you a bit of a boost."

Her eyes finally meet mine. *Shit*, those gorgeous lavender eyes completely undo me.

She squints at me in confusion. "You have healer magic?"

"Not as good as my aunt yet, but yeah." I hold out my hand. "It should only take a few minutes to give you enough energy to shower, change into these, and get to bed."

With some hesitation, she takes my hand, and I lead her to the couch. She sits down beside me, looking nervous.

Landis plops down on the opposite couch, watching us intently.

I take her hands and hold them over the small space between us. I don't want her to misread my intention to help. However, every cell in my body wants to pull her onto my lap, hold her, and make her feel protected—even if only for a moment.

Instead, I focus on my innate healing magic, feel the tingle over my body, and begin to pour it into her battered form.

"Forgive me if I'm wrong, but doesn't that healing thing work better with more body contact?" Landis asks. This guy just doesn't understand limits or boundaries. He's going to get his ass kicked daily by Rourke, and if not him, I might be inclined to do the honors.

"Yes, however—" I begin, but Shayla stops me with a question.

"Does it?" She looks up at me with her angelic face. Fierce, yet right now, vulnerable. "It isn't like you haven't held me already... Unless you're worried about Rourke?" She bites her lip, and I have to look away before my cock stirs again. "Never mind," she says with a tinge of disappointment.

"Come here." I pull her onto my lap. My arms wrap around her, and she nestles into me, tucking her head under my chin.

"Oh," she whispers when she feels the magic flooding into her. "I can feel the difference."

I glance up and see Landis grinning like a Cheshire cat. I need to watch out for this trickster.

After several blissful minutes of holding her, she falls asleep.

Landis comes over to us and takes off Shayla's shoes. With my druidic sight, which can see energetic connections, I notice that his energy doesn't try to latch onto her. He also doesn't make physical contact, not even the slightest brush of a finger on her ankle, as he slips off her socks.

Interesting. Maybe Landis senses how protective I am of Shayla and is acting innocently for my sake.

He sighs and looks up at me. "We should probably wake her and have her wash up before Rourke comes back."

At least the incubus has *some* sense. Yet, I'm resistant. I don't want to release her from my arms, but she needs to clean up and have a proper sleep. The fight with Rourke earlier drained her when she didn't have any reserves.

"Shayla?" I say gently with a shift in my shoulder to rouse her. "You should probably get ready for bed."

She scrunches up her cute nose and tries to snuggle deeper within my arms. I stand up, still holding her, and carry her to the bathroom. After setting her rump on the counter, she finally cracks open her eyes and blinks at me.

"But I don't have my stuff."

"You can use my soap. It's sandalwood, and my shampoo and conditioner don't have much of a scent." I pat the shirt and shorts sitting next to her on the counter. "You can borrow these as long as you need them."

Her face flushes pink. "Thanks. But you don't have to be nice to me just because you found me like roadkill on the side of the road."

Fuck, her words break my heart. She just can't accept a kind deed.

"Hey." I wait to continue until she looks up at me. I brush back her golden brown hair, tucking it behind her ear. "You're my long-lost friend. And now, I'm blessed to be your *friend* again. Okay?"

Her lavender eyes begin to well up with tears, and she looks away. "Thanks. I should get showered before your boost wears off."

I help her down from the counter so she doesn't fall. I worry when she wobbles a bit. "I'm staying with you."

Shayla's eyes widen. "In the shower?"

"I'm turning around. You can undress and get in by yourself. But I'm not letting you fall down on my watch."

I turn, and I can hear her stripping off her clothes. *Goddess, help me.* This was a bad idea.

Her hand catches my elbow when she tries to take off her pants. She stabilizes herself and says, "I guess skinny jeans for today weren't the best choice."

"Do you need help?" I wince inwardly.

Did that come off like I'm too eager?

"Um, yeah... I guess. Sorry." She sounds defeated.

"No need to apologize." I turn, trying to avert my gaze. Shayla's in a sports bra. Okay, that's like a crop top tank. No biggie. I can handle that. Well, maybe not *handle* that.

I refocus and kneel down to help her out of her jeans. And end up at eye level with her tiny white cotton panties. Simple, yet sexier because of it. She doesn't need lace to dress up her body. She's fucking perfect.

Goddess, I almost blurt that out.

I rest my hands on her hips to steady her and see the yellow bruises. I wince. Those bastards will pay for what they did.

I rub my thumb over older scars... burn marks. It has to be her mother's abuse. I curse the pathetic excuse for a fire mage.

Carefully, I lift Shay and place her on the counter again. I kneel down, slide the tight hems of her jeans over her ankles, then drag the jeans down her calves. My eyes follow the glorious sight of her legs, taking in her soft, exposed skin.

When I look back up to see if she caught me ogling, she's blushing and covering her face. "I think I can manage from here."

To avoid the awkwardness I just created, I race over to warm up the water for her shower.

I help her down from the counter again, but I don't let her go until we reach the shower stall.

"Thanks," she whispers.

I sense how hard it is for her to trust—to be vulnerable. And I'm honored that she has trusted me so much already. I'm certain trusting me would've been more difficult had we not known each other from our childhood.

Does she sense how much I care beyond our fleeting friendship a decade ago?

When I felt her energy in the woods today, I was drawn to her like nothing before. The forest called to me to find someone. For a brief, joyful moment, I believed it was the call to find my *dyad*—my druidic mate. But when I caught sight of Shayla's damaged state, it broke my heart to see her hurt like that. And also because I'd heard Shayla is the dragon's fated mate. She isn't meant to be mine.

Shayla clears her throat and brings me back to where we are now. She gestures for me to turn around again, and when I do, she removes her bra and panties. I hear her enter the stall, and I wait patiently for her to finish showering. When the water cuts off, I hand her a towel over the frosted glass.

After a moment of patting herself down, she cracks open the door with the too-small towel wrapped around her beautiful body. Her hair is dark from the water and even more enticing with its curling locks.

"I think I got it now." She waves me out like I'm a pest.

I grin because this is her way of reclaiming the situation. "Understood. But just call out if you need me."

I join Landis on the couch and wait impatiently for her to appear.

A minute later, Shayla's voice filters through the bathroom door. "Arden?"

Landis raises an eyebrow in interest.

I ignore him and race into the bathroom.

She's slumped on the tile floor, utterly drained. The towel barely covers her body. Her hand is hiding her face in shame. "I can't…"

"I got you," I promise. And I do. No matter what happens with Rourke, I won't abandon her again. Not that I had much choice as a kid, but it killed me, leaving her behind all those years ago to the whims of a tyrant. And there's no way I'll let anyone cart her off to the asylum.

That place has already claimed someone I love. Never again.

I keep her towel in place as I pull the clean shirt over her head. I help her thread her arms through the sleeves. I lift her until she's standing, and the shirt drops down like a dress to cover her mid-thigh. Holding her close so that her knees don't buckle, I pull the towel free.

I use it to towel-dry her thick hair.

"Are you okay without the shorts for now?" I adjust the shirt so it isn't dropping off her shoulder. It's worse than I anticipated—seeing her in nothing but my shirt makes me ache for her even more.

"I don't need them," she whispers.

I pick her up and carry Shayla to her bedroom. After tucking her in under the sheets, I kiss the top of her head before thinking it through. "Feel better, Sparkles."

I place the shorts on her nightstand for the morning.

As I shut the door to her room, she murmurs, "Good night."

A moment after that, Rourke and Branden saunter back into our common room from the halls. I swear they're attached at the hip. I rarely see one without the other.

Rourke's eyes sweep over Landis and me. He relaxes a bit when he notes that Shayla isn't in the main room. Without a word, he disappears into his room, the first on the left. And Branden slips into his room in the middle.

"I'm heading out to the commissary. You need anything?" I

ask the incubus because I'll need an ally in this dorm assignment.

Landis' eyes flicker to Shayla's room with amusement. "Make sure you get her size seven Mary Jane shoes at the shop. And her bra size is a 34C. Medium in panties."

I growl. "How do you know her bra size?"

"Dude, relax. It's *literally* my gift to know these things."

I huff and storm out of the dorm, asking myself if I'm that easy to read. I thought I was shielding my emotions from the incubus' empathic power, but apparently, I'm not doing a great job. He even knew what I planned to buy for her.

Just thinking about picking out her panties has me hard. *Dammit*. I need to shove this attraction down.

I can't let Shayla know I've never forgotten the girl next door who had an equal amount of pain and hope shining in her eyes. I fell for her then because I know exactly what that precarious balance feels like.

Earlier, when she confessed that she had cried after I left, I almost shattered. I had been the only kid on that block who was kind to her. And over the years, I don't know how many times I almost reached out to check on her. But I had my own problems. I didn't want to drag her into my own trauma when she already had so much to deal with.

Now, I know how big of a mistake that was. But I'll never let her slip out of my life again—even if it means taking Rourke out of the picture.

FIRST DAY JITTERS

SHAYLA

I crack my eyes open and startle. I forgot that I'm at the academy now. After a rough first day in this place and Arden's healing, I slept harder than I ever have.

I deeply inhale Arden's warm sandalwood scent covering my body. It feels strange to be in his oversized shirt but also comforting. The broken-in fabric slides over my skin like silk. I shiver with the sensation, remembering how Arden's massive, muscular arms held me close last night—and how he undressed me.

I could get used to those arms wrapped around me.

The hem of his shirt is now wedged between my legs, and I'm tempted to work myself against it. But I shouldn't. Before my shower, he made it pretty clear that he only wants me as a friend. I don't blame him, since Rourke's mate bond with me is a monumental deterrent all on its own. And I'm sure he only sees me as the gawky girl from across the street.

I don't know what has gotten into me lately. Since meeting

Rourke, my libido has been fully awakened. I'm attracted to Landis and Arden—even the quiet vampire has his appeal. Before now, very few guys caught my notice. My current count is up to four. And this goes beyond knowing that they're hot. I *want* them.

Ugh… and of course, I'm now living with all of them. This is going to be torture.

I stretch and notice the hand-me-down academy uniform skirt and shirt hanging in the closet. The hems are worn, and they have a few stains. Oh, well. I can put those on after I investigate the amazing breakfast smell coming through the door. For now, I slip on Arden's shorts and cinch the drawstring tight around my waist.

As I step out of my room, I trip on a box. "What the—" I catch myself and glare at the offending hazard. I lean down to study it and wonder what it could be.

It's either a gift or a prank. Both possibilities make me uncomfortable.

"What are you doing, love?" Landis asks, coming up behind me a bit closer than I feel is appropriate as I am bent over.

I quickly stand upright and try not to blush at what I imagined. When I look, Landis isn't even that close, but his energy is so potent that it feels like he's on top of me.

"I was listening for ticking, in case it's a bomb," I joke without much humor. "It would be my luck. I'm pretty sure I've been hexed since birth."

"At least it didn't affect your good looks."

"Yeah, whatever," I scoff. He's just doing his incubus schtick. Since his smoke-gray eyes are drawing me in, I refocus on the package left at my door. "What could it be?"

"I think the trick is to *open* boxes to see what's inside them." He grins, flashing his perfect teeth and making my heart pound.

Begrudgingly, I open the large box to reveal a new academy uniform, a new pair of shiny black shoes, undergarments—all in my size. At the bottom are a full set of toiletries and new toothbrush and hairbrush. I sift around inside to see if there's a note but find nothing. I look at Landis suspiciously. "Where did this come from?"

"Not me!" He puts his hands up since he can see that I'm flustered. "I think it's a welcome package for a new student. Nothing to worry yourself over."

"Did you get one?" I ask.

"No, but this is my second year. And my mother already bought me everything I need."

"Oh, maybe Rourke's estate paid for it since they're footing the bill for this whole mating charade," I guess.

"Hey, you hungry, Sparkles?" Arden calls from the kitchen area.

"Starving. I didn't eat yesterday."

Arden lowers his eyebrows, looking irritated with me. "Why didn't you say anything last night?"

"My stomach probably couldn't have handled anything last night with my nerves so rattled."

"Sit. Eat," Arden orders.

I do as he says. Why argue with free food?

The giant druid sets a hot plate on the table in front of me. "Coffee?" he asks.

"Yes, with a teaspoon of sugar and a couple splashes of cream, if you have it." I begin to shovel food into my mouth. I see no reason to appear ladylike in front of these two since they can only be friends. And if that's the case, they will need to deal with me being me.

Landis stares while I inhale my food. Then grins when I notice him watching. "I like a woman who has a healthy appetite."

I pause in my chewing to make a point. "*Oh, please*, I'm sure you like everyone for just about every reason."

He shrugs but doesn't argue.

A beautiful cup of coffee appears before me like magic. Well, not magic, but it's pretty miraculous to have someone taking care of me. I can't remember the last time that happened. I have mostly fended for myself since I was eight. At an early age, I learned how to make basic meals, or what I usually do—graze on snacks. Even during the time I spent at Myra's, I always helped out, cooking and cleaning.

Arden sets a plate down for Landis and one for himself, and they also begin eating.

The door to Rourke's room opens, and he comes out in only pajama bottoms. And *holy fated mates*, I remember why I was tempted that night. He's truly gorgeous. His toned chest and abs are a perfect balance between buff and lean. His skin is sun-kissed and radiant. Or maybe it's his dragon shining through. He heads to the kitchen and opens the fridge, ignoring me the entire time.

I prefer it to his anger and threats. Suddenly, I feel weird wearing Arden's shirt and shorts. Is it guilt? Am I worried for Arden's sake? I don't know. I've never had to care much for anyone's opinion of me. Myra is the only one whose feelings I've ever considered before. Even that has limits, since we don't always see eye to eye.

But if Rourke takes out his anger on Arden, I will lose my shit.

Before Rourke notices and gets pissed about my borrowed pajamas, I snag my coffee and head to my room, scooting the box inside and closing the door.

After another sip of coffee, I strip off Arden's clothes and try on the stuff from the box. The simple cotton underwear and bra fit perfectly, as do a dark gray and black plaid skirt and a red button-up shirt. Someone must have gone through my things and checked for my size. The same goes for the cute doll-like shoes, which are a perfect fit. I look at the full-length mirror hanging on my closet door and barely recognize myself.

The skirt is shorter than I would like, but it isn't *too* short. I look like a real academy student.

I notice a package of women's pajamas consisting of flannel shorts and a short-sleeved shirt—very modest.

As I empty the box, I pause when I see the shampoo and body wash. It's the same scent as what was damaged during my attack—vanilla and berries. Is that a coincidence? Or did someone at the academy notice my damaged items in detail? Was it Ms. Boyd? I find it all a bit creepy, but my days of semi-privacy are probably gone forever.

I hear Arden and Landis in the showers next to my room, and my cheeks flush with the idea of them lathering up just on the other side of my wall. My heart rate spikes.

I'm going to have to get used to that. But, right now, all I can think of is how Arden's huge, muscular body might look naked and wet. If I really want to know, all I'd have to do is walk a few feet and peek. I wonder if I had asked him to join me in the shower last night, would he have stripped down and entered my stall?

I chide myself. I already have to get rid of one mate. I don't need to get attached to anyone else. I have to keep them all at a distance. But it will be hard when Arden and Landis both have something about them that makes me want to let my walls down just a bit.

Yet, I have to keep myself in check. I don't think I would be able to handle it if Arden were to reject me.

Friends? Not sure if I can handle *that* either. I will have to draw lines. Keep them only as friendly acquaintances.

I look at my new toothbrush and realize that I have to brush my teeth. However, I wait until I hear them turn off the shower and give them a couple of minutes to dry off.

The door is cracked open when I walk over. I knock on the door. "You guys decent?"

Landis chuckles. "Am I really ever, love?"

"Fine." I sigh. "Is it alright if I come in and brush my teeth?"

"You can do whatever you want in my company," Landis purrs.

I hear Arden swat Landis. Then he says, "You can come in, Sparkles."

Opening the door, I almost faint as all my blood pools to my core. Both are still glistening from their showers, their backs to me, and only a low-slung towel is wrapped around each male's waist.

They are… *ridiculous.*

I catch myself staring and avert my eyes, focusing on the available sink between the two males as they brush their teeth.

The sink is officially my lifeline now. Otherwise, I might succumb to my hormones and make an awkward attempt to seduce them.

My body heats with the vision of their rippling muscles seared into my mind. Both are so different, yet each is delicious in his own way.

I get a glimpse of Arden's druid tattoos, his solid, towering body, and broad shoulders. He's like a giant, and I'm curious about what's hidden under the towel.

Landis is far more muscular than I could discern with his clothes on but still built like a swimmer or dancer. I sense that he's both powerful and agile. A dangerous combination for his prey. On my way to the sink, I had caught a good look at his calves, and damn, I didn't know I was a calf girl until I saw his sculpted leg muscles.

My face feels hot, and I look into the mirror to see my blushing cheeks. My breath is coming in short pants. My pussy is throbbing with the vision racing through my mind of them both dropping their towels and flipping up my tiny skirt, pulling my panties aside and…

Breathe.

I splash water on my face, then attempt to stare myself into submission.

Over my shoulder, I see Landis standing behind me, checking out my new clothes.

"Looks like a perfect fit for a perfect woman."

I roll my eyes. I'm confident I'll be getting a lot of eye exercises with him around. This is his default setting—the Flirt.

I nod and adjust my skirt. "I suppose someone did a thorough job snooping through my things to get my sizes."

Arden clears his throat. "Um. You better hurry up, or you'll be late for your first class. They'll dock you points. Don't give Rourke any excuse to mess with your future."

I nod, rinse my mouth, tie my wild hair up in a ponytail, and head back to my room to grab my schedule. I read over the first-day instructions, which are mostly a bunch of stupid rules. It also states that all coursebooks will be handed out during the first session. Professors' office hours are listed, too. I note Mr. Hollis' name and his office hours. I only have a one-hour window to meet with him after my last class.

My schedule alternates between the same classes. On Monday, Wednesday, and Friday, I have my magical or academic courses. I have physical education, hands-on labs, and tutoring scheduled on Tuesday, Thursday, and Saturday.

My first class is Magicology 101. "Which way is the Ryven Building?" I call out.

"I'm going that way." Landis appears in my doorway, smiles, and is somehow already dressed. His auburn hair is still damp and messy, but he looks put together otherwise. I'm sure the messy hair is exactly how he planned it. "I'll show you."

I grab the spiral-bound notebook and a pen from my gift box. As we leave the dorm, Rourke's vampire friend heads to his bathing suite and quietly glares at us. I suppose I should learn his name.

Once we are down the hall and near the stairs, I ask, "So, what's the deal with Rourke's buddy? Does he talk?"

"Branden?" Landis shakes his head. "He doesn't talk much. And he's great at shielding his emotions. So, I know… almost nothing about him."

Worried that he can feel when I'm lusting after his body, I ask, "Can you read *most* people pretty easily?"

"Most people, yeah." He cocks an eyebrow and glances at me. "You want to know how much I get off of you?" When I nod, he continues, "I get flickers of what you feel, here and there. But I don't get as much as I should from someone who claims to have little to no magic. Did someone train you in shielding, or is that one of your innate powers?"

"I don't really believe I have magic at all."

"No indications of magic *before*... your mate thing?"

"Not that I can say for certain. I had an incident with my mom after I was with Rourke, but she might have staged the whole thing to make me come here and claim the rich asshole so she could mooch off of me."

Landis is quiet for a moment, considering my last confession. "It would be weird if you *don't* have powers and have a fated mate."

I shrug, not wanting to talk about it anymore. We fall into a comfortable silence, and he guides me toward the large building to our left.

"The classes are mostly held in the Ryven building and some in the first admin building—the one you first entered when you arrived." Landis goes into full tour guide mode with a polished, deeper resonance to his voice, and I grin. "The building directly across the beautifully landscaped quad is the other dormitory. It isn't as luxurious as ours. It also houses the teachers' apartments."

"What did you mean that the academy picked you as Rourke's roommate?"

"The magic of the academy has a random lottery and spits out the dorm roster. Some say it's a bunch of nonsense, that it's just the admin trying to break up the species' cliques. Especially the wolf shifters. They form packs and can become isolationists. Often, a few or all of the dorm mates develop into a magical coven. Although, usually, they don't put males and females in the same dorm unit anymore. So that's a nice treat for me." He winks.

I know a bit about covens. They're a group of supes who rely on each other for magical and political networking. Although, more supes are going solo—like my mother did. Often upper crust supes are now bonded to covens as a power play. And the concept of a coven circle of fated bond mates doesn't happen anymore—as far as I know.

Fate… If Rourke is any indication of Fate's bad choices, then I understand people going against fate for someone they actually want.

I glance around the quad to survey the other students heading to class. I scan the area to see if Myra is anywhere, but with no luck.

I spot some flower faeries zipping around the wild flowering shrubs. Their presence makes it finally feel like I'm in another realm. Landis smiles when he catches me with my mouth open in wonder.

I quickly drop my awe when I realize I have an audience. "Can you keep your eyes and ears out for my friend, Myra Hurst? She's about my height, shoulder-length blonde hair, blue eyes. A mage. It's her first year too."

"Not much to go on, but I'll keep a lookout. There's a good chance she'll end up in one of your first-year classes."

I notice girls giving Landis flirty smiles and little waves. Then a gorgeous shifter says, "Hi, Landis. I hope I'll see much, *much* more of you this year." She gives him a sweeping, lust-filled gaze, taking in his fine body.

And then I swear that my eyes turn from lavender to envy green.

What the hell? I might not be his girlfriend, but I *am* walking with him. I want her to back the hell up.

"Have a good day, Chara," he says pleasantly enough, but I sense he doesn't want her approaching him right now.

We keep walking, and more girls act the same as the first. All are beautiful.

"So you…" I wave and make an awkward gesture, mashing

my palms together, loosely referring to having sex. "With them?"

He studies my hand gesture with confusion and then chuckles. "If you think that represents sex, you've had rather poor lovers. I should give either you or Rourke a lesson." He raises a hopeful eyebrow.

I make a noise between a growl and a sigh. "So... have you been with *all* of these girls?"

"No need to be jealous, love." He purrs and throws an arm over my shoulders, more like a buddy than a lover, but still, my heart thumps with his proximity to me.

"I'm not jealous. I'm..." But *what am I?* "I'm curious. I don't know much about cubi. Do incubi and succubi group together like shifters do?"

"No. Mostly, we avoid each other and everyone else, unless we need to feed."

"But you haven't been avoiding me..." I make a just-got-it face. "*Oh,* because you want to snack on me," I say as the realization hits me. "I'm just your next meal."

"What?" He drops his arm and stops me from walking by jumping in my path. "I haven't been nice to you just so I could feed on you."

"Then why?" I demand.

"Can I not just want to get to know you?"

"You just said that incubi don't do that," I counter.

Landis sighs and rubs his face. Then his fingers comb back his messy auburn hair. "Yes, I would like to one day... *taste* you, but that isn't why I approached you yesterday."

The way his hunger radiates through the word *taste* sends shivers down to my core. But I reaffirm my resolve and glare at him, waiting for his explanation.

"I felt you. And it tore me up."

Did he feel my utter anguish concerning my life? Or just the pain in my body?

"*What* did you feel?"

"Everything. Like a truck slammed me in the chest."

"Why didn't you run the other way?"

"I know what it feels like to be hurting." With a flourish, Landis opens a classroom door. "And now, *you* must learn to be a supe."

I guess this is it—my first day of magic school.

My instincts scratch at my insides, urging me to run.

MAGICOLOGY 101

SHAYLA

I set Landis' comment about understanding emotional pain on my 'to be investigated' pile in the back of my mind. My entire focus is needed to pay attention in class.

I don't want to be here, but I have to be. Rourke wants me to fail, which alone makes me want to ace my courses. Until I figure out if it's in my best interest to get kicked out of this school, I will study hard. If nothing else, maybe I can find a loophole to get me out of the magical mate contract. Of course, that's unlikely. If there were a simple way that didn't entail sending me to the asylum or killing me off, Rourke's family magistrates would have known about it.

I'm still hoping the incident with my mother was some kind of trick and my mate bond is a mistake. I pray I'll be found lacking in magic. That would mean I would have to go through the painful severing of our partially bonded souls, but I'm fine with that. I'm used to pain. I'm thankful for my pain management skills now or I wouldn't be able to handle the bond's constant torment.

From what I've been told, the only reason Rourke's family just hasn't ripped us apart is that they believe Rourke will be hexed for the rest of his life if he separates from his mate without proven cause to do so. So... yeah.

Shaking off my nerves, I enter the classroom and find an open seat in the back row. A bell chimes, which sounds like it comes from the ethers, and class begins. Talk about cutting it too close. I was almost late for my first class.

Standing at the chalkboard, a tall, lanky man clears his throat. "Welcome to Magicology 101. I'm Mr. Grays. I'm sure that most of you think you know everything you need to know. But I'm here to make sure that is true. Most students will find they have holes in their knowledge."

Yeah, I have a Grand Canyon-sized hole in my knowledge. I'm just a step up from a regular human norm. My mother taught me almost nothing, not caring about my ability to function in a magical world. Ironic, since she's the one who shoved me into it as soon as my betrothal to Rourke was on the line.

"We'll start with our founding mage and her Elven consorts."

I begin to take notes. I have no clue about where we come from.

"The first mage was born a human with magic. Over a thousand years ago, with her consorts, she created the first supernaturals as we know them today... With her magic and the bond with her mates, they unleashed the magic that allows for Elven-human pairings and offspring. If it wasn't for them, we might not have any of the half-Elven mages—or shifters, vampires, cubi, druids, and many others."

A shiver runs through my body. I had heard of *her*. I'm supposed to be distantly related to her. Maybe I only inherited the human part?

"From these new hybrids between humans and elves, over the centuries, we have come to establish particular traits inherent in each branch. Some, but not all hybrids, will develop abilities outside of their traditional set. Vampires, for example, have influence or what some call compulsion, but some vampires are also able to wield magic like a mage would, such as casting spells or having a talent for prognostication."

My skin prickles with goosebumps.

Seeing the future... I've had dreams that have come true before. Was that really magic? Or coincidence? Or was my mind making an educated guess about the results of a series of events?

"Incubi and succubi, or cubi, are known for reading other people's feelings, and some can send and receive thoughts with those with whom they have bonded. A few can even communicate without a bond and outside of a feeding."

I don't like the idea of Landis reading my mind. Or my heart. Neither would make for happy reading. Besides that, I want my privacy. Especially with the thoughts about how stupidly hot he is.

"Shifters are the most varied. As you know, wolves, dragons, big cats, bears, and foxes are the most common examples. They can only change into one animal form. But there are also the rarest of shifters—the *shapeshifters*, able to change their form into a variety of people and animals. We believe they are limited to beings they personally have interacted with so that they can mimic a person's shape and their energetic signature."

Sitting next to me, a smart-looking girl raises her hand. "How common is that? I've heard that currently, there are only three shapeshifters known to exist. Is that accurate?"

"From my sources, that is true. However, some believe that there are far more shapeshifters who hide from our ruling Council since they're widely feared and closely monitored in secure facilities."

"*Shouldn't* we fear them?" the girl asks.

"Wary? Maybe. But from what we know, they do not have any abilities beyond the physical shift and heightened senses such as smell and hearing."

"But we might not know the full population," she argues. "And there might be some with abilities we know nothing about."

Mr. Grays sighs. "This is all speculation. And in my class, we deal with facts."

The teacher drones on about the historical dates and beginnings of the different species. I take notes without paying much attention to the words.

The idea of evil shapeshifters is a bogeyman story. One my mother liked to frighten me with so that I would behave.

When I was little, she tried to convince me that she was a shapeshifter and that she was always watching me—as a man on the corner, a cat on a fence, or one of my friends. I was paranoid for a long while until Arden told me it wasn't true. He explained that his grandma would have warned him if my mother were a shapeshifter. She is only a fire mage and a pathetic one, with just enough juice to frighten and torture her daughter.

At least school got me away from her grasp, even if it's not where I hoped to be.

However, if I can prove that I'm magicless, I'll be free. Screw Rourke and this stupid life.

As class finishes, I glance at my schedule and see that my next class is Arcane Magic 101. The smart girl next to me seems like she would have mapped out the entire campus already, so I smile at her. "Hi, I'm Shayla. I was wondering if you knew where Ryven room 118 is?"

She smiles smugly, "I do."

When she doesn't immediately continue, my heart drops. Being the school reject will be grueling if Landis, Arden, and Myra are the only ones who are even polite to me.

She stuffs her new Magicology tome into her bag and zips it up. "I can show you. It's my next class too." Her golden eyes glint happily at me, and I relax a bit. "If you didn't catch it during roll call, I'm Katniss. But I prefer Kat." She whips her long, silky, black locks back. She looks like she just stepped out of a shampoo commercial. Then Kat saunters out the door.

Grabbing my textbook, I hurry after her, feeling a bit like a lost puppy. I hate that. But I like having someone show me the way to class. As we walk, I check the room numbers to see if she's taking me in the wrong direction. I can't be too careful, although all appears to be okay... so far.

"Are you the fated mate everyone is talking about?" she asks, already knowing the answer.

I sigh. "I suppose I am." This is going to be tiresome.

"Sorry to hear it. Sounds like you got a bad deal. I can't imagine finding my soulmate and then getting dumped."

"Zero stars. Don't recommend," I say flatly.

Kat smirks at my joke and keeps striding like a runway model. I must look ridiculous next to this young woman dripping with sophistication.

Attempting to change the subject, I ask, "Are you a shifter?"

She eyes me and finally says, "Yeah. A fox. Go ahead, poke fun. Kat the Fox. Everyone does."

"Seriously?" I ask in disbelief. "Who makes fun of *you*?"

She stops abruptly and glares at me. "What do you mean by that?"

Stunned by her sudden hostility, I hurry to explain, "You're gorgeous. And smart. And you move with an elegant grace."

Her shoulders relax, and she palms her face. "Sorry. I'm not sure if you caught that outburst, but I also have a temper," she says sarcastically. When she removes her hand, she gives me a chagrined grin. "I was an awkward nerd until last year, so I guess I haven't come to terms with my new appearance."

"No need to apologize. I guess we're both a little prickly. I can handle it."

Her smile is wide and stunning. If I were into women, I could see myself falling for her.

"I can handle it, too. I have five older brothers who drive me nuts." Kat pauses outside the classroom. and we double-check the number. "Here we are."

The only seats available are in the front row, and we both take a seat side by side after we grab a textbook from the tall pile on the teacher's desk.

Just as the etheric chime rings in the air, a tall, dark, and handsome teacher bursts through the door. My mouth instantly goes dry. His black hair is streaked with gray at the temples. Golden eyes, much like Kat's, survey the room as a predator would, calculating and thorough.

When his gaze lands on me, my breath hitches as our eyes lock. In these few seconds, I know that he's a force of nature. He embodies alpha maleness and powerful magic. It's intimidating as hell. But I don't back down and avert my eyes—partly because I'm stubborn and partly because I'm stunned by his presence.

He sniffs the air, almost imperceptibly.

Does he smell how my body just responded to him?

He's a shifter. They might be able to do that. Although, I doubt I was the only one in the room to have that kind of reaction to this male.

Finally, he breaks our eye contact. It feels like he has cut my tether, and I fall back into my seat.

Holy crapola. I'm done for. I can only pray that I can focus enough to pass the class.

When he speaks, his deep, authoritative voice jolts me out of my fantasies, commanding every ounce of my attention. "Mr. Randall is unavailable for the foreseeable future. So I will be taking over this class until further notice. I'm Quade Hollis. I usually have the privilege of teaching more advanced magic studies, so pay attention. I hate repeating myself over the basics. Got it?"

The class is dead quiet.

"Got it?" he demands that we answer.

We all startle in our seats. "Got it!" we say in unison.

Hollis... Great, my personal advisor is a hot drill sergeant. Just what I need to make this hell complete.

As he runs through roll call, I debate whether I should ask for another advisor. How am I supposed to handle all this sexy in a teacher *and* an advisor?

"Myra Hurst?" Mr. Hollis calls, and I snap out of my internal debate. "Myra Hurst?"

Whipping around in my seat, I search the room for my friend, but I don't see her.

What's going on? She's supposed to be here. Myra had been accepted into this academy and excitedly anticipated attending.

I run through a whole list of reasons why she might not be here. If she were a human, she might have a cold, but that doesn't happen to a supe. Maybe her grandmother passed away. I know that she wasn't doing well. To calm my nerves, I rationalize that there must be a simple explanation, but my fears continue to nag me. Something bad must have happened. Could she have been hurt like I was? Attacked because she was my friend? I will have to swing by the healer, Ms. Boyd, and ask.

I'm vaguely aware as Hollis continues through the roll call. "Katniss Kincaid?"

"Here."

My mind spins, wondering if there's a way to communicate with her parents back in the mortal realm.

"Shayla Willows?" he calls.

Kat bumps my foot, and I jump. "Here!"

Hollis blinks lazily at me like a perturbed feline, but I know he's probably a wolf shifter. "Don't be late for our meeting after school," he warns with a bite to his voice.

"Yes, sir," I breathe out, feeling stupid. Yeah, this relationship hasn't started off on a good foot. He thinks I'm an idiot. And why did I use the word *relationship*? But for the life of me, I can't think of another word to use.

I take notes as he begins his lecture. Worried about Myra, my mind barely engages as he explains the different kinds of magic.

Innate magic—what a species naturally inherits—includes self-healing and shifting.

Arcane magics consist of things such as spells, potions, and sigils.

Prognostication and illusions can be either innate, arcane, or a mix.

"Innate magic obviously relies on the strength of the supernatural being wielding it. Some natural talents, such as healing, can be amplified by arcane tools like potions. Divination can be a useful tool for any magical practitioner, but it's dangerous for many reasons. First, the future's not set, and to believe it is, makes it set. So, like that old adage, as above so below, what we hold true inside ourselves can manifest in our reality. The second reason divination is dangerous is that it can be used as a weapon. If you know where your enemies will be or what they plan to do, you can stop them."

My mind is reeling with the info dump.

Mr. Hollis pauses and gives us a grin. The small act reinvents his already beautiful face into something mesmerizing.

Fuck me. I'm toast.

"Now you're asking yourselves why is stopping your enemies bad?" he continues.

I wasn't thinking about anything. My mind has gone blank. But yeah, sure. Go on, explain.

"Because your enemies could use it to stop *you*."

Without realizing that I'm interrupting, I ask, "But couldn't it be used in a positive way? Like… to find a missing person?"

His laser-like focus falls on me, and I cringe. By the look on his face, he doesn't like his lectures to be interrupted with annoying questions.

"That would be a location spell... which falls under...?" he prompts.

"Um, arcane magic?"

"Is that your answer or a question?" he asks.

I straighten my shoulders, my ire beginning to rise with his frustration. He is a teacher, after all, and I wasn't off-topic. "That's my answer."

"Correct." He steals the class's attention back from me and paces away, staring out the window. "Yes, to your question. Any magic can be used with ill intent or with good *intentions*. However, if we allow power to consume us, we might lose our moral compass and harm others in what we *believe* is a cause for the greater good. Many tyrants, supes and norms both, have thought they were the heroes of the world and not the villains they truly were."

At the end of his lecture, he dismisses us with an assignment to read through the first chapter before our next class.

"What do you have next?" Kat slides her book into her pack.

I check my sheet again. "English 201. Main Hall, room 209."

"That's back at the main admin building, to the left, up the stairs," she informs me and then pulls me out of the way as Mr. Hollis barges past me and out of the classroom. "Wow."

"Yeah, wow." Then I look at her. "Wait, what do *you* mean by wow?"

"You."

"Me?" My eyes widen. "What did I do?"

She pulls me close and whispers, "You have the hots for the teacher."

"No, I don't!" I jerk my arm back. "He's handsome, sure, but—"

"I could smell it. So could he, I'm sure."

My face turns bright, flaming red. "Kill me now. I couldn't be the only one to react to him?"

"Fortunately, no." She smirks playfully at me. "But I suggest sitting toward the back for our next class."

"That's not going to help during my private tutoring sessions," I groan.

Kat shakes her head in amusement. "You're so screwed... or you want to be!" She snorts at her own joke, and I clearly see the nerd hidden under her glamorous exterior. "Well, on that note, we'll both be screwed if we don't get to our next class. Want to meet up for lunch? I could meet you outside of the admin building in the quad?"

"Sure," I call out as I race down the halls to the Main Administration Building.

13

LUNCH

SHAYLA

*E*nglish 201 is uneventful and familiar.

Our teacher, Ms. Waithe, asks us to write an essay on what magical life we see for ourselves after graduation. Strolling down the halls to meet with Kat, I contemplate my precarious future. If I were to remain in the magical world, what would I want to do?

Would I end up with Rourke, having a contentious marriage, rotting away my years with someone who despises me? Or would I be able to sever our bond and run off as I originally planned to do?

Fantasizing about my limited options, I let my guard down as I stroll down the halls. Suddenly, a blunt object hits my lower back, and I fly forward and fall to the ground. My books and papers sprawl out in front of me, with students intentionally trampling on them.

Awesome.

Several snickers come from behind me. I pull down my short skirt, thankful for my new clean, full-coverage underwear.

I try to pick myself up onto my hands and knees. Another force slams me down flat again. I whip my head around to see who is messing with me.

Of course, it's Millie and the same nasty group who jumped me when I arrived in the fae realm. Several other students pass me by, some giving me curious or disgusted glances. Some ignore me altogether, as if I were not even worth a glance.

I have to get out of this school. Maybe I can convince Rourke to let this whole charade go. Maybe he'll help me escape if I promise never to show my face in the magical world again.

Ms. Boyd appears in front of me and begins picking up my things. She eyes the snickering gang behind me and says loudly, "Shayla, when I find out who attacked you when you arrived, I'll make sure that they aren't just expelled from school but that they are committed to the Ravenhollow Asylum for illegal use of magic and attempted murder."

I stare at Ms. Boyd, wondering if she would do such a thing. Her gentle face has taken on a hard edge, and her kind eyes glare at the gang with a fierceness that makes me shiver.

Reminder—don't get on this woman's bad side.

The gang quickly disperses after the all-too convincing threat.

"Thanks," I mumble as I attempt to take my gathered things from her grasp.

Ms. Boyd holds on to them. "Was that *them*? Was it Millie?" she whispers.

"I just want to survive long enough to escape this place," I answer instead of confirming her suspicions.

"Very well." She lets go of my things. "If you aren't going to call them out, then you need to be more aware of the dangers surrounding you."

My jaw clenches. It feels like she's blaming the victim. But I should have been more vigilant. It's just... I'm so damned tired. I'm tired of constantly being on alert for danger.

When will I be able to relax without expecting the worst from everyone and everything? I fear the answer may be never.

"How are you recovering?" she asks while inspecting me with her healer's gaze.

"Much better today, thanks." I shrug. "I should go."

"Do you want me to clean up your scrapes?" she asks.

"I'm fine." I wave her off. "It's nothing."

She sighs. "Okay, but I want to give you a checkup tomorrow after your classes, alright?"

I nod curtly and hurry off to meet up with Katniss.

When she sees me enter the quad, Kat's eyes widen. "What the hell happened to you?"

I glance down at myself and notice that my knees are bleeding from the fall. It looks much worse than it is. Although, now that I tune in to my body, I feel the sting.

From out of our dorm building, Arden appears, carrying two large, brown paper bags with the Heritage Café dragon logo stamped on them. His eyes lock onto me and then slide down to my bloodied knees. In a flash, he storms over, faster than I thought he could move. I guess those long, powerful legs aren't just decorative and for my viewing pleasure.

He comes to a halt a few inches away, towering over me. "What. Happened?" He growls low. I'd think he was a wolf shifter if I didn't know better.

I crane my head back to look up at him. "I fell." There's no point getting into this. I don't need him retaliating and getting kicked out. "It's just a couple of scrapes. No biggie."

His vibrant green eyes narrow on me. He knows I'm holding back.

Kat clears her throat and cuts the odd tension. "Um, Shayla, did you want to go to the cafeteria and grab something?"

Arden turns and studies Kat with suspicion.

"She helped me find my class earlier. Kat's cool," I assure him.

After probably confirming with his own senses, Arden nods once, acknowledging me. He lifts the two large bags. "I have food. There's enough for all of us."

I blink. Did he buy lunch for me? It's one thing for him to make me breakfast, but it seems excessive for him to buy a ton of food when we didn't even plan to meet up. But I'm assuming, and maybe he had bought it all for himself. "You don't need to share your lunch."

"It isn't a big deal."

"It is." From my skirt's tiny pocket, I remove a twenty-dollar bill. "They take mortal money at the academy, right?" I offer him the cash. "Here."

"Put that away." Arden hands me a bag. "I'm not *sharing*. I got this for you."

Katniss raises her eyebrows and glances at the two of us appreciatively.

To stop her assumptions, I introduce them. "Uh, Arden, this is Kat. Kat, this is my childhood *friend*, Arden." I emphasize the word friend, so she'll take the hint.

They nod a greeting.

"I saved us a bench," Kat offers. As we head over to the spot she claimed with her backpack, she informs me, "If you need to buy stuff, purchases go onto your school account."

"But I don't have an account."

"I'm sure Rourke's estate has set one up for you. Although it might be a measly amount," Arden explains.

I make a mental note to look into an account in case the school doesn't take my cash. I can't allow Arden to foot the bill for my meals. I'll pay everyone back for what's spent on me, even Rourke. I was planning on surviving on my nest egg when I ran away, but I'll just have to use it here. I don't want to owe Rourke anything, even if he can afford it.

"I can't have you buying my meals anymore—" I begin to lecture Arden, but he frowns as if he were a bit hurt, so I amend. "I already feel like a burden. Please don't make me feel like a charity case. I have my nest egg. I'll pay you back."

He doesn't say a thing but instead looks down at my scraped knees. "I'm going to mend your wounds." He doesn't wait for my permission and places his giant hand on my thigh above the knee.

My core instantly heats with the contact. Why does a simple, innocent touch make me react like a nymph? My cheeks heat up, and I know that they're now pink. I squirm. "Uh, it's not that bad."

His hand tightens on my thigh, firm and authoritative. This only makes me want to squirm more and have him move his fingers higher. His warm, electric touch would feel like heaven between my thighs.

With that arousing thought, my panties are ruined.

Kat pulls some of the food from the bag Arden offered and begins to eat and watch our interactions like this is her new favorite TV program.

A few moments later, the lacerations are sealed, and he removes his huge hand. I kind of wish he had left it there, but no. I remind myself—*friend*. No. Friendly acquaintance.

Arden pulls a napkin from his bag, then wets it from a water bottle in his pack. He wipes the drying blood, taking his time with long, slow strokes.

I grab the napkin, feeling so weird about my reaction. I love that he's taking care of me… a little too much. "I got it. Thanks! I'm not a child."

Right then, Landis shows up with two lunch bags. "Now it's a party." He looks at Kat for a moment longer than is necessary. They exchange names efficiently. I wonder if maybe he wants to feed on her, too. I don't like that thought one bit.

He quickly shakes himself out of his inspection of my new

friend and says to me with a dimpled grin, "I brought you something." He swings a bag as if to tempt me.

"I already got her something," Arden says with irritation.

"Well, you can *never* have too much of a good thing." Landis smiles and winks at me.

"That is the opposite of the expression," Kat says with a chuckle.

"Not in an incubus' world." Landis waggles his eyebrows. Such a flirt. He hands me the bag and sits down on the grass in front of us. Then he notices the blood on the napkin, my scuffed shoes, and my damaged books. He tenses—all humor evaporated. His gray eyes grow a shade darker. "What happened?"

Arden glares at me, daring me to lie to the empath.

"I... fell."

"While that is technically accurate, I don't believe that is the whole story, love." Landis narrows his eyes and then flicks a knowing look at Arden.

"It doesn't matter." I shrug and scrounge inside the lunch bag for something to distract myself. "I have bigger concerns. Is there a way to contact the mortal realm?"

"Why?" Landis asks, sounding concerned.

"My friend should be here. But she wasn't in the class I was supposed to have with her."

"Maybe she switched classes?" Arden offers. "Sometimes schedules shift last minute during the start of the semester when students' needs are still being worked out."

"I don't know..." My eyes scan the quad. "I just would have thought I'd see her by now. Landis, did you ask around about her or see anyone matching her description?"

"I kept an eye out, but my classes are more advanced. And there's not much crossover to freshman classes."

"You could check with the administration," Kat offers. "They might tell you something. But to contact the mortal realm directly takes a lot of magic, and they don't use it on what they might consider a trivial thing."

"Besides, she might be here already," Arden says, but I hear doubt leaking into his words.

"If I don't run across her by tomorrow, I'll ask the staff," I say, hoping they're all correct—that there's nothing to be worried about.

14

OFFICE HOURS

SHAYLA

*A*fter lunch, I have Sacred Geometry, which is supposed to satisfy my college math requirements. And Potion Fundamentals, funnily enough, qualifies as Chemistry for the mortals' accreditation our administration has set up. For both classes, I'll be able to get a passing grade since they don't rely on magic to pass.

They should be uneventful, based on the course curriculum. However, I worry about my Potions *Lab*, where practitioners must have innate magic to activate spells. And since it's assumed that I'm a mage until proven otherwise, I must take it. For the lab, I know that I'll fail miserably since I don't feel any magic inside me.

My gut clenches as my last class lets out. Now I have to face Mr. Hollis up close and personal. My pulse races with that thought—worried about how my body might react to being so close to him and because he's intimidating as hell.

As for my libido, I try to remind myself that he's probably a raging jerk. And I'm full up on my jerk quota. That thought brings my body back under my control. I just hope it stays that way throughout our meeting.

Standing outside his office door, I stare at it. For so many reasons, I don't want to go inside. First, he might tell me I'm indeed magical and must complete the bond with Rourke. Second, my body might react to his presence the way it did in class. Third, I will definitely make a fool of myself no matter what.

A presence crowds up behind me from nowhere, and a deep voice asks, "What are you doing?"

"Stars!" I yelp, completely caught off guard. I was so in my head that I hadn't felt the presence until it was too late. This isn't like me.

I flinch away, and I hear a sniff. Dropping my books, my hands come up to fight whatever weirdo assault this is.

Mr. Hollis.

He smirks at my weak attempt to fend him off, looks at my discarded books on the floor, then to my surprise, he corrects my fighting form. "Hold your arms like this and twist a bit." He shifts my shoulders.

Stunned by his actions, I let him correct my form. When he nods his approval, I quickly shake out of it and drop my arms to my sides. I back away until I am pressed against the door.

"I don't recommend submitting to your opponent until all avenues are exhausted," he says in his lazy teacher's voice that vibrates down my body.

Dammit. He really is disarming.

My wits come back to me finally, and I glare at him. "Is that what you are? My opponent? I thought you were supposed to teach me—be my advisor." I cross my arms over my chest, feeling vulnerable under his intense gaze.

"Everyone is an opponent. If you don't understand that, you will soon enough." He nudges my shoulder with the back of his hand, indicating that I move out of his doorway.

I do, and while he mutters a chant to unlock his office, I pick up my books.

Mr. Hollis strolls in and sits behind his desk. He leans back in his chair and casually laces his fingers behind his head, eyeing me as I walk in. "Close the door," he orders.

I gulp as I turn back to the door. It feels like a trap. But it's probably just my anxiety about this meeting and his aggressive behavior.

Sitting down, I place the stack of school books on my lap.

Mr. Hollis looks relaxed, but I see the hidden tension in his graceful, muscular body as he watches me like the predator he is. At a moment's notice, he could easily spring on me, shift, and rip out my throat.

Although seeing him with his jacket off, rolled-up sleeves revealing his corded forearms, and his shirt stretched tight over his biceps, I realize that he could probably rip out my throat *without* his beast.

Unwittingly, I rub my neck.

His pupils dilate, taking in my movements.

Will this guy talk already? I suspect the uncomfortable silence is for intimidation. He's probably willing to let it drag on until I crack and say something.

Yet, the stubborn part of me that wants to avoid this entire conversation keeps my mouth shut.

Hollis stares down his nose at me. "What *are* you?" he finally asks with a hint of distaste.

"I thought that was what you were supposed to tell me." I return his cold stare. "I'm a null."

"Don't think so." He unlaces his fingers and sits forward, elbows on his desk. "You passed the entrance test."

"Fluke." I lean back. This guy doesn't have a clue if I have any magic. Why was I worried that he would tell me that I did? "I have elven blood... the portal must have responded to that."

"Not everyone with elven blood has magic, and those who don't, can't get in."

I shrug. "I've never displayed magical abilities before."

Hollis glowers at me. "Not what I read in your file. You blew up your kitchen."

"I believe that was my mother's trick, trying to convince the Lewellyn family that I'm bonding material." I roll my eyes, look out his window and gaze at the forbidden forest beyond the academy wall. Perhaps I could escape and live out my days there in peace?

He cuts into my daydream, "Speaking of which, your magic initiated a mating bond with a damned *Lewellyn*? You're quite ambitious."

I whip my gaze back to him. "One, I didn't even know his name when *we*..." I stumble at confessing my sexual history with this male. Then I recover, "When *we* accidentally initiated the bond. And two, that *might* suggest I have magic, but it's inconclusive."

He chuffs and shakes his head. "Why the games? The *I-don't-have-magic* angle doesn't get you any closer to all that money and power." He leans forward even more. His golden eyes seem to glow with magic. This conversation reminds me too much of my mother's attacks.

"Screw you!" I snap.

He launches himself to his feet and zips around the desk. His hands land on my armrests, bracketing me in but not touching me. His face is inches from mine. I can feel his heat, his breath. His scent reminds me of vanilla and leather-bound books.

It takes all my emotional strength, but I don't flinch from his intimidating stance. Bullies, like my mother, keep coming when their victims show weakness.

"What *are* you?" he growls, and his teeth elongate.

He's on the verge of a shift.

"Nothing!" I snarl back, but my reaction doesn't have the same resonance and power as his voice.

He sniffs me again, and his eyes flare brightly with magic.

What did he just sense about me?

"I don't want power or money," I continue. "I don't want to be entangled with Rourke or his family. I plan to prove my null status and get the hell out of here."

"So you just spread your legs to some nameless stranger? Is that a common occurrence for you? I notice you also have your sights on both the druid and incubus."

I shove at his chest to make him back up, but my weakling human form doesn't have a chance of budging a powerful shifter. With the contact, my fingers tingle as if I was zapped by an electrical outlet. It must be a ward or his innate protective magic.

"Back off!" Tears well in my eyes, but I don't let myself cry. This is all too much. Everything has been too much. I feel hopeless as he glowers at me. Judging me. Thinking I'm a power-hungry, gold-digging whore and manipulator. "Landis and Arden are my dorm mates. That's it! I'm not *after* them."

"Hmm." Slowly, Hollis backs away, studying me the entire time, not even blinking. "Not yet."

I move to get up and leave. Hollis flicks his hand, and a focused blast of wind tosses me back into my seat. Whoa, he has some powerful air magic. At least it isn't fire.

I can't leave, so I defend myself with words. "Even if I was after all of them, which I'm not. So *what?* Are you Rourke's lapdog?"

He leans over me again, making me lean back in my chair. "I'm no one's *dog*, especially not the Lewellyns."

"Then why are you coming at me like *I'm* the asshole here?"

"Because you're playing some strange and dangerous game with one of the most powerful and ruthless supernatural families. You're either stupid, or you're *greedy* stupid."

"I guess I'm just plain ole stupid stupid," I say with an even tone. "What the hell has you so riled up about this? I thought you were supposed to help me with my magic. Not get involved in my sex life." Shit, did I just say it like that?

All the steam in him hisses out, and he pulls away, walking to the window and staring out into the forest. He sighs wearily. "I was trying to bring forth your magic, trigger it to protect you."

I sit quietly with that thought for a moment. "That might be partially true, but you seem to have something against the Lewellyns too."

"The Lewellyns are bad news." He turns around to face me again. His eyes are their usual amber now—his magic packed away for the moment. "As far as your magic goes, I can sense that you have some, but not exactly *what*. If I had to guess, it would be that you are a mage like your mother."

My blood boils at the thought of being compared to my mother. "I hope I'm *nothing* like her."

"Well, since you don't know who your father is or was, we don't have much to go on. Not without you presenting some affinity."

"Is that why you keep sniffing me? To catch a scent of my magic?"

"It's a specialty of mine. I've pretty much ruled out a shifter or a vamp. I suppose you could be a succubus."

"Oh, yeah, because I'm so loose, since a nameless dragon took my damned virginity?" I blurt out sarcastically and turn red when I realize what I've said.

"*Took* your virginity?" Hollis' eyes flare golden again. "Did he force you?" His voice is restrained, but I sense that his beast is barely controlled. His body is locked, coiled, and vibrating.

"No. Not like that. It was… consensual." I look down, and embarrassment floods every cell in my body. I'm uncomfortable talking about my sex life, and it feels even weirder telling my hot professor the details. "I need to explain. Rourke is a… jerk, but he didn't force me. I thought I met a nice human guy—who was actually attracted to me. We flirted and kissed. We decided to keep it casual, without knowing each other's names. I agreed since I was planning on escaping my mother and the magical world. We were at a norms party, and neither of us realized the other had supernatural origins, until…"

"Until the bonding magic happened." His voice is more gentle now. He strides forward and moves my hair away from my neck to check for a bite. "He didn't mark you?"

"His teeth grazed me several times, but no, not a *mating* bite."

"That's why they think they can sever the bond," he says to himself. Something changes in his demeanor.

Maybe he doesn't see me as the bad guy.

Mr. Hollis sits on the edge of his desk and clears his throat. "Uh, did he have… a knot? Did he… Were you compatible… physically? He didn't injure you?"

I flush pink again. "I was able to, um, take it."

Mr. Hollis swallows down the awkwardness and slips back into teacher mode. "That indicates you have dragon or wolf shifter somewhere in your lineage."

I sigh. "So that's another strike against me getting out of the bond, isn't it?"

His intense gaze locks onto me in such a way that I can't look away. He claims every ounce of my attention. "Do you realize his family intends to prove that you're unstable, unable to control your magic, and commit you to Ravenhollow so they can maintain their honorable pretense and safely break this bond without a curse?"

"I got that impression, yes."

"Miss Willows, you have magic. Maybe not much. Or maybe it hasn't manifested properly yet, but you have enough to no longer be considered a null." He rubs his perfect hair, mussing it, and adds, "Do you know how bad the asylum is?"

It can't be as bad as they say, right? Wouldn't supes throw a fit if the inmates were abused? I shrug. "My mother threatened me with it all the time."

A growl rumbles in his throat. "Supernaturals who end up at this so-called mental hospital don't come out. Yet, it's more than a prison. It's a death sentence. If the supes weren't insane when they go in, they are within a short time. And for everyone's safety, they're put out of their misery."

I believe him. He has no reason to lie to me that I know of.

A chill runs down my spine. All the stories, all the warnings, they are real. "*Killed?*"

He nods. His hand cups my shoulder in the act of consolement. "I realize that's the last thing you want to hear, but if you are to survive this, you must access and master your magic. Or you *will* be sent away... and *never* heard from again."

I don't know if it's because he's acting so compassionately, but I'm tearing up. My dreams of freedom have been ripped away from me, and I now feel hollow.

"And if I master my magic, then what? For the rest of my life, I'm supposed to be chained to someone who hates me?" My voice cracks with the thought.

"Maybe." He sighs. "Or maybe there's another way to dissolve the bond contract. For now, let's just focus on bringing out your magic and controlling it."

15

ANOTHER DAY

SHAYLA

I have no appetite when I return to my dorm room. Fortunately, Rourke and Branden aren't here, and Arden and Landis don't press me to explain why I look like I've been crying. Perhaps everyone cries after visiting Mr. Hollis.

"I have lots of reading to do," I say, which is the truth. I'm behind most students with what I know. I will have to work much harder now that I know I won't be allowed to leave.

I have magic.

Mr. Hollis' words bounce around in the empty cavern where my dreams of freedom once existed.

A bit later, as I come out of my room to use the bathroom, Arden steps in front of me. "Hey," he says softly.

"Hey." I drop my gaze to the floor.

"I know you want to pay your own way, but I know you haven't had a chance to buy anything at the commissary yet. So let me get dinner and breakfast for now, and you can get me back another time."

"Okay." I finally look up at him, and his earnest, vibrant green eyes undo me. "Thanks." I feel myself about to cry. Why can't I handle someone actually being nice to me?

"Sparkles, what's wrong?" His huge hands cradle my face.

I want to deflate and dangle from his hold like a rag doll. Instead, I lean forward, and he captures me in a hug. His powerful arms encircle me, and I want to live in this embrace forever. His presence is so huge that I wonder if I can hide from the world, safely tucked away in a friend's hug.

"I'm making a casserole," he says, and I chuckle. "What's so funny?"

"You look like a Viking god, and you're doing something so... domestic."

He tightens his hold playfully. "I thought it was *strategic*."

"How so?" I ask, nuzzling into his chest, listening to his pounding heart. Why does it always sound like it's thrumming too fast, or beating too hard? Maybe because he's so tall.

"Well, I figure we can eat this, then have leftovers for a couple of days. Leaves more time for other stuff."

Reluctantly, I pull back to look up at him again. "Very smart. A warrior's move." I smirk.

"Damn straight." He drops a kiss on top of my head, and my skin warms from his attention. "Now, go clean up. Food's almost ready."

When I come back out of the bathroom, Landis has joined Arden in the kitchen. He's heating up something on the stove.

"How was your first day?" Landis asks.

"A lot." I look around to see if I can help, but Arden has already set the table. "Anything I can do?"

"Yes, you can sit and relax." Arden gives me a panty-dropping grin. "Let me do my *warrior* thing."

I plop down at the end of the table and watch Landis and Arden move fluidly around the kitchen. I notice an easy camaraderie developing between them, which eases my aching soul.

In the morning, Arden's back in the kitchen.

Exiting my room, I see a new box sitting near my door. "What's this?"

"Delivered this morning. Probably stuff someone forgot to put in your welcome package," Landis says, strolling past me to the bathroom.

I peek inside and see a backpack, a set of gym clothes, and sneakers. "I suppose I need to look into my mysterious school account soon." This stuff doesn't look cheap. I don't look forward to dipping into my nest egg to pay back the Lewellyns.

"Don't forget your appointment with the healer." Arden smiles, mentioning his aunt.

"I won't." I sigh. "I just don't know if I should go before or after my next session with Mr. Hollis."

"Don't piss off Hollis. See him first." Arden warns, "He's... moody."

I give him a wry expression. "I've noticed."

After shoveling down breakfast, I grab my uniform and rush to the showers. I place a towel on the outside hook and strip down inside the center stall, tossing my pajamas over the frosted door, so they don't get wet.

"Wow. Kind of feels like a burlesque show," Landis says, walking by my stall.

"Yeah, a low-budget burlesque show," I joke, turn on the water, and he does the same in his stall.

I hear Arden step into the third shower stall. *Fuck.* They are both so close to me, naked and rubbing their bodies... I choke down a groan. With Landis' incubus powers, can he sense that I want my hand to drop between my legs and relieve this tension?

"It's *hard* for me," Landis says, echoing my inner feelings.

Oh, Goddess, he knows that I'm lusting after them.

"Landis!" Arden warns. "Knock it off."

"What? *I* believe in being *honest.*"

There's something else going on with his comment, but I don't have the mental focus to figure it out. Maybe he's hinting about how I secretly feel about them?

"Well, you don't need to vocalize every damn thing that comes to mind," Arden grumbles.

"Oh, believe me, I don't." Landis chuckles softly.

"I'm going to get out and get dressed," I announce as I pull the towel off the hook outside my shower door and wrap it around my body. "Can you give me a second?"

Dripping wet, I race over to the counter where my clothes are set on the vanity. The towel barely covers me, and I jump when Landis turns off his water.

"Has it been a second?" he asks as his shower door swings open.

I shield my eyes, even if every other instinct tells me to look.

As I hurry to the toilet room for privacy, I trip on my own wet feet, twist, and crash to the floor.

"Shit!" I squeak out.

Landis and Arden are both crouching over me, soaking wet. Their towels are dangerously close to revealing their family jewels. I avert my gaze, swatting Arden away when he tries to help me up.

Dangling from Landis' fingertip is my underwear. I snatch it back and glare at him.

Arden gathers the rest of my clothes from the floor. "Are you okay?"

"I'm fine," I huff. "I might have bruised my ego and my ass, but I'll be okay."

"You should probably heal that right now, Arden," Landis says with a twinkle in his eye. "Remember, direct contact is best."

Arden glares at him. "Maybe you should stop being such an in—"

Landis cuts him off with a snap, "An incubus?"

Arden shakes his head and sighs. "No. An *inconsiderate* jerk. Shayla obviously feels uncomfortable about our housing arrangement. You don't have to make it *more* awkward."

Landis bites his lip and then finally nods. "Shayla, I was just teasing you. I didn't expect you to get hurt."

"I know." I wish I could open a portal and fall through to avoid this awkwardness. "I'll just get up earlier and take showers before you guys, so I won't make it weird."

"Fuck," Landis hisses. "I'm sorry. I wasn't thinking. Usually supes don't think much about nudity. I guess this has to be hard on you with… your mate so close."

"Thanks." Hearing a genuine apology from someone makes my eyes misty. "But I don't want you to be uncomfortable either. It's just that I don't know how to act around other people. Well, with *guys* and with…" I wave my hand in their direction. And then quickly adjust my towel when it begins to slip. "…all this flesh."

Their eyes flicker over to my exposed skin.

"Uh, I better get dressed." I thumb toward the door. Clumsily, I scramble to my feet, grab my stuff from Arden, and rush out of the bathroom, my clothes clutched in my hands.

Rourke is on his way to his own bathroom and catches sight of my barely concealed body. I'm sure my eyes are wide and my cheeks pink with embarrassment. His eyes dart to the open bathroom door with Arden and Landis talking inside. "You just run around naked with them now, huh?"

"Don't." I throw one hand up to emphasize my statement. "I'm not in the mood for your bullshit."

"Bullshit?" He stops and glares at me. "You are *my* mate."

"Yeah, and I'm here in this mess because of you. Besides, I'm not doing a damn thing but going to school. I'm sure you don't want me in your bathroom. So leave me the fuck alone right now." When I walk a couple of steps to my room, I have a slight limp.

"Hey." Rourke blinks at me, and then he growls, "Did they hurt you?"

"Nothing happened. I'm sorry to inform you that your rejected mate is a klutz. Deal with it." I slam my bedroom door shut and exhale when I hear him enter his bathing suite.

On Tuesdays, Thursdays, and Saturdays, my first class is Physical Magic, which is basically P.E.. I thought I was done with sweaty locker rooms, but no, the fun never ends.

Landis offers to escort me to the far end of campus so I don't get lost on my way to class.

As we stroll through the halls, girls drool over Landis—yet again. I attempt to ignore his admirers and my unjustified possessiveness, and instead scan the sea of students for Myra.

Trying to sound casual, I ask, "So, Kat's cool, huh?"

"Wow." He laughs. "You're really bad at this."

"At what?" I ask innocently. "She's nice to me. And she's gorgeous."

"I didn't realize you were into the ladies," he mocks, knowing it isn't true, based on his innate incubus magic.

"I'm not, but *you* are into females, right?" I prompt.

"I lean toward the feminine, but I've been attracted to males too," he confesses.

"Really?" My eyes unfocus as I imagine how hot that would be.

Landis clears his throat, and I jerk back to our conversation. "Pawning me off already? You didn't even try my wares."

"Your *wares*?" I laugh. "Is that what you call *it?*" I nod toward his groin.

"You can name my cock anything you want as long as you cry out my name too," he says seductively.

And now, all I can think of is what he looks like naked and how he might make me cry out.

Then I remember that I shouldn't get involved. Not with anyone. Rourke will hurt them out of pure dragon spite.

Landis senses my mood shift. "Your new friend is cute, but I'm good."

"Already have a meal lined up?"

"I've been eyeing a certain menu. But I'm not sure if I can afford it." He glances up and down my body with a dark, hungry gaze. "However, I might sacrifice everything just to have a *taste* of something so damned sweet."

Holy Shadowcock.

I suppose all women feel this way around an incubus... like I'm the center of his world in the moments we share. But then I remember, I'm not. Even if I could be with him, this is just his nature. Being intimate with Landis wouldn't *mean* anything more to him than feeding his power.

And my heart would be broken for the second time this year.

Fortunately, the welcome box that arrived this morning had a pair of white sneakers, red gym shorts, and a gold tee-shirt—our school colors. Yeah, school spirit!

I'm assigned a locker to hold my clothes and bag. While half-naked and changing into my workout gear, someone slams into me so hard that I fall off the bench.

"Back off," a fellow female student warns.

When I look up to glare at my attacker, I recognize her from Landis' many admirers, Chara. I wonder if they have something going on.

"Back off of *what* exactly?" I ask, not assuming I know what she means, since it could also be about Rourke. I stand up and don't bother to hide more than what my bra and underwear cover.

"Don't play dumb," she snarls. "You claimed the dragon, and now you're going after *my* incubus."

"He didn't mention he was taken." I shrug. "And I didn't *claim* either male. Have them both. I don't give a shit." I cross my arms. "Are we done with the theatrics?"

Chara narrows her eyes, reading me, but I'm sure I'm only giving screw-off vibes. Part of me *wants* to claim both males, the animalistic, sexual aspect of my nature. However, my rational brain says, *Run.*

"Landis is *mine*," she growls.

"Message received." I drop my hand to pick up my gym shorts. "But you might want to let him know."

"Chara, we're going to be late for class," her friend calls.

She huffs, leaves me to slip on my gym clothes, and follows her friends to the training field.

A tiny, super sporty shifter female calls the whole class to her in the center of the track and field area. I glance around to see who else is in the group and spot Kat. I maneuver over to stand next to her. She grins when she sees me.

"Hello, class! I'm Ms. Banks." Her medium-length blonde locks are tied back in a high ponytail. She has a whistle around her neck.

I'm having flashbacks to high school, and my stomach twists.

"We're going to discover your level of health and endurance. To practice magic, you must be of a fit mind *and* body. During your entire attendance at Shadowcraft, you'll continue your fitness and combat training. Occasionally, I will have guest teachers drop in to teach a skill they're particularly knowledgeable about. But mostly, this class will be about enhancing your basic physical fitness with me."

Looking at the large mass of students, a mix of males and females, I search again for Myra, but I don't see her.

"We're going to see how many times you can make it around this track in the next hour," Ms. Banks announces and blows her whistle.

"Great," I mutter.

Kat giggles. "You can't hate running that much."

"Oh, yes, I can. I'm pretty sure running is a shifter preference. Whatever I am is diametrically opposed to such behavior."

"Come on. I can help pace you," Kat offers.

"I appreciate the offer, but you shouldn't. Get a good mark on this. I'll only hold you back."

She frowns but sees the wisdom in my words and takes off at a quick pace. I begin to jog. If I have to do this, I should ease into it. As I pass close to the woods, I feel a creepy sensation that someone is watching me. I don't doubt that I'm being watched by Chara and her jealous, possessive cronies. But this feels strange. I shake it off when I can't pinpoint who's watching.

Even though I pace myself, after an hour, I'm flushed and winded. Running is so not my gig.

"Willows," Ms. Banks says as I pass her. "You need to pick up your overall time. It was… unimpressive."

"I don't run," I say through gasping breaths.

"If a predator is chasing you, you'll need to run," she says.

A chill runs down my spine. I glance at my fellow students. Many of them qualify as my predators. "I get it. I suppose that's why this class exists, huh?"

"You may want to train on your off days to catch up with everyone else."

I grimace but don't argue. I won't be doing that… unless my Mr. Grumpy-Pants Advisor makes me run during our private sessions. I sense that he's cruel enough to do just that.

Kat walks over like she hasn't been running full tilt for an hour straight.

"What do you call a fox bitch?" I joke.

She smirks, "A vixen."

"Ugh. Even that sounds hot." I roll my eyes and clutch my sides in pain.

"I have to make up for all the nerdiness I have going on." Kat laughs, throwing her head back. It should look over the top, but she still looks like a supermodel while I pant like an overheated pug.

Chara and her gang walk by, giving me hateful looks.

"Friends of yours?" Kat asks.

"Besties." As I say this, I feel a prickle of anxiety. *What happened to Myra?*

We head back to the locker rooms. Fortunately, the showers have stalls with doors, so I don't have to be scrutinized by Chara and her friends. But they seem not to bother me when Kat is around. I suppose Chara doesn't want witnesses to her insecurities concerning Landis.

I'll have to ask him about her. If they do have something going on, I'll have him back off because that isn't cool to flirt so much with me, even if it's in jest. And like I don't already have enough problems with Rourke, his fan club, and a potential permanent stay at the asylum.

As I slip on my shoes, Kat saunters down my locker aisle, fully dressed. "What do you have next?"

"Potions Lab. Then the dreaded tutoring with Mr. Hollis." At the mention of his name, I break out in a cold sweat.

"Girl, you have it bad," Kat teases.

"No, I don't. He just makes me nervous. I thought he was going to bite me when I went to his office yesterday."

"Were you disappointed when he didn't?"

I glare at her without much heat, because she isn't wrong. For some stupid reason, I'm attracted to him. It isn't just because he's drop-dead gorgeous. I've seen strikingly handsome males of the supe world. They're literally a dime a dozen. But something about Mr. Hollis draws me in. I hope it's some deeper quality that I have yet to pick up on, and not that I'm so damaged by my mother that I'm drawn to assholes.

But he can't be all bad, can he?

"Fae to Shay?" Kat snaps her fingers in front of my face. "Wow. Were you imagining how he would look naked?"

"Ha ha," I mutter flatly. "No. I was wondering why he's an asshole."

"From what I heard, he had some trauma years ago with his coven or something like that. Must have had a falling out since he's covenless."

Kat walks with me on the way to Potions lab.

"What do you have now?" I ask.

"Finessing Shifts." When she sees the question on my lips, she explains, "It's a hands-on course for shifters, to learn to half-shift, so I can just bring out my claws or canines. It's useful. I can do it a bit, but it helps to have an expert guide us."

We say our goodbyes, and I enter the Potions lab. It's exactly how I imagined it. Cauldrons rest on work tables, herbs, and even some frighteningly *identifiable* items in jars sit on shelves along the walls. An older, wizened woman nods at me as I take one of the last open spots. My seat is next to a young man I don't recognize. I hope he isn't on Team Rourke.

"Hello students, I'm Ms. Zane." She paces back and forth in front of the class, quite spryly, given that she looks to be about a hundred. "This is where you will put to use your knowledge from Potion Fundamentals. This is a pass or fail course."

I'm not the only one who groans.

Ms. Zane pauses and grins at the class, her eyes twinkling. "Don't fret. I'm quite generous. Since some of you cannot enhance your potions with your innate magic, I will take into consideration both your species and your level of giftedness. However, you must be precise with your attempts. You'll learn how each potion tastes, smells, and feels to your magic. And you will be quizzed on that as well. Even if you cannot recreate the potions on your own, you should learn to identify them in your daily life and know how they are made. It could mean the difference between dying from being poisoned or not. Or knowing what antidote to use."

Awesome. Now I need to start worrying about being poisoned. How far would Rourke's fan club or his family go to get rid of me?

Just with the thought of him getting rid of me, my heart clenches so hard I worry I might pass out. This fated thing sucks.

"Today, we'll run through the basic tools of the trade: cauldron, stirring utensils, ingredients, measuring tools, proper storage containers, and safety protocols—of which there are many."

Apparently, almost anything can be dangerous here, depending on the recipe.

The guy next to me barely talks, but I think he's just shy. I prefer it. At least I don't have to be in battle with my lab partner.

16

BACK FOR SECONDS

SHAYLA

*W*hen I arrive at Mr. Hollis' office, there's a note pinned on the door. "Meet me in the west side recreational yard."

I stare at the note for a good, long minute. Is this note for me? Or is this a note for him from someone else? He could have at least written my name on it or signed it.

It's like this guy lives to push my buttons.

I knock, just to make sure. Maybe he forgot to take this note down, and he's inside, waiting for me.

No answer.

Off to the side yard I go. Hopefully, the big bad wolf won't eat me.

My face flushes with heat with all the innuendo that comes with that thought. I'm so happy that he can't read minds, since I don't have a handle on my newly-awakened sexual self.

Oh, no… He can't read minds, can he?

I have to find that out asap. Exiting the admin building to

the side yard, I don't see a single person... or animal shifter. I check my surroundings... Yes, I'm on the west side of campus.

What kind of game is Mr. Hollis playing? So he's back to the jerky Mr. Hyde version.

A bench beckons me right beside the building. I sit down to wait for him to show up, and rest my back against the hard plank. I gaze out across the grassy expanse roughly the size of a football field. Through the dense treeline and all its shadows, I can't see the wall that keeps the rest of Elfhame out. I wonder about the dean's warning to stay within the walls. Is it dangerous to travel from the portal to the campus gates?

Is that what happened to Myra? I barely made it myself, but that was due to Rourke's fan club.

The dean made it sound like something sinister lurks outside. Or was that all scare tactics to keep us from wandering off and causing the school problems?

I'll have to investigate what it all means.

But right at this instant, the ache in my muscles and exhaustion from P.E. hits me. Now that I have a moment to rest, my eyes drift closed.

"Wake up, runt!" a male yells, inches from my ear.

"*Fuck!*" I fling my fists in the direction of the voice even before my eyes fully open.

But Mr. Hollis is already far out of my range.

I launch myself off the bench and brace myself for a physical attack, arms up, crouching, and ready to spring away. This time, I'm in the correct fighting form.

"Nice defense reaction. With those reflexes, I might have guessed a shifter." Mr. Hollis eyes me, studying every inch of me for what I assume is a clue to my supernatural nature.

But my body doesn't know what to do under his scrutiny. I feel insecure and important all at once. Important, because a powerful mage like him deems me interesting enough to study. Insecure because I will be found lacking any magic of interest.

"I can't smell shifter on you... yet."

"Yet?" I blink but don't relax my defensive stance.

"Perhaps you've repressed your magic so much that it might never come forth properly. Or maybe you simply don't have much." He shrugs and walks toward the center of the open yard. "Which do you think it is?"

I grab my bag to follow him, but he calls back without looking, "Leave the bag."

Hesitantly, I drop my bag onto the bench and cautiously move toward him. He inspects me as I walk, and I'm sure I'm going to stumble under the pressure of his gaze. We're in the dead center of the field, and I stop at a safe distance, three long strides away from him.

"Who hit you?" he asks.

"Today?" I think back to remember if I've been assaulted today... it's becoming par for the course. "I was shoved off the bench in the locker room. Does that count?"

His eyes widen barely a millimeter. It's so subtle that someone who hasn't had to be constantly on alert for emotional cues for survival might miss the gesture.

"You had to think about that?" he asks.

"Well, I don't know if you've heard, but I was attacked on my way from the portal to the gate. And then yesterday, someone shoved me down with their magic during lunch break."

Hollis grimaces. "I suppose nothing really changes around here."

"Bullies are everywhere." I glare at him pointedly, trying to remind him that he's in bully territory. So what if he's a teacher?

"And was your mother your bully growing up?" he asks.

"The most consistent one, yes. But she had a revolving door of assholes to help her with *keeping me in line,* as she would say." I don't mention that I also was harassed by the supernatural kids growing up.

Rubbing the stubble on his chin, he considers my words.

"She used her magic on you," he prompts.

"Yes. She uses magic to hurt me. Fire."

He winces with that word—*Fire*.

"And yes, I see the irony that I'm fated to an asshole fire dragon. I don't think Fate likes me all that much."

"I'm not a fan of Fate either," Hollis grumbles. His hand sweeps back through his silky salt and pepper hair. "Sit."

I don't move. "Why?"

"You must refrain from asking me insubordinate questions. I'm supposed to be your teacher."

"Yeah, but you also assaulted me. So, are you planning on doing that now?"

Hands falling onto his hips, his head tilts back to the sky—I assume to gather his patience. "No. I'm going to try another approach because I now think your magic retreats with threats."

Satisfied with his answer, I sit cross-legged on the ground. My hands fall between my legs to keep my skirt from fluttering up and flashing him my goods.

"Shoulders and spine straight," he orders, and I comply. "Close your eyes."

I narrow my eyes instead.

He takes the hint that I don't trust him not to attack and sits down. "Take a deep breath, mentally counting to four. Then hold for seven. Then release for eight counts."

"Why?" I ask.

"Do you always argue this much?"

"You seem to bring it out in me."

"I feel so honored," he says flatly. "Now, do as I say."

I close my eyes and remind myself that it appears he's trying to help me. Just because I hate everything about it doesn't mean I shouldn't attempt whatever this is. If it keeps me out of Ravenhollow, then all the better.

But I'm also afraid that this will trigger me. I don't want Mr. Hollis to think that I'm some weakling or a whiny brat. Although, I kinda feel like both right now.

"Can you read minds?" I ask.

He chuckles. "If I could, my life would have been a whole lot easier." He points to his graying hair. "And I believe you're only causing me to grow a few more grays with all your sidestepping."

Fine, I can play along. I relax my shoulders while also keeping them straight. Breathing in for four counts, then holding and releasing.

"Good, just like that. Repeat until I say otherwise."

I'm not sure why his praise hits me hard, but maybe because I don't usually get it from authority figures in my life. I push away the welling up of emotions and focus on my breath.

After several cycles, he guides me in a meditation. "Do you have a place you go to in your mind or in real life to feel safe?"

I nod, immediately thinking of an imaginary place I've envisioned since I was a child. It's where I went mentally when bad things were happening.

"Go there now." He pauses for me to settle into my imaginary world. "Now call your higher self—the part of you which exists outside of time and space. This is the part of your soul which observes your life and nudges you when you need guidance."

I mentally call for this 'higher' self, but no one arrives. Maybe I don't have a wiser aspect of myself. That tracks.

"You're not separate, not really," he says, sensing my frustration.

Suddenly, a being that feels a lot like me but much more radiant and confident sits across from me in my mind's eye.

"Now, ask her what your power is."

I do, but her mouth opens and closes without sound. Of course, I wouldn't be able to hear her.

After a few moments, he asks, "Anything?" I shake my head, and he redirects me. "That's okay. Try to tap into the feeling or sensation you have when you look at your higher self. Usually, one's magic sits along one's spine in our chakras. Go from your root, at the base of your spine, all the way up through to the crown of your head."

Halfway through my mental journey, I get a buzzing sensation.

It grows until it vibrates, on what feels like a cellular level, and rattles me until…

I lose all conscious thought.

17

A WOUNDED WARRIOR

QUADE

*T*he moment I set eyes on Shayla, I knew there was something special about her. She was walking across the quad with the incubus. And then, as fate would have it, she ends up in the class where I'm the substitute teacher. Her sweet, seductive scent—honey and ripe citrus—made it almost impossible for me to stay focused on my lecture.

When I realized she was the same student assigned as my mentee, I nearly charged down to the dean's office to change it. However, I'm the best at drawing out a student's gift, and it would be unfair to potentially prevent her from discovering her magic.

She needs me. Or that's what I tell myself. But there's more to my attraction to her. My wolf wants her. He's convinced that she's our mate. But the last female I thought was a mate match broke my heart and destroyed my future. If it hadn't been for that mistake, I'd be out with the other Mage Enforcers, investigating the missing supes. Instead, I'm stuck at this school.

I can't allow my wolf to bully me into falling for Shayla—my student, for fae's sake. I've never crossed that line and don't intend to do so now. I feel like an asshole for being attracted to her at all.

I thought my senses would be muted by dragging her out to the open field, but her scent still drifts toward me, ensnaring my thoughts and causing my body to respond to her soft curves and soulful lavender eyes.

In those eyes, I see a reflection of myself—a wounded warrior.

I guide her through a meditation, asking her to sense her own power. There's a tremble in her very spirit at the thought of accessing her gift. She hates magic. Or hates the idea of having it.

Breaking down the walls that her mother helped create won't be easy.

Her body shakes as if someone were rattling her. I open my magical perception and scan our surroundings to sense if someone with the gift of mind control or telekinesis is assaulting her, but I feel no one.

Shayla falls backward. Fortunately, her head lands on the soft, lush grass.

I scramble to her side, looking her up and down to understand what's happening.

I feel magic churning and grinding inside her body. She *does* have power. A lot of power. My wolf is correct—at least about her being my equal or even my better.

"Shayla?" I call.

Her body vibrates and shakes as if she were having an epileptic seizure. I turn her onto her side and hold her against my chest, hoping she'll come out of this fit soon.

My hand automatically strokes her cheek to soothe her.

Finally, her body settles.

"Mr. Hollis?" her voice cracks.

"Quade," I correct. *Shit.* Why did I do that? I need to back away, not race forward.

Shayla squints up at me, her head resting in the crook of my arm. "What happened?"

She registers how close we are, and her eyes widen. I know it's not out of fear of my embrace because her gaze drops to my lips, and I scent her natural perfume.

Rationalizing to myself that I shouldn't immediately release her because she might relapse, I keep holding her. "You had a sort of seizure. Did you sense anything about your power?"

Shayla groans. "It hurts inside." She closes her eyes, trusting me to continue to hold her close while she's so vulnerable. The implications of that make my head swim.

I'm floored by her openness with me even after I acted like a dick.

Does she feel the tug of a mate match too? Or is the attraction she has toward me merely physical?

Sucking in a breath, I remind myself that it doesn't matter. I can't have her. She's bonded to a *fucking* Lewellyn.

I know their bond won't end well for her. And if the Lewellyns discover my interest in her, it will be even worse for both of us.

Chastising myself for getting lost in her tantalizing presence, I move to let her sit up on her own. "How are you feeling now?" I ask.

"Drained," she says, slumping into a sitting position. "What *was* that?"

I scent her fear now. She knows what it was but still doesn't want to believe it.

"Your magic… It can't get out."

Shayla's eyes well up with tears again, and she tips over onto her back so I can't see them.

I crawl over.

"I'm so pathetic." She covers her face.

"Why would you think that?" I ask, softening my voice.

"I keep crying around you. I *don't* cry. And my magic is so screwed up it makes me pass out. They're going to throw me into the asylum."

"Hey." I wait for Shayla to look at me. I'm hovering over her, and my hand caresses her cheek, my thumb wiping away a tear. This is so intimate... a lover's moment. I need to pull away, but I must also convince her that she's strong. She finally looks up at me, and I say, "Crying is not weak. Tears are there for a reason. To allow us to release the tension and pain we have inside. You've been strong for so long, trying to keep all those tears hidden. And you *are* powerful. Powerful enough to restrain and hide all the magic you possess. And from what I sense, it's quite a lot."

"It is?" Shayla bites her lip, studying my face. "Why do you seem worried about that?"

"Because if you had very little power, Rourke would likely find a way to sever his tie with you. But maybe he'll change his mind now."

"You think he'll want to keep me if I have as much power as you believe I do?"

I nod, seeing my future chance of being with her slipping away. "You can't tell anyone yet. Okay?"

She nods, eager to keep this a secret as well. "I won't."

I glance around to see if anyone's watching. "We'll need to continue your lessons in private from now on so he doesn't find out about you."

Shayla swallows and glances away, breaking our intense moment.

I sigh. The weight of her future pulls me down too. "I should see you to the healer now." Everything in me wants to scoop her up in my arms, but I only allow myself to help Shayla to her feet.

18

RED TAPE

SHAYLA

I'm hyper-aware of Mr. Hollis… *Quade's* energy as we head into Ms. Boyd's healer wing. Something shifted between us, maybe a few times, during our session.

He currently appears quite reserved, but I sense his magic surrounding me.

Is it only to ensure I'm all right before he hands me over to Arden's aunt?

Ms. Boyd eyes us as I shuffle in. "You were supposed to be healed up the next time I saw you," she chides. She watches for Quade's reaction.

"I was trying to use my magic, and I think I pulled a psychic muscle," I joke.

"Hmm." She helps me up onto the examination table, then turns to Quade. "Anything I should know?"

"Her magic is trying to come out, but she's resisting. It drained her."

"You can go." She waves him off.

He bristles but gets the hint. "I'll see you in class, Miss Willows."

I don't like the distance in his voice or how he calls me Willows. "Sure thing, Professor," I say coldly.

When he's long gone, Ms. Boyd finally asks, "How are you?"

"After the day I had, I could use a year-long nap."

"I'm going to psychically scan your body for any injuries lingering from your attacks and today's exertion." After a few moments of scanning me, she smiles. "It appears that you're still healing, but you *are* healing. I know you need to bring forth your magic, but you can seriously hurt yourself if you try to push too fast. And if you have no experience with how to control or channel your energy, you might hurt others, too."

Riled because it feels like she's blaming me for following Mr. Hollis' orders, I say, "I was only doing as my *advisor* instructed." I look at the exit. "Can I go?"

"Why the hurry?"

"I was hoping to talk with the admins about my friend."

"What friend?" Ms. Boyd searches my face. Maybe she wonders if I'm upset with Arden.

"My best friend from back home, Myra, hasn't shown up to school. It doesn't make sense. I'm worried that something happened to her."

Ms. Boyd hums, acknowledging my words, but I sense she's holding something back.

"What is it?" I grab her arm in desperation. "Do you know what happened to her? Please, I have to know."

"I don't know what happened to your friend specifically." She looks away and sighs. "But I've been hearing things."

"What? Please tell me!" I'm holding back a screech in my throat. My newly awakened power stirs in my belly.

"The admins won't tell you about it, but supes have gone missing."

"Missing?"

She hurries to add, "But I don't know if that's what happened to your friend. Maybe she had a family emergency or any other number of things. This school isn't cheap. Maybe she couldn't make the entrance payments."

"Her schooling was already paid for. I know that much." My head spins with the thought that Myra has been taken by some mysterious entity and what could be happening to her right now.

"Mr. Randall. He didn't show up for classes. He's one of the missing, too?"

She ignores my question, but I can see the answer on her face. "You have to keep this under wraps. Or, at the very least, don't mention my name."

"I won't." I slip off the exam table and plod out of the healer's wing.

I realize quickly that I'm not okay. The overload of magic took too much out of me. I'm not sure if I'll make it back to my room on my own. I just hope that I won't run into Rourke's fan club.

Fortunately, the halls are quiet. It seems most students are still in class or back in their dorms.

Then I feel the itch of someone's gaze between my shoulder blades. I try to hurry my steps, but it's no use.

I turn back to find a huge male rushing toward me.

He pins me to the wall by my shoulders, knocking the air from my lungs.

His humongous hand goes to my throat. I pull on his wrist to stop him from crushing my windpipe.

I look up to see who it is. I have seen him around, on the periphery of Rourke's groupies. He's part-troll, and doing nothing to live down his species' violent reputation. Would he go so far as to murder me on campus?

"You have no right to be here," the guy hisses.

Suddenly, he's flying away from me, and I tumble as his grip pulls me along. Fortunately, we break apart, and the guy scoots away from me.

His face fills with fear.

I look up to see who he's staring at. I expect to see Arden or Quade, but I'm shocked when I see Rourke's best friend, Branden.

"You have no right to touch Rourke's female," Branden snarls, his fangs descending.

Grasping my damaged throat, still on the ground, I lean away from the vamp. But his attention is not on me.

"Leave," Branden orders, and the guy runs down the hallway as if his life depends on it.

I wonder if it does.

Then Branden's black orbs for eyes lock on to me.

I flinch, then try to steady my nerves. However, even with the boost of adrenaline, I'm fading.

Standing stock-still, his handsome face is blank while he inspects me, probably wondering why I'm just a pile of flesh on the floor.

I won't thank him, not yet. I'm not sure if he just wants to do the honors of killing me himself. We're all alone right now. This would be his chance.

"Can you walk?" he asks.

I make an effort to get to my feet but only manage to lean on the wall.

Before I see him move, he gathers me into his arms and begins carrying me toward our dorm. After the shock wears off, I take a moment to finally and truly look at him. His jet black hair matches his black irises. His skin tone and facial features suggest Hispanic lineage. He's another stupidly gorgeous male.

"Why did you stop him?" I ask before I lose my nerve.

"Would you rather I didn't?" he asks without looking at me. He feels a million miles away, except for the power I sense bubbling under the surface. He has magic beyond his innate vamp gifts.

"No. But it's clear you hate me. And Rourke hates me."

Branden finally looks at me, and I shiver from his intensity. "You have no idea what we feel."

He's right. "Maybe I don't, but you both definitely appear to resent me. I'm pretty certain he wishes he never met me."

"That's closer to the truth." His eyes don't veer away from me, even as he carries me up the stairs. "But isn't that the same way you feel about him?"

"Uh, yeah." My dreams of escape crumble in my heart all over again. "If it wasn't for what happened with him, I'd be free now. I'd be a thousand miles away, far from all this bullshit. But instead, I'm under the threat of death or being committed to the asylum. And after how he treated me? I don't want to be near him."

"That's what you claim."

Before I can gather enough energy to argue, the door to our dorm flies open. Landis, Arden, and Rourke shoot out, and all of them appear angry.

Rourke orders, "All of you, inside. Now."

Branden follows everyone and gently sets me on the couch on my half of the common room. Landis and Arden sit on either side of me. Rourke perches across from us, leaning forward, elbows on his knees, eyes narrowed. Branden paces back and forth behind Rourke.

They all appear so tense and almost crazed. I ask, "What's happened? Am I in trouble?"

"Depends," Rourke growls.

My head flops back against the couch in frustration. "What now?"

Then I glance at all of them. Their newfound lack of aggression toward each other is weird. "When did you all buddy up? Or was the enemies thing an act to trick me?"

"We're... putting aside our animosity for a *brief* moment," Landis explains.

It doesn't feel like a lie, but what if that's a skill they all possess? Blocking is a talent many supes have, and if they all come from powerful or wealthy families, then it would make sense that they would know how to block an untrained person like me.

"What happened with Hollis?" Rourke bites out.

"What the hell do you care?" I snap back.

"He was crawling all over you in the yard, pawing at you."

No matter how confusing Quade's actions were, I must downplay all of it—my magic and how he made me feel. I roll my eyes. "I was training."

"For *what* exactly?" Landis asks with an edge to his voice. Strange coming from an incubus. I thought he would be amused by a potentially sexually charged moment.

My eyes dart over to look at him. "His job as my *tutor* is to bring my magic out so I can learn to control it properly." I study the four males surrounding me. "Is that the problem?" My glare settles on Rourke. "Do you want me to go to the asylum? I get that you want to sever our bond. But do you really want me to just disappear, rot away in the dark? You really did fool me that night. I thought you had at least an ounce of kindness in you."

He grimaces but doesn't argue. "What did Quade do to you?"

"He didn't do a damned thing. I just sprained my brain trying to access my pathetic magic." I rub my head and my bruised throat. I feel like the rest of my energy will give out any second.

"William attacked her in the halls. That's why she's out of sorts," Branden adds.

Rourke growls. "Tell them all to back the hell off. It doesn't look good."

"Oh yes, we wouldn't want it to *appear* like you want me dead." I sneer. "You need to be more *nuanced* about ending my life. We wouldn't want any fingers pointing back at you when I *disappear* like the others."

Rourke freezes and stares at me. "What do you know about that?"

Everyone else tenses up.

Suddenly worried, I glance at each of them in turn. "Nothing. My friend is missing. One of my teachers is gone. Something's going on."

"Drop it," Rourke orders and storms out of the main door. Branden follows behind him.

Landis turns to me, searching my face. "Seriously, what's going on with you? I can read you fairly clearly right now—although it's a chaotic mess."

"Welcome to my heart," I say sarcastically, trying to stand.

Arden helps me up. As he walks me to my room, he asks, "Did Quade do anything… inappropriate?"

"No. But why were you going along with Rourke's interrogation?"

"Branden saw him touching you in the side field while you looked like you were passed out. Apparently, Quade has bad blood with the Lewellyns, and Rourke thought he might try to take it out on you."

"It's only for *appearances* that Rourke acts like he cares. It would look bad if he didn't try to prevent it," I huff out.

"Maybe. Or maybe he's conflicted with his mate bond. It's pulling him to you."

"Whatever, I have no more fucks to give right now."

"Yeah, I sense your exhaustion," Arden says. "And your pain on many levels."

"Between hurting myself with my magic, being assaulted, learning my friend is probably a missing person case, and you all ganging up on me, I think I have a right to be exhausted and in pain."

"I wasn't suggesting otherwise." His large fingers skim down my throat. Then he helps me sit on the edge of my bed. "This needs attention, or you'll be black and blue tomorrow."

"Yeah. Wouldn't want anyone to think Rourke's behind my constant attacks," I mutter.

Arden gives me an exasperated grimace. "Stop it. You know I only want to help you."

Landis appears in my doorway. "I get why you're pissed. But we're all worried. I don't think Rourke's only concern is for his reputation."

"Why are *you* siding with him?" I demand.

"I'm not. But I don't like how you feel the entire universe is out to get you."

"Isn't it, though?" I pout. Ugh. *Goddess, how whiny do I sound?*

"Sparkles, will you let me heal you?" Arden begs.

Looking into his glittering emeralds for eyes, I concede. "Fine." I kick off my shoes and wait for him to begin his work.

"Lie back. I'll sit right here, and you can just drift to sleep." Arden helps me by pulling down the covers to have me crawl in fully clothed. I'll be a crinkly mess tomorrow. Whatever. I don't give a damn about how I look anymore. Not that I gave much of a damn before. I have more important issues to worry about.

Myra might be dead or worse. She could be held prisoner and tortured.

And Rourke just wants me to drop it? Screw that.

"In the morning, if you don't have your natural psychic blocking back in place, I'm going to teach you a basic method before class," Landis informs me. He stands, arms crossed, leaning against my door frame. His face is hard right now, unreadable. It's disturbing that the playful incubus persona has fallen away completely. Is he *that* worried?

"Are you really that upset about Quade?" I ask him. "Can you sense something that I'm not?"

"No," Landis confesses. "But he's an extremely powerful mage. I would have to force my way into his psyche, and I won't do that."

"Just be wary of him," Arden adds.

"Don't worry, it's my default setting." I close my eyes, relaxing and negating what I just said. I trust them. Maybe not much, but I do.

Arden's electric touch tingles as he strokes my neck. I drift away, allowing fatigue to take me.

19

NO MORE

SHAYLA

*W*hen I open my eyes, it's morning. Arden and Landis are no longer in my room, but I'm not surprised.

Feeling much better, most likely due to Arden's healing, I stretch and look down at my wrinkled clothes. I notice a button missing on my shirt, ripped during the troll's attack. I suppose I'll be wearing the worn hand-me-down uniform in the closet.

I open the door to the common room, and I smell a sweet temptation… pancakes. Arden's pancakes.

As I poke my head out, he turns, flashes me that dazzling grin, and points to the stack he just plated. I swear that if he keeps feeding me like this, soon I will have to buy a uniform in a bigger size. But I'm not complaining.

I see an official-looking, sealed school envelope pinned to my door—and another box. I peek inside and see a new uniform and a light jacket. I suppose soon enough the weather will change. "Does the academy *know* when I need new stuff? Like how it tries to set up potential coven mates?"

"Magic works in mysterious ways." Arden shrugs and pats my unofficial chair at the end of the long table.

Rourke's seat is at the opposite end. But he isn't around for breakfast. "Is he still out?"

"I didn't hear him return," Landis says as he comes out of his room and runs his fingers through his long auburn bangs. Goddess, help me... he has no shirt on.

I can't pull my gaze away from his sleek muscles until Arden asks, "Butter and maple syrup? Or fresh fruit?"

"All of it? Why choose?" I grin and plop down in my chair while opening my school letter.

My heart sinks as I read the contents.

Landis rushes to my side. "What is it?"

Overcome by emotion, I hand him the letter instead of reading it aloud.

"Mr. Hollis will no longer be available to mentor you privately," Landis reads. "When the school finds an acceptable replacement, you will be informed. In the meantime, please use your tutoring hour for auditing any classes. Signed Dean Cranish."

I rip the paper from his hand and stare at the words as if they might change. "It doesn't say why."

"Maybe Rourke complained because he didn't like Hollis being alone with you?" Arden suggests.

"Or your aunt," I say. "She saw me right after I fritzed out my magic, and she wasn't pleased with him or me for trying to push my magic too hard."

"Speaking of which, your walls are back up this morning, but not as solid as they were before." Landis peers at me, attempting to read me. "I felt you when you got upset just now with the letter. So, try not to react emotionally when you're in public."

I glare at him. "Yeah, I'll just keep my shit locked up nice and tight so that no one thinks I might be a real person. We wouldn't want them to know that the punching bag has feelings."

"Shit, I'm sorry." Landis rubs his face. "I didn't mean it to come out like that. I'm just worried that someone will use your vulnerabilities against you."

I sigh. He has a point. "What was that technique you were going to show me?"

Some of the light returns to his smoky gray eyes as he sits down next to me. "First, imagine you're in the center of a bubble. Next, make it solid like glass. Then, imagine..." He points to the butter melting on my pancakes. "That this butter is on the outside, and no one's psychic tendrils can grab onto you."

I bark out a laugh. *"Really?"*

I look to Arden, who is shoveling food in his mouth, for confirmation that Landis isn't pulling my leg.

He nods and swallows his mouthful. "It's real. Basic, for kids, but it's a good start. No spells needed."

I try it out, feeling silly, but Landis hums his approval. "Good. Just hold that image in your mind and reinforce it whenever you can. It'll become second nature."

Before my classes for the day begin, I visit the administration offices.

A fussy little fae goblin sits behind a tall desk. Her haunting eyes and dark red hat make me shiver when I think of the legend that says they dip their hats in the blood of their slain enemies. They wouldn't have a murderous fae running the front desk in their office, would they? Although, when I think about it, that's probably the type I would hire so I wouldn't have to talk to anyone.

"May I help you?" The tone in her voice conveys that she means to *not* be very helpful.

"I have a few things I'd like to discuss with the dean." I wave the ridiculous letter in my hand.

With recognition clearly apparent in her eyes, she shakes her head. "I'm sorry, but he isn't available right now."

"Then when can I see him?"

"What is this concerning?" she asks, as if she doesn't know what I'm holding—my unofficial asylum sentence via the lack of a proper magical tutor.

I take a deep breath and solidify my magic bubble so she can't read how I want to strangle her. "I need to talk to him about Mr. Hollis no longer being my mentor."

"Mr. Cranish plans on resolving that as soon as possible."

Okay, I'm getting nowhere with the mentor thing. So I switch gears. "I do have another question. My friend was supposed to be attending school. However, I know she's been absent from at least one of her classes."

The goblin shrugs. "Perhaps she changed her schedule."

"I don't think so." I glance at the filing cabinets behind her. "Do you have a record of her showing up?"

"Those records are classified. You wouldn't want me sharing private information about you with random students, would you?"

"No, but—"

The little fae goblin cuts me off. "Then you can't expect me to just give you that kind of information. I don't even know if you're her friend."

Frustration brews inside me. I understand the need for privacy, but I also know something isn't right about Myra's absence. "I would like to contact the human realm."

"We cannot allow that at this time."

"Why not?" I clench my teeth.

"Is it an emergency?" She gives me a condescending smile.

"I don't know, dammit!" I snap. "It *might* be an emergency!"

"Ten points will be deducted for disrespecting your elder."

I close my eyes and calm the swirling magic in my gut. Why is that happening now? I didn't call upon it. I need to chill out, so I don't blow another fuse in my brain. "I'll be back to discuss getting a new mentor."

I walk away before I get more points docked.

I dread attending my Arcane Magic class and seeing Mr. Hollis again. Will he be there? I didn't voice my concern with Arden and Landis, but I wonder if Mr. Hollis is the one who put in the request for his removal.

I believe he might be drawn to me, as I'm drawn to him. Maybe he worries that, as a tutor, he can't remain professional with me. Or the most likely reason is that he senses how much *I* want to kiss him.

Claim him.

Holy crackers. Did I just think that?

Perhaps our separation *is* for the best.

I hesitate outside the classroom door. Kat, who has been quietly walking next to me, asks, "You okay?"

"Yeah. It's just been a rough couple of days." I don't want to say more, in case Mr. Hollis is inside. His hearing probably is keen enough to hear me.

Throwing the door open, I see that Mr. Hollis is there, leaning against the chalkboard. He pretends to not notice me, but nothing gets past this shifter. Kat takes the lead and walks to the back of the class. Thank goodness it looks like her idea to sit as far from him as possible.

During class, Mr. Hollis ignores me. His gaze never lands on me as he scans the room while lecturing. I take notes but have a hard time focusing.

At the end of class, Mr. Hollis calls out, "Dismissed." When I shove all my notes into my pack, I hear him say, in a distant, formal tone, "Miss Willows, a word?"

Kat's eyes widen, and she mouths that she'll be right outside.

I wave her off and shake my head.

"Then I'll meet you for lunch at our bench." With one last glance at Mr. Hollis, she leaves me to my fate.

Walking up to the front of the class to face him, dreading every step, I cross my arms and wait for him to begin.

"Did you get a letter this morning?" He finally looks at me briefly and then stares at the door.

Now, with his cold demeanor, I assume it's Mr. Hollis, not Rourke, who ended our tutoring sessions.

I hate to admit it, but I feel the sharp pain of rejection… again. First, my fated mate, now him. But I have no right or rational reason to feel this deeply about Mr. Hollis pulling away.

"So you decided to toss me aside?" I say before thinking my words through.

"Excuse me?" His attention lands back on me fully. His golden eyes feel like they're ripping me to shreds.

My cheeks redden from a combination of embarrassment and anger.

"I had nothing to do with that." He explains, "The dean called me in last night and told me that *you* complained about my methods… that I was a bit too *hands-on*."

"Fucking Rourke," I curse.

Quade's entire body ripples with a barely held back shift. His eyes burn with a golden glow. Magic crackles over his skin. He bares his teeth and snarls, "*Lewellyn* did this? He *really* doesn't want you to survive this bond."

Instead of being turned off by his magic rising to the surface, I'm drawn in, since he wants to protect me, not harm me.

"I *suspect* it was him." But with Quade so obviously angry, I worry he might run off, attack Rourke, and get himself in trouble. "Maybe. I don't know for certain. But when I got back to my dorm last night, he was waiting to interrogate me about our tutoring session. Apparently, Branden had been watching us. He acted as if it bothered him how you held me when I passed out."

Quade grimaces and turns his head away. After a few long, deep breaths, he says, "I apologize for that... if I made you uncomfortable."

"You didn't," I say softly. "I was upset and in pain, and you were only trying to make sure I was all right. If you sensed I was uncomfortable, it's just that I—"

Quade looks back at me. "What?" he asks when I don't finish.

"I'm not used to anyone but my best friend being worried about me."

His gaze slowly takes me in. "Maybe it *is* for the best that you find another tutor."

"Oh." I pick at my fingers and try to endure the strange shattering sensation happening inside my heart. It makes no sense, but his pulling away feels almost as intense as with Rourke. Perhaps my emotions are just so on the surface after years of hiding that any little upset feels like devastation.

So naturally, my default defense mechanism is triggered into action—anger. "Yeah, well, I probably belong in an asylum anyway, right? I just have screwed-up magic because of my screwed-up mother. I should just go admit myself now. Save everyone the trouble. Because my mate has it out for me. This whole gives-a-damn act he puts on is only so he can look innocent while having me locked up. Did you know the dean didn't even bother to give me another advisor? I'm taking that as a bad sign for my future."

Overwhelmed and close to tears, I race for the door. Just as I reach it, Quade grabs my arm and spins me around to look at him.

He looms over me, eyes flashing brightly. He hisses, just above a whisper, "You're *not* going to end up in the asylum. Do you hear me?"

"Whatever. You don't have to act like you give a crap about me anymore." I try to yank my arm away, but he doesn't let me go.

"I care more than I should," he grits out, still in hushed tones. "We're going to continue your lessons… in private. I'll meet you in the wooded area beyond the side yard at our appointed time."

Looking up at him, I study his face, so close to mine. I can see a turbulent storm behind his fierce look. I sense that he's both conflicted and determined. I shake my head. "I know you said in class that the future isn't set, but in my case, it might be."

"If you think that way, then it will make it…" he begins to say.

I cut him off. "I call bullshit on your theory. I believed I was going to escape the magical world and all its assholes, and I was only dragged further into it."

"That doesn't mean you should give up. I *will* help you."

"No. You'll get in trouble. Like you said, the Lewellyns are too powerful, and I'm not worth it."

Sadness flickers in his eyes. "Saving your life will be worth any punishment I might receive."

I swallow down the lump in my throat. We're frozen now, gazing into each other's eyes. The sounds of students approaching the classroom shake us out of our trance.

"I should go."

"Next session," he says, releasing his hold on my arm.

"Next session," I agree and dart out of the room.

When I look down the hallway, I see Branden casually

leaning against the wall, watching me with a heated scowl. Instead of what I should do when seeing a surly vampire, I storm toward him. I stop when I'm right up in his face. "What the hell? Are you following me?"

His face reveals no emotion. Does this guy even have emotions? "Someone sure thinks she's the center of the universe."

"I am the center… to me." I clench my jaw. "And that wasn't a denial."

"Just making sure Hollis backs off," he explains. "You were in there with him for a while."

"He was just explaining that he didn't remove himself as my advisor and tutor. And that he would make sure I had someone to help me with my magic soon."

"You aren't his problem anymore."

"Yeah, I don't suppose I'll be anyone's problem soon enough. Not when you all get your way, and I either get locked up or go missing."

He aggressively steps toward me, closing the already short distance between us. His body is almost pressed against mine. I crane my head back to look up at him, not backing down or away.

"Drop the missing people topic," he warns.

"No." I glare back into the dark abyss of his eyes. "My friend is gone."

"You don't know that," he corrects.

"Yeah, and I want to know what *did* happen."

"Fine," he growls. "What's her name?"

I blink. Why would he help me? Is he pretending to, in the hopes of shutting me up? Anyhow, I don't know how it can hurt to tell him—she's already missing. "Myra Hurst."

"Be a good girl, and I'll tell you what I find out." He zips away with his unnatural speed.

Dammit. I'm going to be late for my next class.

As I run to English class, I wonder if I should still meet with

Mr. Hollis secretly to continue my training. If Branden discovers us, he might not help me with Myra. But he might not help me, anyway. Yet, something about his promise rings true.

When I get to class, I burst through the door. Ms. Waithe shakes her head as she docks me ten points.

Great.

20

BIRTH DAY

SHAYLA

Fortunately, Rourke's mandate about not harassing me has taken root. No one has threatened me, choked me out, or knocked me over with magic in the last couple of days. So I'll count that as a win.

However, it does feel like the calm before the storm. I don't trust quiet. My mother used to ease up right before she went on a rampage. I know this peace won't last, either.

My nerves itch as I watch the clock. Since my conversation with Branden, I've been worried about what I should do with Quade... *Mr. Hollis*.

In Potions Lab, I proudly don't blow anyone up with my first attempt at brewing a sleeping aid made from ground sloth claws, lavender, camomile, valerian, and dust from an oleander fairy. Ms. Zane warns us that we should use the potion rarely and only in small quantities due to the poisonous oleander. I feel a bit sluggish after taking a drop of it, and I don't like the sensation, so I'm not planning on ever making this again.

Fortunately, no magic is needed to activate this elixir.

After Potions Lab, I walk toward the admin building to meet with Mr. Hollis. But as the side yard comes into view, I don't want to risk Branden not telling me what he discovers about Myra, so I turn around and hurry back to my dorm. It's probably for the best. I can barely face Mr. Hollis with all my stupid emotions and my frustrating attraction to him right now.

No one is in the dorm, but I shut myself inside my room anyway. I make a weak attempt to study, but my mind keeps circling through all my problems: Rourke, the mate bond, my broken magic, my impending incarceration in the asylum, Hollis, Myra, and whether it's wise to meet with Hollis and risk Branden not giving me information about Myra. I'm so mixed up right now, and I can't focus on any of it to work it out.

I realize I could wait a few more days to see if Branden comes through for me. If not, maybe I can still work with Mr. Hollis. That's *if* he forgives me for standing him up. But even if he doesn't forgive me, then I need to take control of my future, learn about my magic—help or no help—and investigate Myra's disappearance on my own.

During my next class with Hollis, I don't look up to see the potential glare of disappointment in his eyes. Instead, I write a quick note, explaining that I have to avoid him for a few more days because Rourke and Branden are watching me too closely.

When the class ends, he locks eyes with me. I rush forward

and hand him the note. I race out before Branden, if he's watching, can suspect that I'm communicating with the professor.

As I burst forth from the classroom, Branden nods and saunters off. That asshole better hand over some information soon.

All's quiet for a week. Sensing my irritation at their intrusion into my situation with the professor, Landis and Arden have all but left me alone. They speak sparingly to me. After working out the currency exchange, I buy my own food with my own money.

Landis hasn't walked me to class either. Honestly, it's been a relief. All my feelings for them confuse me when I need to focus on understanding my power and studying for my classes. Although I miss our time together, I know I must keep my wall up for all our sakes.

I've been trying the meditation techniques Hollis taught me. But my higher self still isn't talking. I'm a bit nervous about pushing myself and having another magical blowout.

Since I don't want to have a magic meltdown, I've mostly been immersing myself in my studies. I need passing grades to avoid the asylum as well. Nothing motivates someone to pull an all-nighter like the threat of a padded cell.

The one time I almost catch Branden alone to ask him about Myra, he evades me with his super speed.

After lying awake in bed for hours, I finally need to face the day I had hoped would be my salvation. I rub the fatigue out of my eyes and get up.

I sigh, pressing my forehead against my bedroom door before opening it. Today is my birthday. Fortunately, no one seems to know... which is perfect. At home, I hated my birthdays because my mother was always extra horrible to me. She felt that I was some sort of cosmic punishment, and she would take it out on me. I thought not long ago that this birthday would finally be different—I would have my freedom. But it turns out I traded one set of shackles for another. I seem to have upgraded from a pathetic drunk fire mage to an asshole fire dragon mate.

While slipping out of my room to head to the café and then P.E., Landis calls to me. "Shayla, please. Can't we be friends again?"

I freeze at the outer door, my hand on the handle. Without turning, I ask, "Were we ever really friends?"

"What about me?" Arden asks from the kitchen. Hurt rings clearly in his voice.

Slowly, I turn. "So what was all that possessive, alpha-hole behavior concerning Hollis? You took Rourke's side. The guy who rejected me, wants me to fail, and have me locked away so he can find his perfect little life partner match."

"For me?" Landis answers, "I was acting out of pure jealousy."

"Cubi don't get jealous." I scoff. "And of what? You and I aren't a thing. And Rourke would kill you for touching his discarded toy. Besides, your only interest in me is part of your incubus schtick."

"Schtick?" His gray eyes turn dark. "What's that supposed to mean?"

Realizing that I'm offending his core nature, I backtrack. What I said isn't kind, no matter how irritated I am. "Sorry, that came out wrong. I meant that it's in your nature to seduce, even when you don't really *want* someone for... more."

"So, according to you, I'm incapable of having real feelings and desire someone for more than a power feeding?"

"I didn't say—" I protest.

Landis cuts me off. "You kind of did." He stalks across the room until he presses me to the door, but without making any physical contact. He leans down and whispers in my ear, "I want more than a feeding from you, love."

As he pulls back slightly, my gaze drops down to his lips. Then I remember Rourke's threats. My eyes dart to my mate's door.

Landis calms me by saying, "He's not here."

"We can't—"

"No one needs to know." He grazes his lips over my cheek, a molecule away from actually touching me.

I shiver with need.

What would a creature notorious for their sexual prowess be like in bed?

From the other side of the room, Arden interrupts the beginnings of my fantasies. "Shayla? Do you want him to back off?"

"I'm fine."

"Would you like to eat here this morning instead of at the café?" he asks as I duck away from Landis.

All the irritation I had stored up against them dissipates. "Uh, okay."

"Are you going to the party?" Arden asks as he piles some eggs on a plate for me.

"What party?"

Of course, I have no idea.

"A welcome back party in the woods."

"On this side of the wall?" I ask with a bit of fear, thinking of the dean's warning.

"Of course." Landis smiles. "I thought I could take you... as friends."

"I guess a party could be interesting. Rourke's fan club hasn't bothered me lately, so it shouldn't be traumatizing."

"Good. It's a date!" Landis' eyes twinkle.

"Landis..." Arden warns.

"Friends have play dates!" he argues.

"Hey, have you heard anything more about supes going missing or about Myra?" I ask.

Both of them tense their shoulders.

"Something's going on," Landis tells me. "I heard rumors of four other students who never showed up at the academy."

"What could be taking them?" I ask, my imagination running wild with monsters scarier than the supes that I know about.

"Has anyone gone missing from campus?" I wonder aloud.

"Not yet, but we shouldn't wander off alone," Arden says.

"You mean *me*." I huff.

"He has a point," Landis agrees and sips his orange juice. "Have you accessed your magic yet?"

"No," I say, gritting my teeth over the predicament I'm in.

"Then how are you supposed to fight off anyone? Unless you have some secret weapon that I don't know about?" Landis points out.

"Fine. I'll be careful."

As soon as I arrive for P.E., Kat jumps up and down and tugs on my arm. "I know you've been bummed out about not finding answers about your friend, but you have to go to the party with me tonight."

"I'm going." I calm her down with a settle-down motion.

"Landis told me about it this morning. He says I have to escort him. We can make it a group thing, so Rourke doesn't get weird."

"Sure, Landis is cool." Kat grins. "Is Arden coming too?"

"He is." I study her for a second, jealousy rising in my chest that she might want Arden and *get* him. But he isn't mine and never will be. "You like him?" I ask, not truly wanting to hear the answer.

"He's damn hot." She rolls her eyes. "But there's no way he's into me."

"Uh, I think you need to look in the mirror again," I say to boost her self-confidence. And maybe Arden, having a girlfriend, would help me strengthen my boundaries. "You're a catch, and not just because you're stunning. You're a whiz in all your courses. Unlike me, even though I'm studying my ass off."

Kat peeks at my backside. "Sweetie, I hate to tell you this, but you still have a full plump ass." She giggles and then waves off my concerns. "You're just doing a bit of catching up because your mom sucks. You'll be a top student in no time."

Then I realize school uniforms are probably not party attire. "All my regular clothes were trashed in the first attack when I entered Elfhame."

"You can borrow something from me," Kat offers.

I laugh and wave my hand to indicate her tall, slender frame and then my much shorter, *rounder* form. "I don't think that's going to work."

"I have some leggings that are short on me. And a stretchy top that will expand over your boobs."

The outfit that I imagine sounds a bit too catsuit for my taste. I might draw *more* unwanted attention, people thinking I'm on the prowl for another mate... and I didn't need the first one. "I think a pair of my jeans might be salvageable."

"You realize there's a small clothing shop right off the admin building?" Kat asks. "They have some cute things."

"You want to meet up after your last class?" I ask. "I'm

seriously *not* a shopper. My friend Myra had to help me pick out my party gear."

"I'd love to!" Kat bounces, just like a fox does when it's excited.

I wish I could be more excited about life. But I guess I'm always waiting for the other shoe to drop on my head and break my skull. Unfortunately, it usually does.

I mentally smack myself. *No more whining!*

For half a second, I debate whether or not to tell Kat it's my birthday. Maybe her zeal for life and celebration will make me appreciate the fact that I'm twenty and considered an adult in the supernatural world.

21

WELCOME PARTY

SHAYLA

*S*hopping is… *fine*. Kat insists that I try on every single article of casual clothing until she finds the outfits she approves of.

With the plan to meet at nine in my dorm's main lobby, we separate to rest and fix ourselves up before the party.

I don't usually wear makeup at all, but I decided tonight I'll make an effort.

The idea of Landis desiring me makes me want to look somewhat attractive. Even if he probably only wants a feeding from me—that's all we could have, anyway. When or if Rourke severs our bond, Landis would likely lose interest in the challenge. I don't really believe the *only* reason he's nice to me is to irritate Rourke, but I think that's part of his motivation. From what I read of the cubi, they often crave those who are unattainable. So, yeah, I suppose that I would qualify as that… currently.

After checking myself in the full-length mirror, I decide

that it's as good as it's going to get. The skinny jeans hug my curves, and a flattering royal purple silky blouse brings out my eyes. I actually make an effort with my wild hair and tame it with a styling product that was in one of my supply boxes. I rock the beachy waves look for the middle of the forest.

I step out of my room, and my jaw nearly drops completely off my face. Landis and Arden are in their street clothes, which I rarely see, and they look incredible. Not to say that they don't look gorgeous in their uniforms, but what they have on now flatters their personalities and enhances their natural beauty.

The six-foot-four druid wears his long wavy hair down, framing his masculine but kind face. A dark green long-sleeved henley shirt grips his massive, muscular arms and chest. His sleeves are pushed up to show off his delicious forearms. His sacred druid tattoos peek out at the collar and along his arms. I crave to study them in detail. His jeans are the perfect fit—tight in the ass and around his thighs and loose over his rugged biker boots.

My gaze trails over to the incubus with his auburn hair mussed just enough to look roguish. His charcoal button-up, fitted shirt hugs his muscles without appearing like he's trying to show off. Jeans that look like they cost more than all my clothes combined hang comfortably on his narrow hips and sweet butt. His sleek six feet of polished sex is in stark contrast to the rugged-looking druid. I don't think I could choose if I had to at this moment.

If we were in a love-based coven, I wouldn't have to choose. But those are so rare these days that I don't dare let myself dream I could have it. Besides, I know Rourke wouldn't want a mate coven with me, since he doesn't even want *me*. Although if what Hollis said is true, if I do possess a lot of magic, he might want to keep me around anyway.

But if I were free? Maybe I could be with one of these beautiful males—hopefully, for more than one night.

No, I can't. Arden sees me only as a friend, and Landis sees me as a meal.

That doesn't mean I won't ever fantasize about that Shay sandwich.

"Elfhame to Shayla?" Landis smirks. He's caught me checking him out.

"Uh…? Yeah, right here." My cheeks flush pink.

"You look fabulous," he purrs.

"Thanks. You guys dirty up good, too," I joke.

Arden smiles shyly. "You really have grown up, haven't you?"

When he reminds me of my stupid birthday, tears well in my eyes.

"Fuck. What's wrong?" Landis closes the distance.

Arden leaps over the couch and runs to my side. His hands cup my jaw, making me look at him. "What? I didn't mean to upset you."

"It's dumb." I close my eyes and use my birthday wish to will them away, but it doesn't work. My birthday wishes never come true.

"Sparkles?" Arden calls me. "What happened?"

"It's my birthday," I confess.

They both growl in unison, "Why didn't you say anything?"

"I hate my birthday. My mother was always extra generous with her vitriol."

"We're going to make sure you have your first good birthday," Landis promises, his forehead almost pressing to mine in a surprisingly intimate gesture.

It takes everything in me to pull away from him. I shrug to cover the struggle. "I guess it hasn't been horrible so far. But the night isn't over yet!" I try to sound light-hearted and joke about it.

"Knock that off, or I'll give you a birthday spanking," Landis warns, and my core heats with the image of his hands on my ass.

"We should meet up with Kat," Arden cuts in.

My attention shoots to him, wondering if he'd like to hook up with my fox friend. I tell myself to be okay with that. They both are so kind… it would be a good match.

The weather this evening is perfect since Elfhame seems to be much more temperate than the mortal realm so far. There's a little chill in the air, but I won't need a jacket.

Landis leads the way down the stairs. Kat beams her hundred-watt smile when she sees us. I glance over at Arden, but his eyes flick away from me. Weird.

The third quarter moon is high in the night sky as we cross the open field to the wooded area beyond. I can hear excited voices and the thrum of a bass speaker for dance music. This isn't much different from the human party where I met Rourke.

Speaking of the dragon, when we come to the small clearing where most of the students are congregating, my sights instantly land on his golden hair, highlighted by a small bonfire.

And, as if it needed to be said, Branden is close by, brooding and sipping out of the Elfhame version of a solo cup—a wooden stein.

Rourke laughs heartily at something Millie says—another one of my long list of *admirers,* the one who attacked me when I entered the fae realm. *Great,* makes sense that they are *friends.* They'll both have something to say about how closely Landis is standing by my side.

Then, as if sensing me, which he probably did, he turns and glowers at me. Yeah, lovely welcome. Suddenly, I'd rather be anywhere than here.

"Don't pay him any mind," Landis says.

My brain knows I should hate Rourke, but my heart and soul ache for him. The bond practically demands to be complete.

Arden comes forward and stands in front of me, blocking my view of Rourke. His green eyes glow slightly from being in his element—nature. "Do you want to leave?"

"I have to get used to him, right?" I shrug. "I barely see him in the dorm."

"Anytime you want to go, just let us know," Landis says. When I nod, he runs over to the coolers and kegs to get us drinks.

"Non-alcoholic, please," I call after him.

Rourke and Branden watch the whole exchange like they're stalking prey.

Kat perks up. "Come on, I want you to meet some of my other friends from class."

I follow along, trying to ignore Rourke's attention, and fail. His gaze crawls over me. Maybe this setting reminds him of our sweet moment before fate collided with us.

I meet Kat's friends, two girls and a guy—a male shifter named Douglas. I'm pretty sure she's into him, and he's into her.

Arden stands next to me and gladly accepts the drink that Landis hands him.

Landis gives me a fruity-smelling drink. "What's this?" I eye him, wondering if he got me something with booze in it.

"Goldenfrankle juice. Non-alcoholic. Although you may be the only one who will be sober tonight." He chugs some of his potent ale.

"That's fine by me." I grin and sip my drink. It's freaking delicious, and I take another swig. "I'll be the designated dancer," I say, then sway my hips and lift my arms, attempting to let go.

"Great idea, love!" Landis hands Arden his stein and pretends to reel me out to the impromptu dance floor.

I follow along but don't get too close. Rourke's attention is burning a hole into my good time. I wonder if he'll make a scene even though Landis and I aren't behaving like more than friends. He hasn't touched me once. Myra and I were more handsy than this. A pang of loss hits me, and I slow my dancing to a sway.

"You okay?" Landis steps closer.

"Just worried that I'll never see Myra again."

He nods knowingly and whispers, "I'll help you figure out what happened. Starting tomorrow. Okay?"

A faint smile returns to my lips. "Okay."

Arden's warm presence slides up behind me. I spin around and smile up at him. Then my gaze travels back down as he dances without lifting his feet from the ground. His boots are off, and I swear I see energy extending from the earth, wrapping itself around his feet, then trailing up his swaying body.

"Oh, shit," I say in awe. "Is that—"

"You can see it?" he asks, in what sounds like shock. When I nod, he says, "It's my druid connection to the earth. I'm recharging."

His intricate Celtic-style tattoos are subtly glowing. "It's... beautiful." I almost reach out but realize I shouldn't mess with someone's magic.

"You can touch them." Arden holds out his arm for me to inspect his markings.

"But aren't they kind of... sacred?" I ask.

"You already are in my sacred circle."

Holy eggplant parmesan. "I am?" I whisper. "How?"

"When I healed you."

"Oh." My mouth hangs open in shock. We're more connected than I understood.

"Come on." He grins and pulls me to him, his hands on my hips and making me move with the beat. "We're supposed to be dancing to celebrate your birthday."

I burst out with laughter at his insistence that I have a good time. Then I sense Rourke's eyes shooting daggers at my back. I feel the burn of our mate bond.

What does it mean when I feel the ache so intensely like this? Is he jealous? Is it the male's prideful dragon or the pull of his mate bond that's actually the source of any jealousy? And will I be free of him one day?

I sip more of my juice and realize that I need another serving. "Need more," I say as I break away from Landis and Arden and head over to the drinks area.

Scanning my surroundings, I notice several pairs have broken off to find a bit of seclusion in the woods. Then I spot a wolf in the distance. A shifter with golden eyes and black and gray fur is watching me. I'm reminded of Hollis' intensity and power, and I wonder if it's him. Should I risk walking out there by myself and finding out if it is?

But as I'm considering it, the wolf vanishes.

Suddenly a presence is right behind me, closer than is proper. A deep, husky voice whispers in my ear, "Have you been a good girl?" Branden's blend of sweet and metallic vampiric scent washes over me.

I shiver, knowing that I've been caught longing for my professor.

"Yes," I say without turning or moving away. I won't let him intimidate me. "Are you going to give me what I want?"

He chuckles darkly. "And what exactly is that, witch?"

I don't argue that I'm a mage, not a human witch. He means to poke at me. And is it really an insult to be a regular human with a magical gift? "I want lots of things. Freedom, mostly, from a certain asshole dragon. But I also want what you promised—answers about my friend."

"Not here, but I'll tell you tomorrow."

I flick my hand to wave him off. "Then go back to your master now."

"Oh, sweetheart, as if *that's* how it works."

Something in his tone intrigues me. I spin and study his obsidian eyes. "How *what* works?"

Branden smirks and races off—jackass. A hot jackass, but still an ass. And hopefully, one with answers.

I look back at the party. Landis and Arden are busy chatting up some fellow students. Kat is flirting with Douglas. Rourke is nowhere to be seen.

Taking another sip of my juice, an overwhelming urge has me walking out toward where I saw the wolf to see if it's Hollis spying on me. I've seen a black and gray wolf a few times while running on the track. But when I squint into the darkness with the trees shading the moonlight, I can't see those golden eyes anymore.

I feel compelled to walk farther out.

I idly wonder if Hollis is a potential mate match? It would explain my intense, irrational pull to him.

Fatigue has my eyelids taking their time to open and close. Everything feels slower. My feet shuffle on the ground. My cup drops from my hand.

A root trips me, and I tumble to the ground.

I blink. Two dark shapes loom over me, grab me by the arms, and begin to drag me away.

A warning alarm goes off in my mind. Why am I leaving the party? And heading toward the outer wall?

I jerk my arms to break free. I can't scream for help. I can't even remember how to use my voice.

A male hisses. "Fuck. She should be out cold."

"We were warned she might be more powerful than she appears." Another male.

I don't recognize their voices, but they could be disguised by their whispering.

One male pinches my jaw open, and they force more juice down my throat.

My feeble burst of strength gives out. My head lolls toward the ground, but I force myself to stay conscious.

They take my surrender as their cue to move again. "I can't believe we couldn't sense an ounce of magic off her before. But I can taste it now."

Who *are* they?

Where are they taking me?

22

SHADOWWALK

LANDIS

Shayla. Damn, she can sure shake that fine ass.

It takes all my restraint not to constantly grope her. But the dragon would literally burn my hide if I did—especially if I dared to touch in public what he thinks is *his*. So, I dial it down and stay a safe distance as we dance. Besides, I can't touch her for my own reasons.

She bounces off to get some more juice as she's worked up a thirst.

A friend from Advanced Potions calls me over, and I chat with him, losing all worries about Shayla. She's only fifteen feet away, getting a refreshment. There's no reason to turn around and watch as she bends over and digs out the bottle of juice from the cooler.

What...?

Yes, there *is* a damned good reason to watch her do that. She's all I can think about lately.

Then I realize that I feel muddled.

Compulsion.

Shit. Someone's using compulsion on me. With a muttered incantation, I use my mage magic to break out of the spell. I spin around, hoping to calm my nerves with the sight of Shay's golden-brown locks and her lavender eyes, but I don't find her anywhere.

"Arden!" I bark.

He blinks as if he were waking up. He quickly scans the party for Shayla. "Where the hell is she?"

I expand my senses to feel for her emotions, but she has gotten so much better at psychic blocking that I don't feel a fucking thing.

Is she okay?

Shayla wouldn't have left without telling one of us.

I race to Kat, "Have you seen Shay?"

Confused, she says, "She was dancing with you a second ago."

Arden inspects the area by the cooler, looking for clues.

I hear a shout in the distance, barely audible over the music and chatter from the party. "The outer wall," I say to Arden, and we both charge in that direction.

What I wouldn't give for a shifter nose right now.

The druid moves faster than me, partly because of his longer legs, partly because he's so in tune with nature that he can sense every bump, root, and hole under his feet. That druidic magic is very similar to mine. It's all about energetic entanglement.

"This way," he orders, veering to the right. "I sense a disturbance."

When we near the outer wall, we see Shayla on the ground with a huge black and gray wolf running toward her.

Without concern for his safety, Arden charges forward and rams into the wolf, carrying him away from Shayla. While the threat is neutralized, I race to Shayla, drop to the ground, and inspect her for injuries. She's face down, and I can't tell if she's awake.

"Shayla?"

Why isn't she responding?

I roll her over, careful not to touch her skin to skin.

She's out cold.

Arden slams his massive fists into the shifter's side. The wolf cries out and shifts.

Into... *Hollis.*

"What the fuck did you do to her?" I scream.

Arden pulls back his arm to clobber the naked professor again.

Hollis holds up his hands in surrender. "It wasn't me!"

"If it wasn't you, then what happened?" I demand.

"Two males were dragging her away. I just chased them off when you showed up."

"Sure. What were you doing out here in the first place?" Arden asks, not believing a word.

"Keeping an eye on the party. The school always sends a teacher to watch the students."

"It wasn't so you could spy on *her*?" Arden grabs Hollis around the throat.

"I swear. It's not like that." Hollis pulls on Arden's wrist, and finally, the druid releases him.

"Shayla?" Arden calls as he storms over to us.

"She's knocked out," I answer for her.

"Can I see her?" Hollis asks. "I thought I scented something."

We let him approach, and he sniffs her. "Sleeping draught. A lot of it from what I can tell."

Arden scoops her up effortlessly and races toward the school—to his aunt.

Hollis shifts back into a wolf and runs after him. I'm not as fast as either of them, but I do my best to keep up.

When I reach the healer's wing, Shayla is on a bed. Ms. Boyd uses magic to assess Shayla's state. My sweet mage is still unconscious.

"I can try to draw out most of the toxins," Ms. Boyd says. "But I've never seen a poisoning like this myself. She's in a coma-like state—a magically induced one, and... I fear she might not wake up."

Hollis' wolf whines.

Yeah, me too, fucker.

"I can help," Arden offers.

"Don't push yourself too hard," his aunt warns. "You almost burned yourself out last time."

He turns a steely glare on her. "I will do whatever I need to for her."

Ms. Boyd backs down.

"Do you think I should try to go inside Shayla's mind and wake her?" I ask, feeling nervous about broaching the subject.

Hollis shifts into his human form. He steps in front of me in all his naked, masculine glory, blocking my view of Shayla. If I weren't so freaked out by Shayla's condition, I would admire Hollis' delicious body.

"How skilled are you at shadowwalks?" The professor narrows his eyes at me, reading me with his mage intuition.

"I'm good... very good." I grimace.

Too good.

"We should bring in someone with more experience," Hollis says.

"I won't allow another cubi in her head." I step threateningly toward him. "Got it?"

He studies my resolve and sees my commitment to Shayla's well-being. "I think I do."

Like I do when I feed astrally, I relax on a bed. This time, I'm lying right next to my target. I've wanted to sink into her mind so many times, but not like this. I wanted to be *invited*... by her. I wanted this beautiful, yet broken soul, who has pieced herself back together, to welcome me inside.

"This won't hurt her?" Arden asks as he holds her. Already, he has burned off much of the poison, but she's still stuck in a coma.

"I *never* hurt those I feed on. I *never* feed from their magic, only their pleasure. Besides, I'm not going to feed on her," I grit out, my jaw tight. I understand why he's asking, but it offends me just the same. Hasn't he been paying attention to my feelings? Or maybe they all assume it's my *schtick*, as Shayla called it.

Ms. Boyd's eyes fill with worry every time she looks at Shayla.

She isn't going to snap out of this unless I can help heal her mind and convince her consciousness to wake.

I can do this. I *must* do this.

Laying back, I close my eyes and concentrate. After a moment, I feel the pop of my shadowself detaching from my body. Hovering over her, I give Shayla one last look. She doesn't have the look of someone peacefully sleeping. Her lips are blue from the poison, her skin ashen.

I hate having to use my powers on her without her consent. I had promised myself that I would *never ever* do that—on anyone, let alone her. I never want to be like *him*.

Will I find that I'm truly no different from that asshole? And all my objections and rules were just lies that I tell myself? Will I discover after today that I'm just a monster like him?

I had planned to make Shayla trust me, winning my way into her heart and mind. I fear that she'll never trust me after this breach. With how much she hates psychic invasion, she may never forgive me, that is *if* she wakes at all.

Shoving away the negative thoughts, I dive into her head.

But it isn't as easy as it should be. I bounce off a wall of darkness. Given that I've never entered a mind unwelcome, I don't know if this is what happens when someone's defenses are still up. But from everything I know, it shouldn't be this... dark.

I throw myself against the wall several times, with a growing worry that I've trapped myself in someone's mind. It has happened to other cubi. It could happen again now.

"Shayla!" I call telepathically. "It's Landis. Let me in!"

I smash against her mental walls. Then I feel a strange sensation… a soft burning, but I know it's not *exactly* real. I pull back and wonder if this is her magic. Is it trying to push me away? Or can I pass through… *safely*?

Perhaps the defenses she's reinforced for two decades are too strong for her to drop them for anyone, let alone someone she has only known a couple of weeks.

I press my shadowhand against the barrier. My senses tingle, but the burning sensation has changed into the pins and needles of an arm going numb. Encouraged by my hand's ability to move past the barrier, I slowly step forward.

Immediately, I'm surrounded by a swirling hurricane of magic. *Shit*.

Is *all this* Shayla's power?

I'm a bit frightened. If she can't learn to control this amount of magic, when it finally does break out of its cage, she will hurt herself—or others. And she'll be tossed into the asylum, Rourke's idea or not.

I can't even guess what her innate ability is. It doesn't feel like anything I've tasted before—and I've tasted *almost* every supe there is.

I trudge through the chaos that feels like wind and sand against my psychic form. Something feels wrong. I realize I'm beginning to erode away.

What the fuck?

Reaching Shayla's inner space, where her soul now hides, might be more challenging than I anticipated.

I force myself forward. After a few more difficult steps, I'm in complete darkness.

Did I get kicked out of her mind?

Have I died?

No. I *feel* her. She's close.

A child's whimper draws me forward. Faint figures reveal themselves in the gloom. A woman with hair the same color as Shay's looms over a small girl of about six years old. The girl is curled up in a ball, her back against a wall of sorts, holding her hands over her head to protect herself from any blows.

My heart cracks. This would be hard to watch in any circumstance, but knowing it's Shay... I can barely hold myself back from attacking this woman—her mother. Of course, it wouldn't do any good. This is only a memory. And Shayla has to break out of it herself. Although, I can help. Or I hope I can.

"I wish you'd never been born!" the woman yells and kicks Shayla's side. "He promised we'd have a *powerful* child, and all I got was pathetic trash like you."

"Shayla," I call to her gently. "This isn't happening."

The woman continues to throw insults, but Shayla peeks through her arms at me.

"It's real."

"Yes, it happened, but *this* is only a memory." I slowly approach. "Do you remember me?"

She blinks at me a few times, and the sound of her mother's voice begins to fade. Her red-rimmed, innocent child's eyes freaking shatter me. My own eyes fill with tears.

"Landis?" she asks. She ages to her twenty-year-old self, and the mother disappears. "You look... different. Faded. Like a shadow." She narrows her eyes at me. "Why are you here?"

"You were drugged. Attacked. I'm trying to wake you so you don't die."

Her eyes glaze over for a moment as she remembers. "Those males. The juice."

"Yes." I hold out my hand for her to take. I wobble from my lack of energy. Remaining here drains me since I'm not feeding off her in any way. "Arden and his aunt are working on clearing your system of the poison, but you aren't waking up. I'm sorry I intruded, but I couldn't let your soul drift away."

"I'm dying?" she asks, not sounding particularly upset by the idea.

"Hey." I move forward and hold her hands. "I know life sucks sometimes. But please, let me help to make it better."

She stares at our joined hands. Something I've never done in our physical bodies. Then she searches my eyes. "You're risking yourself to do this, aren't you? Why?"

"I couldn't let you go."

"You need to leave." She pushes away my hands. "I can feel your energy's fading. Go!"

"Not without you!" I grab her hand.

She stares into my eyes. Maybe she sees my sincerity, my desperation. I can't tell.

I'm ejected from her mind, crashing through the darkness and the swirling chaotic magic, and the next thing I know, I'm staring up at the healer's ceiling.

I gasp for breath. Ms. Boyd is nearby and places a hand on my chest so I don't try to launch myself up. I'm glad since I would have fallen on my face. I'm weak.

Dressed in only gray sweatpants, Hollis stares down at me with concern in his eyes. He pats my shoulder. "Rest. You drained yourself." They way he looks at me, like he's proud that I tried, makes me suck in a breath. Goddess, I hate that I like him more than I should. That he sees me as more than my species or my past.

"Shayla?" I ask, trying to ignore what the professor stirs in me.

"Color has returned to her cheeks, but she hasn't opened her eyes yet," Hollis says, all while staring in her direction.

He's distraught. Reading him, not with my powers—they're shot—but just with my mundane senses, I know he cares about her more than a professor should.

Arden calls, "She's waking!"

Ms. Boyd rushes over.

I try to leap up again, but Hollis catches me. "Take it easy."

He helps me up to my feet and moves us closer, so I can see Shay.

Still looking worn, she blinks a few times and studies us with confusion. She looks down at Arden's tight grip on her, Hollis' naked chest, and then my weary face as I lean against Hollis.

"Landis! What happened to you?" She moves to get up and help me but crashes back down into Arden's arms.

"Easy," Ms. Boyd soothes her. "He's just a bit drained from breaking you out of the coma."

"You really were in my head?" Her eyes and voice are vulnerable.

"I'm sorry. I didn't want to invade."

Shayla doesn't respond, but I see a flicker of unease and fear.

Ms. Boyd motions me back to my bed. "You've seen her. Now rest."

While Hollis helps me, Shayla watches me with wariness. Fuck. I didn't want this. But I knew going into it that this might be her reaction. She might never forgive me... might never trust me.

"You can go now," Ms. Boyd says to Hollis.

"No," Hollis says, with no room for argument. "Someone is after her. And I will not leave her alone."

Ms. Boyd hears the same thing in his voice that I do.

Possessiveness.

Shayla hears it as well and looks unsettled by the realization. "But Rourke—" she says softly, apparently not wishing to summon the beast.

"Do you see him here, worrying over you? No! For all we know, he's behind this attack!" Hollis growls. His chest heaves with his fraying restraint.

"You think he would do *that*?" I ask.

"So he can have his *perfectly* packaged future?" Hollis glares at me, his eyes flaring gold with unbridled magic. "Yes. I do."

His guard drops ever so slightly, and I sense his hatred is for

Rourke's family, not so much directed at Rourke himself. Now I wonder what happened between Hollis and the Lewellyns. Especially if he means to claim Shayla, as I sense that he wants to.

Shaking off that concerning thought, my eyelids grow heavy.

My energy gives out, and I fall into oblivion.

23

RETURN TO OFFENDER

SHAYLA

*M*y memory of Landis' trip inside my mind is fuzzy.

I stare across the space between our hospital beds and wonder why he risked himself for me. Perhaps there's more to his interest in me than a flirty friendship and a magic meal.

I *feel* Rourke storming down the halls before I see him. Our bond... I've felt it tug on me before.

I also know when he's *with* someone else. I try not to let it bother me, but the magic link makes it hard to ignore that he has something going on—and has feelings for this person. Was he in a relationship when he hooked up with me?

Or is he following the Elven way of discovering one's sexuality before mating? Either way, the magic within our mate bond doesn't like being uncompleted.

Rourke and Branden burst into the healer's arena.

"Where is she?" Rourke demands. It almost sounds as if he cares.

Hollis springs up and blocks Rourke's path to me. "Was it you?!"

"If I wanted her dead, she'd be dead," Rourke growls in the professor's face and pushes past him. He charges up to my side. His cobalt eyes trail down my body and back up to my face, no doubt seeing how close I came to dying. "What happened?" He sounds more demanding than worried, but a hint of concern pops through. Was it just for his reputation or for my well-being?

"Like you don't already know!" Hollis barks.

Ms. Boyd brushes past Branden at the foot of my bed and comes up beside Rourke. "Being that she is your *betrothed*, I will tell you what happened. Shayla was given a lethal amount of sleeping draught and was being dragged off toward the outer walls. Mr. Hollis was on patrol to monitor the party and caught them before the males made off with her beyond our boundaries. They were taking her toward town."

Rourke's body is tense. He keeps his attention on me but asks her, "How did she survive a *lethal* dose?"

Arden speaks up at his question. "Are you disappointed?"

Rourke's eyes simmer with fire as he snaps his gaze to the druid. "Screw off, tree fucker."

Ms. Boyd cuts in, irritation evident in her tone, "Due to *Arden's* quick response, bringing her here, then draining all of his magic to heal her, and Landis calling her consciousness out of a coma, she was able to make it through."

"Landis was *inside* her?" Rourke shouts.

All the drama finally drains me, and my eyes flutter closed.

"Everyone out," Ms. Boyd orders. "She needs to rest."

Protests are heard all around, but Ms. Boyd stays firm. "Stand outside if you like, but not in here."

Even Arden is forced to leave, since he has exhausted his healing magic.

I'm worried when I realize Landis never roused during all the yelling.

If he dies on me, I'll bring him back to kill him.

When I wake up the next day, Landis is not in the healing wing.

I panic, and Ms. Boyd hears me cursing.

She rushes over and sees my eyes lingering on his empty bed. "Landis is fine. He returned to his room a little while ago."

"When can I leave?"

"You need to remain in bed for the next few days."

"Here?"

Ms. Boyd places her hands on my forehead and reads my health. "If you promise to rest, I will let you return to your dorm room."

As if summoned, Arden appears out of nowhere. "I can take her."

His aunt rolls her eyes but waves him on. He picks me up, despite my protests that I can handle it, and carries me all the way to our dorm. Thank goodness it's early enough that we hardly see a soul.

Rourke, Branden, and Landis appear as if they're all waiting on the couch for my arrival.

"What's all this?" I ask, my heart thumping with what looks like an impending confrontation.

Arden sets me down on the open couch, places my feet on his lap, and drapes a blanket over me. Weirdly, Rourke doesn't complain or seem jealous.

My mate eyes me. "Were they students?" he asks gently. I find it odd that he would ask this if he were behind my attack. Is this some elaborate cover-up?

"I don't think so," I answer honestly. I remember what they said when they thought I was unconscious.

Rourke sees something in my eyes. "What is it?"

"They mentioned they saw me before… and thought I had no magic. Also, I definitely *was* their target." My eyes well up with emotion, my mate bond making me hurt more than I should. "You really weren't behind my attack?"

He sighs, knowing that I have a right to ask. "No."

"Your family?"

"I don't think so. If they were, they didn't tell me. I think they worry too much about a curse to send someone after you directly."

"Then who would want to kidnap me?" I ask. "I'm nobody."

Rourke glances at the group and back at me. "Not anymore. You're connected to *me* now. Also, I think you have more magic than you realize."

Hollis' warning that I shouldn't let anyone know about my power echoes in my mind. "Yeah, because I thought I had zero magic. And it turns out I only have a suppressed wisp of magic." I shrug, trying to downplay what Quade seemed to sense in me.

"I feel a lot more than a *wisp* through our bond now." He levels a knowing look at me.

"What are you getting at?" I try to reinforce my blocking abilities.

"Magic is dwindling. And supes are disappearing," Rourke explains. "I don't know how or if the two are connected. But your attempted abduction is the first concrete evidence I have that *someone is* taking supes, and they aren't just vanishing for supernatural reasons."

"Your friend disappeared on her way to the Elfhame gate," Branden adds. "But from what I was able to find out, there was no evidence left behind. No indications of what species took her or if she just ran away from home."

"She wasn't going to run. That was me. Myra was excited to come here."

"I believe you," Rourke says. "And now, I don't want you going *anywhere* alone."

"I don't get it." I snap, "Why do you suddenly give a damn about me?"

Landis flattens his lips in distaste. "He thinks you might be powerful now."

Rourke glares at Landis and then says, "Yes. I do." He turns to me. "And you're mine... Well, until we can permanently sever our bond. If someone takes you, they'll have a link to me. Does that satisfy your suspicions about my intentions?"

"Perfectly." I scowl. "Wouldn't want me to think you give a fuck about your *fated* mate!" I fling off the blanket and stagger to get up.

Arden is there in an instant and steadies me. "She needs to rest."

Rourke doesn't argue with that assessment and storms out of the dorm.

Branden stands and walks over to the hall door. "Seriously, you need to have someone with you at all times."

"Do you trust Arden and Landis to make sure I don't get whisked away?" I ask, a sneer in my voice.

He cocks a brow, considering my question, and nods. "Mostly." Then he grabs his bag by the door and heads out.

After Arden tucks me into my bed, he looks at Landis lingering at my door, staring at me. The druid gives him a nod. "I'll be in the main room if you need me, Sparkles."

When we're alone, I can't look Landis in the eye. I wave him off.

"Shayla?" Landis asks with such an insecure tone that I barely recognize his voice.

"Hmm?" I refuse to turn my head and make eye contact with the male who rummaged through my nightmare brain.

"Will you ever forgive me?" When I don't immediately respond, he goes on, "I would never have gone into your mind without your permission, but—"

"Shut the door. Sound-seal it," I order.

Landis audibly swallows his nerves. He does as I ask,

waving a hand over the closed door to block our voices from traveling outside the room. It's an incubus' innate gift.

"What did you see?" I ask.

"First, darkness, your shield. Then a fuck-ton of magic, swirling like a class five hurricane. And then… uh, your mother."

"I remember you seeing my mother hurting me, yelling at me. Did you go anywhere else that I don't remember?"

"No. That's it. I swear."

"So now you think of me as some pathetic child."

"What? Never!" He reaches out but quickly stops himself. With only his eyes, he implores me to believe him. "I think you're stronger than I ever realized for having a shit parent like that, and you're still kind and wonderful."

"And broken," I add.

"Aren't we all a little broken?" he asks. I hear the notes of a dark past ringing in his voice. Until now, Landis has always had the lilt and demeanor of a playboy. Not now.

He still looks horrible. His eyes are sunken. He sways ever so slightly.

"Are you okay?" I ask.

"I'll be fine." He tries to square his shoulders and appear strong.

"Did going inside me mess you up?" I ask, feeling guilty.

"I'll recover." He smiles at me, but it doesn't reach his eyes. He turns toward the door.

I grab his shirt sleeve before he can get far. "Why haven't you replenished your magic?"

"I… I did what I promised I would *never* do. I invaded."

"But you only did it to help me, not to benefit you. That's obvious by the look of you. So why haven't you fed? Are you punishing yourself?"

Landis turns back to look into my eyes, searching for forgiveness. "Do you forgive me?"

"Yes. Of course. I'm not happy that it needed to happen or

that you hurt yourself doing it, but yes." He still seems off, so I ask, "Is there another reason you haven't fed?"

He opens his mouth but doesn't answer.

"You literally have a mob of females who want you—"

"I don't want them," he blurts out.

"Then is it Chara? Or are you into guys?" I hurry to ask. "I'm sorry, I shouldn't have assumed."

"You. *I want you*," Landis says, and then his eyes widen, surprised at his own confession. "But I messed that up."

I'm stunned. He has neglected himself because he wants only me. I sit, rattled and confused. "How did you mess it up?" I ask. "Is it because you can't forget the scene in my head? Or because you think I wouldn't want you to feed on me now?"

"That trip didn't change how *I* feel about you. Besides, everyone has their secrets. Believe me. That isn't even the worst I've seen." He rubs his face and refuses to look at me.

"Then feed on me."

He drops his head, sits on the edge of my bed, then finally gazes into my eyes. The gray irises swirl with dark smoke. "My need for you isn't about a meal. Well, not completely."

"Oh." I bite my lip.

His eyes catch the motion.

"I didn't want to assume it was anything more," I whisper.

"If that frightens you…"

"No," I quickly say. "Well, yes. It does. But I want you." I stare off in the direction of Rourke's room. "What about him? He will know. I can feel him when he's… with someone. If he can sense the same with me, he might figure it out and come after you."

"If I use my shadow to *connect* with you, it shouldn't register to his senses. It would be like a dream."

I shiver.

"But we don't have to do anything, love." His darkening gray eyes draw me in.

I know that he isn't actively trying to seduce me. Goddess,

he doesn't even have any magic to *make* me crave him, but in this moment, all I want is him. I think about how he makes me feel, my growing desire for him, and his sacrifice, and I want to give him whatever he needs. If the only way for us to be together is through a shadow dream, then so be it.

Lifting my hand, I reach out to brush my thumb over his plump lower lip.

He pulls away. "We shouldn't touch... physically."

For some reason, I don't think it's just because Rourke will know. And then I think about it, I realize that he has never made skin-to-skin contact with me. "Why not?"

"I'm not ready to talk about it. I just can't..." He looks away. "If that's a deal-breaker, I get it."

"No. I want you. Now."

He sucks in a breath. Then he says, "Don't do this out of pity."

"I've wanted you from the moment I saw you, *dummy*."

"Such sweet seduction." He grins playfully.

"I'm not like you." I blush, thinking about my inexperience. "I'm just a step beyond a virgin."

"It was with *him*?"

"First, last, and only." I frown.

"Tonight then?" He studies my response, looking for any hesitation. "And you can say no at any moment. Do you understand? I'll leave with no expectations."

"But you need to feed," I protest.

"Your comfort will *always* come first. Always. Do you understand?" he demands, his voice taking on an authoritative tone that makes my core melt.

When I don't answer, he asks again, "Understand? If I do something you don't want... I will *never* forgive myself."

"All right. I'll tell you if I need to stop."

24

SECRET RENDEZVOUS

SHAYLA

*T*he thought of being with an incubus… being with *Landis*, an *incubus*, has me worked up all day. I refrain from relieving any tension because I know that he'll feed off this excitement that's building between my legs.

All four of my roommates have taken shifts in the main room to ensure I won't get abducted again. Fortunately, only Arden and Landis try to talk with me. Arden brings me food and water. Landis gives me little winks and hints about what to expect from our rendezvous.

Which is… *anything* I want.

No pressure.

I roll my eyes at myself. I suppose I should be grateful that it will take place in the shadowscape where reality is warped. Maybe I'll even be a gifted lover in this alternate reality. I certainly don't feel good about my *physical* love life.

Rourke. He definitely was great until it all went to shit.

I just hope it doesn't happen now.

Arden says goodnight after checking in on me and closes my door. I can hear everyone in the main room. Then an eerie silence—Landis. He has sound-sealed the door.

Closing my eyes, I allow my mind to drift to sleep. It isn't hard. I'm exhausted. And Landis has assured me that it's safe. He won't feed on my magic or energy from emotional memories, just my sexual pleasure. And in my dreams, I won't be too tired.

I'm waiting for Landis, but I can't wait any longer. My hand slides down my sleep shorts and under my panties to my slick center. I want to feel his hands on me. I've been working myself up all day.

I sense someone watching. *Is it him?*

A shadowy figure emerges from the darkness that surrounds me.

I freeze. At first, I think it's due to fear.

"It's me, love."

"Landis?" I suddenly realize I can't move except my mouth and eyes. "Am I asleep? What's happening?"

"You're asleep—like a lucid dream. And the paralysis is a side effect when I feed. I'm sorry about that. Do you want me to leave?"

"No. Wait! You're just going to leave me like this?" I use my eyes to indicate my hand down my panties, the other hand up my shirt, squeezing my breast.

"Impatient little thing," he chides playfully.

"I've been *very* patient—the entire day."

I feel his gaze on me even if I can't truly see his eyes. While he appears to be contemplating what to do to me, I study him. He's a ghost of himself. I'm able to see right through him, but somehow I still see a twinkle in his eye, amused by my compromised position.

"I suppose *ghosting* takes on a whole other meaning for an incubus," I smirk.

"You aren't afraid of me?" he asks. Somehow I can see worry etched in his wispy form.

A bit of doubt rubs at my conviction. "Should I be?"

"No." He moves closer. "However, I'm going to pleasure you so thoroughly that I ruin you for anyone who dares to tempt you away from me."

"I'm not afraid. I just didn't realize the legends were accurate—that I'd be unable to move."

"Unfortunately, they are true."

"Will I be able to feel you?" I ask, a pout in my voice.

I gasp as a shadowy tendril extends from his form and strokes the side of my face.

The sensation is like velvet, lighting up all my nerve endings.

It skates over my pert nipples, down my arm, and grazes my sex.

Desire. Lust. Need.

This is all in my mind, but it feels so real. I realize this is happening in a space that exists outside my normal understanding of reality. But it feels... so natural.

His tendril slides next to my fingers and skims lightly against my clit in the most delicious way.

"Stars!" I pant.

Two more tendrils pull up my shirt until my round breasts are revealed.

His *eyes* sparkle in his shadow form.

I hate not seeing his beautiful physical body. But I understand if this is all we can have... *for now*. Our secret moment.

His appendages loop around both of my nipples, pinching them, and making them pebble. Then he tightens his hold, tweaking them in the most exquisite way. A tendril slides down my panties and caresses my inner thigh but has yet to give me the attention I crave.

"Landis, I need more," I whine.

His entire form slips down and covers me completely. Tendrils of shadows skim along every damned inch of me, even where my body touches the bed.

A mouth of sorts presses over my lips. I part them and allow a shadow tongue to tangle with mine. If I close my eyes, it's almost as if it were his physical body on mine, his weight on top of me.

"Let's move this hand," he says as he pulls my hand from my wet center.

Then my shorts and panties slide down my legs.

"Are you going to…" I breathe out.

"Yes. I'm going to give you what we both need."

Frozen in place and helpless to his whims, I feel like I shouldn't be as turned on as I am, but his touch is so gentle yet confident that I can't help but get lost in his control over my body.

His mass shifts downward until his face is level with the apex of my thighs.

Tendrils wrap around my legs, pulling me completely open to his hungry gaze.

I cry out when his light touch brushes my pussy, skimming over me again and again, driving me insane. I try to wiggle and squirm for him to press harder, but I can't move.

"*Please…*" I moan.

After my plea, he latches onto my clit with his mouth, and a tendril slides inside me—stroking in and out, slowly probing deeper. It begins to thicken. He's stretching me, hitting all the places inside. His tendril undulates and almost feels as though it were vibrating.

All the sensations are driving me insane.

A tug on my nipples makes me cry out. "Landis!"

"It's fucking beautiful to hear my name on your tongue like that."

"Please," I beg. I can do nothing to return his affections, just bask in the bliss that I feel.

All my pent-up sexual energy over the last few weeks crests inside me…

I'm pretty sure I see actual stars, not just the burst behind my eyes, because it feels like I'm launched into the cosmos.

The wave of my orgasm hits me so hard I double over from the force of it.

A guttural cry escapes my lips.

When I blink, Landis is gone.

I know I'm in the real world again.

Sweat glistens on my skin as I pant. I look down to see I'm fully clothed. My pussy is still tingling from my orgasm.

I half expect the guys to burst in here from my scream, but I remember Landis has sealed the door. Unless…

Branden, Arden, then Rourke burst into my room, looking around for the source of my cry. Landis leans against the door frame with a heated gaze until the others turn. I hope no one noticed his lustful look.

"What happened?" Arden asks.

"It was only a dream," I say.

Rourke narrows his eyes at me and sniffs the air. "A *bad* dream?"

Whoops. He can smell my arousal.

"A none-of-your-business dream." I wave them out of my room.

Rourke glances at Landis, perhaps suspecting something. "I think it *is* my business."

"Oh, so we're playing that card? Then you want to tell me who you've been having sex with?" I snap out.

Rourke trades a look with Branden. The vamp barely moves a facial muscle, but I can see it in his eyes. He's warning Rourke to back off.

"Fine. Have your *dreams*." Rourke huffs and storms out. I can smell the angry smoke wafting off him.

Branden gives me a lingering inscrutable look, then zips out of the room.

The druid stares at Landis, then at me, shaking his head. "Be more careful."

"Of what?" Landis asks innocently.

"You appear *much* better, Landis. I suppose you found a source to feed?" Arden knocks the incubus' shoulder as he passes by to leave.

Landis blows me a kiss and mouths the words *thank you*.

As he closes the door, I whisper, "You do look better."

The following morning, Landis stays behind to keep an eye on me while I recover, as the other three leave for class. He looks like his usual, healthy self again. He runs a hand over the outer door so that no one can hear us from the hallway.

"We need to talk," Landis says as an opener.

My stomach drops. My heart races, pounding in my ears until I don't think I could hear him if he said a word. Here it comes... I'm about to get rejected once again.

My brain reminds me that I never wanted a mate, but my heart doesn't give a damn in this moment.

"I get it." I stand up to hide in my room, just in case any tears decide to come out and make me look like a sappy fool. "You can save your breakup talk. Your chase is over. It was what it was—a feeding. Well, I guess now we're even."

"*What?*" Landis rushes to block me from escaping to my room.

His hand slides up to cup the side of my face, but he doesn't touch me. This no-touching rule of his is starting to drive me insane. I need to know what his hang-up is.

Is it me? Or did something happen in his past? *What?*

His gray eyes dull as if I hurt him when I beat him to the breakup sucker punch. "That wasn't at *all* what I was going to say."

"*We need to talk?*" I huff. "I might not have any experience with boyfriends, but I know a brush-off when I hear it. Don't try to smooth it over now."

He looks at the ceiling, frustrated. "Shit. I guess it came out like that."

"Okay, then what is it?" I cross my arms, not believing him completely.

He guides me back to the couch. "It's about last night... which was amazing, by the way," he adds quickly. "But I have a confession... I accidentally tasted some of your magic when you came so hard that you knocked me out of your mind. By the way, getting tossed out of the shadowrealm like that has never happened to me before."

"Don't you usually *taste* a person's magic when feeding?"

"Not like this," he explains. "When you orgasmed, you threw me out. I crashed through your magic and absorbed a bit of it. As I did, I got a better sense of it because your magic wasn't trying to fight me off, per se. It was like nothing I ever sensed before."

"Is it... bad?"

"Bad? No, I'd say *intense*. Scary, powerful, turbulent."

I shiver with the thought. "*Am* I a threat to others? *Should* they lock me up?"

"Well... you might have the potential to be a threat if you don't get a handle on it."

"But Mr. Hollis has been ordered to stay away from me. And the school won't assign me anyone else to help—probably on Rourke's orders."

"I think you need to ask Hollis to work with you—in secret."

Landis says softly, "And I might be able to help in my own way. Especially if he's able to identify what power you have."

I don't mention Hollis has already offered to help in secret. I think I can trust Landis, but I need to be cautious. Branden threatened to withhold any news about Myra.

Then I remember that Branden hasn't given me any information beyond that she's missing. Rourke told me that magic is vanishing, and so are supes. I already knew that. Besides, I need to fix my magic before I disappear, too. If I get locked up or abducted, I won't be much help in finding Myra, anyway.

"After you were poisoned and I entered your mind, you were in a memory about your mother," Landis prompts. He winces as he remembers his uninvited visit.

I nod. "She was hitting me and yelling."

"She mentioned your father... and that he claimed you would be powerful," Landis reminds me. "Did she ever say what kind of supe he was or why he told her that?"

I think about anything she might have said about him but come up with nothing. The memory Landis witnessed was buried deep in my subconscious. I hadn't thought about it until now. "Not that I can remember." Then I ask, hoping for more insight, "What did my power feel like it *could* be?"

"I don't know." Landis leans forward, almost brushing his lips over mine. He enjoys driving me insane with lust. He promises, "But I'll help you find out, love."

Arden is the next to watch over me, as if I needed babysitting.

Fortunately, when it's Rourke's and Branden's turn, they sit in their rooms with the door half shut.

I hate to admit that I feel better knowing my abductors

would have to go through one of my roommates before getting to me. If only I could wield my mysterious power, I could fight back. This is the first time I want to claim my magic. And it worries me now that Landis describes it as a hurricane.

What if I am dangerous?

Having gone through the rotation today, Landis gives me a wink goodbye behind Arden's back as he heads off to his last class.

All the thoughts swimming in my head have drained me. Besides, I'm still not a hundred percent yet. I intend to go back to class after tomorrow, regardless of their protests.

I wander toward my room so that I can lie down.

"Come here," Arden orders gently but firmly. But he meets me halfway and holds the sides of my face with his large hands, inspecting my eyes and my coloring. "You're improving, but you need more healing."

"Arden." I place my hands over his wrists, which still hold me. "I know you're wearing yourself out doing that. You need to save your strength. You need your magic for your studies, too."

"I powered up in the forest before I headed back here. I'll be fine." He drops his hands, scoops me into his arms, and carries me over to the couch, setting me on his lap. My side presses against his broad chest. I'm only wearing a thin tank and sleep shorts and feel practically naked in his arms.

"You know, I'm not a doll to carry around," I huff, but I really don't mind it that much. I feel safe and protected in his embrace. It's truly the first time in my life I can say that and really understand the meaning behind those words.

"You aren't a doll, but you are stubborn."

"You're one to talk." I glare at him with no heat behind it.

With one swift motion, Arden slips off his shirt. My body

heat rises instantly, by about a million degrees. Why does my best friend have to be so hot?

I try to avert my gaze before I begin to drool over his bulging muscles and silky skin dusted with light brown hair, just enough to tickle my skin and stimulate my senses. But I can't seem to look away.

His cheeks turn pink when he sees my widening eyes gawking at his chest. "Uh.... Skin to skin. It'll be easier on my magic."

"Do you do this for every girl who gets a boo-boo?" I joke.

"No," he says succinctly.

With his strange tone, my eyes dart up to take in his forest green irises. "What is it?"

"Nothing. I just don't really share my healing with others."

"I guess the way you do it, it's kind of personal." I drop my head and tuck it under his chin. My hand slides over to his hulking arm draped over my hip. "I'm honored you chose to share your gift with me."

"Uh, I suppose I should've told you the first time that there's a bit of an energy *exchange*... small but *some*. I'm sorry that I didn't mention it before."

"I don't mind that I'm connected... to you." I trail my fingers closer to his sacred druid tattoos. "I want to have a closer look at your symbols. Is it still okay for me to touch them?"

"*You* can."

I run my finger over the intricate art of his Celtic knots, which swirl from his wrist to his shoulder, then over fine lines that trail up into his hairline and end, from what I can see, behind his ear. Then I lightly trace the outline on his outer pectorals, moving down his side, all the way to his waist.

He jerks.

"Did I tickle you?" I perk up and look at him.

"Don't you dare," he warns. "I'm supposed to be healing you."

"But isn't high morale good for my health?" I bat my eyes in an over-the-top fashion.

He chuckles. "No, *Sparkles*."

My childhood nickname… I blush bright red, thinking how stupid I was to have a crush on him for all these years. He will always see me as a broken kid. I suppose I am.

"Hey, what's wrong?" he asks, his electric healing pauses, or maybe I don't feel it due to my embarrassment.

"Nothing."

"Will you tell me?"

"Fine." I look at my fingers instead of his face. "I was thinking about how I was such a silly, broken thing when you knew me. You must've thought I was so dumb for getting excited that you gave me a sparkly pen." I don't tell him I still have that pen—one of my few mementos attached to a happy moment.

"Is that why you think I call you Sparkles?"

"Isn't it?"

"No. Whenever you had strong emotions, there were sparkles all around you."

"Was it my magic?"

He glances away. "Well, I thought it was your inner beauty shining through."

I blush again but for a completely different reason than I did previously. The way his emerald eyes glow when he remembers me makes my heart hiccup.

I smile, wanting with all my being to lean forward and kiss him. But that would make him feel awkward and ruin our friendship. "That's sweet." I sigh as I relax back into his arms, absorbing the affection from this beautiful male.

25

BACK TO SCHOOL

SHAYLA

I return to my classes. I'm grateful it's the academic day, not P.E. and tutoring.

Landis and Kat fuss over me. But I finally convince them that I'm fine.

I dread the idea of begging Mr. Hollis to train me in secret. After I blew him off and the awkward being drugged-and-dragged-off fiasco, I don't want to face him again, but I will.

"I can't believe Mr. Hollis fought off your attackers," Kat whispers as we enter the room.

"He's in fighting form." I wistfully remember his exposed muscular chest during a rare conscious moment after the attempted abduction.

Kat eyes the professor with new appreciation as we sit down in our seats.

He catches my attention with a nod of his head. "Miss Willows, did Miss Kincaid give you a copy of my class notes?"

"Uh, yes, sir. I should be caught up." I smile gratefully. At least, I hope that's the smile my face is making. It might be a grimace. Whenever I'm around Quade... *Mr. Hollis*, why do I feel like a baby fawn staggering awkwardly with my limbs wobbling everywhere?

"Good to have you back," he says, and my cheeks flush hot. Thankfully, he looks away before seeing the charge his words have on me. "Class, today we'll talk about *how* a mage uses their magic to cast an arcane spell. First, a mage has to be identified as such. How many here are full mages or have some mage magic?"

Several hands go up—half of the class. Even Kat raises her hand.

"Yes, some mages, like Miss Kincaid and myself, are also shifters. Or they can be druids. Even cubi or vampires can have mage abilities. So what does that really mean? We're all magical, right?"

A murmur of agreement goes through the room.

"Well, some supes only have the inherent magical abilities that come with their birthright. They cannot channel magic for uses such as enhancing a potion, or say, creating a ward, or using telekinesis, to name a few." Hollis sits on the front edge of his desk, his legs stretched out before him, looking every bit the casual, sexy professor.

"Miss Kincaid, when did you first notice that you had magic beyond your shifter abilities?"

Her eyes widen for a second, surprised he called on her, then she shrugs her shoulders, "I electrocuted my brother when he was trying to steal my book away from me."

"Remind me to never touch your books," I say out of the corner of my mouth.

The room chuckles, even Hollis, which lights up his face in such a beautiful way that my heart wants to explode since I put that smile on his mouth.

"Very good. Yes, emotions are often how we access our magic for the first time. It can be a positive emotion like joy or excitement or what we consider a negative emotion, such as fear or anguish."

I raise my hand, and he calls on me. "What do you mean by *we consider* fear or anguish as negative emotions?"

"Humans, and those of us partly human, have labeled fear as a negative emotion. However, that isn't the only way to look at it. Fear can be a healthy thing when used correctly. Having a healthy fear of heights when standing on the edge of a cliff will help you not fall off. Or if you have a fear that someone might be out to hurt you, then you might be more aware of your surroundings or what they say and do."

I nod, thinking about my fear of my mother. My heightened awareness of her got me out of a lot of bad situations because I avoided them.

Mr. Hollis explains, "At first, a mage learns to channel their magic with emotions. Then, as they become more adept at accessing it, they don't need to rely on their emotional state to trigger their magic. As I'm sure you learned in Basic Magicology 101, there's innate magic and the arcane. But truly, they're one and the same. Arcane magic is just focused, redirected innate magic. The problem is that innate magic can be wild and unpredictable, especially with a newer practitioner or someone who doesn't work with their magic very often."

Mr. Hollis glances at me and continues, "As you know, a big part of why this academy exists is to ensure you all have a firm grasp on your innate magic and learn how to wield it. Studying arcane spells can help you understand the flow of magic. And if you have mage abilities, how to redirect magic if you have too much built up inside you or how to use it to protect yourself from attacks."

His gaze lands on me with that last phrase. I squirm in my seat. If I had been learning to bring forth my magic, I might have been able to fight my attackers myself.

"This is why you all are here. To learn. To grow. To control your magic. So you can function happily in life." Mr. Hollis begins pacing slowly back and forth in front of the class and continues his lecture about creating wards with arcane spells.

His words today were meant especially for me. He's reminding me that I must control my magic or I'll be locked away. He doesn't realize I already planned on talking with him.

When class is dismissed, I tell Kat, "I'll meet you for lunch. I have a question about some of the stuff I missed."

She smirks playfully but agrees with a wink.

Hesitantly, I walk up to Mr. Hollis as the classroom empties out. "May I speak with you for a moment?"

His golden eyes lock onto me. I'm reminded of his predator. The self-preservation voice in my head says run. But I can't. I won't.

"Of course, I'm always available for my… students."

When we are alone in the room, my mouth races to get all the words out. "I don't know if you still have time or not, but I need you… or *someone* to teach me. I'm sorry I didn't take you up on your offer before. And thank you for stopping those men. But if I'd had my magic, maybe I wouldn't have been taken… and Branden didn't have any real information for me anyway. So I'm not going to let him coerce me anymore. I need help. But if it's you, we'll have to hide it from Rourke."

I gasp to take in a breath.

Hollis stares at me, unmoving. "Branden promised you information so that you would back away from me?"

I nod slowly. "He must have figured out we were going to meet in secret. And I wanted information about my missing friend Myra."

"Did he tell you anything at all?"

I glance at the door, half expecting Branden to burst in and tell me not to spill the beans about what they know. "Just that other students are missing."

"And what about magic itself?"

My eyes widen so much that I'm afraid they'll fall out of my face. I can't believe he's confiding in me. But I don't admit anything. "What about magic?" I whisper.

"Magic is dwindling in Elfhame, but oddly enough, you seem to have an ample supply swirling inside you—more than most."

"But hasn't Elfhame's magic been slowly shrinking for centuries?" I ask.

"Yes, but it's accelerating... exponentially. At this rate, we might not exist a decade from now."

"Fuck," I breathe out.

"Fuck, indeed."

"So, wait a sec. Why did you mention magic with the missing students? Do you think they're connected?"

I study his stunning face. There's a light stubble he's allowed to grow over the last few days. As he considers my question, his salt and pepper hair falls forward over his brow. For a moment, I forget that I had a question.

"I have no proof... not yet. But my instincts? They say yes."

"And you know that my friend is indeed missing?" I ask, my fear of the answer filling me with dread.

He sighs. "Myra Hurst is among the missing."

My heart breaks, but I try to hold it together. "What can I do to find her?"

"Without your magic? Nothing." He shakes his head. "Not even if you *had* your magic. Even our trained agents can't find them... *yet*."

I hate his resigned attitude.

"I'm sorry, Shayla."

"Sure, yeah." I realize I'm in danger of being late for my next class. "Should I find someone else to tutor me with my magic?" I ask, determined to master my power and find Myra.

His body tenses ever so slightly. The way my senses are tuned into his slightest movement, perhaps I am a shifter or vampire.

"Do you really believe I would trust anyone else with you?" His voice rings with possessiveness as well as protectiveness.

"I didn't know since I kinda blew you off." I shrug and frown.

"I understood why—Rourke's vengeance. But I was prepared to demand that you meet with me secretly as soon as you healed from this latest attack."

"I guess we're finally on the same page."

He grimaces, then nods. "Meet me behind the gym at our usual time."

"I'll be there," I say as I race out of the classroom to get to my English class across the school grounds.

My heart's pounding. I thank the goddess when I don't see Branden lurking outside. I suppose he believes that I'm done with Hollis—that he's successfully lured me away.

A hand grabs me from out of nowhere and stops me in my tracks. Another hand covers my mouth, keeping me from crying out. I'm pulled out of the hallway and into a shadowy alcove.

I smell Branden's heady vampiric scent. But my fear does not ease.

"Don't scream," he whispers into my ear. His hand drops from my mouth and instantly clasps my throat. He could snap my neck or rip out my jugular before I could say *mother-sucker*.

His nose sniffs my pulse. "Your magic is stronger, but it's still hiding, little witch."

I steel my voice before I dare to speak. It's icy when I ask, "What do you want?"

His nose lightly trails over my jugular. "You."

I suck in a breath. "What?"

In response to my shock, his hold on me tightens. "I mean... I need you to meet with Hollis and have him train you."

"But I thought—"

"It's different now." He presses so close that my body reacts to his power, craving his touch and his bite.

I want to lean into his hard lines and feel his length against my backside. I shake my head to clear my mind. "Why? What's your angle now?"

"You have power," he says.

"So what?" I wiggle, and he lets me break away to turn and look at him. "I'm still a nobody. The Lewellyns will put me in the asylum or maybe even in the ground to keep me away from Rourke. From everything I've learned in the last few weeks, they don't want someone like me muddying their bloodline."

"If you've been paying any attention, then you know that I do what is best for Rourke—not the Lewellyns—and often that *isn't* the same thing."

"So... are you saying you want me to *be* with him?"

"We'll see. First, claim your magic. Then we'll move forward with a plan based on what you have to offer. But you need to keep your progress quiet. Make sure Hollis knows that."

"Does Rourke know about your machinations?"

"Machinations?" He chuckles darkly. "So you aren't as simple as you first seemed."

"Yeah, I've read a book or two." I cross my arms. "But you're still an asshole."

"Guilty." He smirks. "But an asshole who might be your savior?"

"I doubt that." I roll my eyes. "I'm going to be late for my class now. You know I can't afford to lose a single point, or I'll be thrown out of this stupid—"

Before I can finish my sentence. I am flying down the hallways... in Branden's arms.

Holy blue ovaries, he's fast. The scenery flashes by, and I feel motion sickness.

When he screeches to a halt, I almost hurl. After setting me on my feet, I sway and bend over to catch my breath and make the world stop spinning.

"What the—?" I ask and almost fall over.

Branden shows me mercy and stabilizes me with a strong

hand on my lower back. I tense at his touch. I still don't trust him, even if he says he might want to save me.

"Thanks for the rollercoaster ride, but don't do that ever again." I stand up and glare at him.

His obsidian eyes twinkle with mischief. Damn, if it isn't a good look on him. "No promises." Then he zips off to wherever the hell he goes when he's not harassing me or being Rourke's personal bodyguard.

With unsteady steps, I walk into my English class exactly one second before the bell rings.

"He *wants* you to meet with Hollis?" Landis asks with doubt.

Arden and Landis crowd inside my tiny room, making everything look small. I don't worry about the others coming into the common room and hearing us, since Landis has sound-sealed the door.

"But what's the catch?" Arden asks.

"Either he wants me to piss off Rourke, or he's playing the long game. But I think he wants to use my magic for Rourke's benefit."

"He believes your magic is that powerful?" Arden asks, shaking his head.

"It might be," Landis says quietly.

I hate it when he's serious, and my incubus looks deadly serious right now.

"I don't know what I have to offer, but I need to control it whether or not Branden has designs on my abilities."

"True." Arden tightens his jaw, and his arms flex with restrained irritation. "But with Hollis?"

"You know he's the best mage here," Landis argues. "Besides, he won't do anything to hurt Shayla."

"How do you know that?" Arden turns to Landis.

"Because his wolf wants to claim her."

"What?" My mouth gapes. "That's ridiculous."

"Is it?" Landis cocks an eyebrow. "You feel a pull to him, too."

"Sure, he's very handsome and all that, but that's not what's happening." Even I can hear the lie in my words. "And with him, he's just protective of his students."

"Yeah, sure. And I'm a monk." Landis grins.

"It doesn't matter. Nothing's going on, and nothing *will* be going on. I already have one grumpy mate. I don't need two!"

"He won't claim you, but he *wants* to." Landis watches closely for my reaction, his smoky gray eyes swirling into charcoal.

"It doesn't matter either way." I shoo them out of my room. "I won't let anyone claim me again."

Landis spins and grabs me by the waist, pulling me close to his lean, muscular body. I feel his arousal through his pants, pressing into my stomach. He whispers over my lips, almost grazing them. "Don't make promises you won't keep."

Although my body craves to finally taste his lips, I yank myself out of his hold. Anger stirs and boils at his assumptions that I'm weak and will cave to Hollis or any other male's wish to *claim* me. "You don't know who I am, so don't assume you do."

Arden grabs Landis by the scruff of the neck. "Leave her be. She doesn't want you to provoke her with your bullshit."

26

LESSONS

QUADE

a day later, Shayla's scent still lingers in my nose. Or perhaps I'm just haunted by the blasted female.

Why her?

It's official… my love life is hexed.

Twice now, ruined by the cruel and vicious Lewellyns.

I wait for her behind the gym, like a couple of high school outcasts. In some ways, we are… outcasts, at least. We both come from poor backgrounds—the magic world against us.

But I had training. Sure, it wasn't ideal guidance, since it was in the form of an overly disciplinarian father. He would beat me to be better. Learning all the tricks, I pushed so much magic through myself that, at times, I thought I would die.

I almost did a few times.

Thankfully, I found someone else to help guide me when I was in my rebellious teens so that I could manage my anger. My unexpected mentor saved me.

I feel Shayla's presence before my heightened shifter senses can pick her up. *Goddess*, I'm doomed. My wolf knows her energy and claims that we're meant to be.

Not now. Maybe not ever.

First, I must focus on keeping her out of Ravenhollow Asylum. Second, I will find a way to break Rourke's claim on her. After she has passed her trials and is free to leave, *then* I can pursue something... *if* she doesn't just run for the hills the second she's freed.

Shayla slips around the corner. She doesn't know it, but I feel that she's used a bit of her magic just now. *Invisibility*. Well, not true invisibility, but the ability to pass unnoticed.

Interesting. Perhaps an innate gift? Or perhaps she created an impromptu spell of sorts to keep her mother's attention off her.

Good. That means not *all* her magic is locked away. Just shoved so far down that it feels like it exists in the center of the earth.

"Hi," Shayla whispers. She glances around as if expecting someone to jump out of the bushes in this remote, isolated location and attack her. And to be fair, it could happen.

"Come with me," I say without more than a hello back. *Distance*. I have to keep my emotional distance until this is done. Until the timing is right. *If* it ever is.

"Branden knows," she says, hurrying to keep up with my long legs. "So does Arden and Landis."

That makes me stop in my tracks and look at her. "Are you worried that I might do something to you?"

"What?" She chokes on the word. "Should I be worried?"

"No. Of course not. But it sounded like a warning that others know I'm with you, in case anything happens."

She gulps. Now I've got her worried. Perhaps I'll be able to tap into this and access her magic later. She charges up through emotions. I just have to break through the walls she's built up to keep her mother out.

"Branden caught me after our chat yesterday. He *wants* me

to work with you—almost insisted on it. He wants me to hone my magic."

"That's worrisome." I clench my jaw and plow forward to our remote and hidden destination.

Her eyes land on the taller city buildings not far from the school wall. From this far side of campus, one of the few remaining fae cities is only a quarter of a mile away. "Uh… where are we going?" she asks, panting to catch up.

"The bomb shelter." I bend down and open a hatch on the ground.

She steps back, leery of our new venue. "A real bomb shelter?"

"It's only what we call the safety room. Where some of the more powerful spells can be tested out while keeping the school safe. It keeps the bombs *in*… not out."

I scent fear on her. She's frozen in place. I can almost see her anchoring herself into the ground. Maybe she has an earth affinity?

"What is it?" I ask.

"I don't want to go down there." She won't look at me, her eyes locked on the open hatch.

"I promise I'm not going to hurt you."

She chuckles darkly, with no humor. "Yeah, that's not it… exactly."

"Then what?" I step closer, but she holds up her hands in a plea for me to stop.

I do, but everything in me screams to gather her into my arms and make her feel safe. But maybe that gesture would have the opposite effect.

I've been there when she has been at her most vulnerable. Maybe she associates me with the attack at the party… and with her weakest moments?

Maybe doubt still lingers that I had something to do with it. I hold perfectly still, waiting for her to trust me enough to let me know what's wrong.

"It's tight spaces—like closets. Being locked in."

"Shayla," I call to coax her to look into my eyes. "It's actually quite spacious down there. And the door will be closed but *not* locked." I pause when she continues to look unsettled. "We can go somewhere else, but this is the most secure. And I didn't think you wanted to go back to the woods or to my apartment."

"Uh, yeah, no, on both of those options." Her cheeks shade pink.

"Maybe you can take a peek down there, and if you don't think you can handle it, then I'll find another option. Maybe working at night, when everyone is asleep, we can have one of the classrooms to ourselves."

"I can *handle* it," her voice simmers with the fire that I've heard before. "I've handled more than most."

"I don't doubt it." I descend the narrow stairs ahead of her and allow Shayla to follow me at her own speed. What the fuck did her mother do to her own child? I shudder, knowing exactly how brutal a parent can be.

It seems so unfathomable to me that someone would hurt a girl with those sweet, lavender eyes. But I know better to think that innocence would stop a tyrant. I've seen the ugliness that exists in the realms. I suppose I always minimize my own childhood abuse, as if I had somehow deserved the punishments. But no child deserves to be tortured.

Her shoulders relax when she sees the open space of the room. The only major difference in appearance between a regular classroom and this space is that there are no windows down here. Beyond that, the wards are as thick as the two-foot concrete walls of the shelter, successively layered within them as the safety room was being built.

My body relaxes as all the psychic noise from the world dissipates.

"It feels… um, quiet in here," she says softly like she thinks it's a dumb observation.

"It is." I smile and nod to reassure her. "The wards prevent others' magic from coming inside or pushing outward. It's just our energies in here now."

It feels intimate. I both love and regret that feeling.

She quickly turns her head away from me and walks over to a cabinet with various magical instruments on the shelves.

"Okay, let's do it," she huffs out.

My heart sputters, wishing she meant the words I desperately want to hear.

She turns back and frowns. "I just want to get it over with."

That was the slap I needed to bring me back to reality.

"Sit. Center of the room," I order. It comes out a bit more gruffly than I mean it to. I'm angry at myself, not her.

She raises her eyebrow. I'm sure she sees through my aggressive display—the flimsy attempt to distance myself emotionally.

I hold my ground, crossing my arms and waiting for her to obey.

Shayla gives me an obstinate glare.

Damn, if the alpha in me doesn't want to kiss that defiant look right off her beautiful face.

Fortunately, she does as I say without argument before my wolf finds her rebellious nature as an excuse to come forth.

BUNKER FUN TIMES

SHAYLA

I've met with Quade... *Mr. Hollis*, at what, ironically, I now call Bunker Fun Times, for three evenings in a row.

And nothing. I have nothing to show for it except that my attraction and repulsion to him grow in equal measure with each visit. My body wants him—the primal call to couple with a virile male, no doubt.

Biology. Not a big fan at the moment.

I have repulsion because he has begun to give up on the idea of using positive reinforcement to access my power.

I stand in the center of the room with my arms extended and eyes closed, trying to feel the energy within me, with no luck.

"*Again.* Go inside. Just like when you ask yourself if you're hungry. Check in and feel the swirling power of your magic." His voice is heavy with irritation and disappointment.

I try. I really do. But for whatever reason, all I can see is a wall—a dark, shadowy wall, just like what Landis described.

I let my arms drop to my side. "This is useless. Are you sure I have any power?"

"I can smell it, feel it. From what you told me, Branden senses it in you. And Landis has seen it!" he snaps. His magic stirs the air inside the bunker, making my hair whip around my face.

I flinch. I'm triggered to remember my mother's rage when I inevitably disappointed her.

"If I have it, why can't I access it?" I practically scream with my frustration at myself.

Quade paces like a caged wolf. "I've tried everything that has worked with former tough cases. You make no sense at all!"

That's it. I'm fully triggered. "Forget it! This is a waste of time. I'm sure Branden plans to use my magic against me, anyway. So maybe it's better if it stays hidden."

I storm toward the exit, wondering if I could run from this school and find someone to sever the bond.

A curse on the Lewellyn family is exactly what they deserve. I should figure out a way to sever the bond myself. I'm already cursed, so it can't hurt me much.

But then my traitorous heart cracks with the idea of separating from Rourke.

Stupid bonds.

Quade catches me by the arm and spins me around to look at him. "You can't give up." His amber eyes flare with magic, anger, and probably disappointment.

Goddess, I hate all of this crap. Why do I want his approval?

"Not to be the voice of reality or anything," I snarl, so fucking tired of life treating me like a punching bag. "But do you see a world where I don't get thrown into the asylum, whether I can access and control my magic or not? You hate the Lewellyns for a reason. And even though you haven't trusted me enough to tell me why, it can't be because they're sweethearts. They'll find a way to make me go away after their due diligence to the mate contract and for keeping up appearances to the supe community. I should run."

"No. They aren't sweethearts," Quade says, and his free hand circles around my waist and pulls me closer. He loosens his grip on my arm... and now has both hands on my hips. "Shayla," he whispers. His eyes soften. His face is so close—*too close* to mine. "Please don't give up. I couldn't..." He doesn't continue.

My breath comes in short pants with him so close. Everything in me wants to slam my mouth onto his and kiss him.

Claim him.

Goddess dammit, I don't need a mate. And a male like him wouldn't want a defective one.

"You couldn't *what?*" I prompt him to finish his sentence, so I won't do something stupid like lean forward and brush my lips over his.

He closes the already narrow distance between us. His nose bumps mine. He's still staring into my eyes, and I'm hypnotized by his intensity. "I won't *let* you be sent to the asylum."

"But that isn't up to you," I breathe out. "Is it?"

"No. But—" He squeezes my hips with his strong hands, and his eyes glow gold. His wolf is close to the surface—I can see it. "I would help you escape," he confesses.

"That's a kind offer, but I wouldn't make it very far on my own. Not without my magic and more training. They'd find me." I avert my eyes to avoid his golden gaze that reduces me to a quivering mess of lust.

I realize he's only acting like this because his wolf must see me as pack since we've spent so much time together. But why is he letting his shifter side take over and act so protective of me? I didn't take him for one to lose control.

His hand moves up and cups my jaw, forcing me to look at him again, to make me hear his words. "I'd go *with* you."

He *can't* mean that. I'm light-headed with the idea of us

running off into the sunset, exploring my attraction for him. But that can't be what he's suggesting.

"*Wait, what?*" I lean back and stare at him in shock. "You don't mean that. You have your whole life here."

"A life I don't want."

"You wouldn't want a life on the run with some inept dependent. I can't give you anything but trouble," I argue.

A brief look of amusement flashes over his features.

"I could teach you... if we had enough time together." Quade rushes to finish, "You could learn to control your power. We could find a way for you to break the bond with Rourke, and we could return. We could clear your name and secure a real future for you."

"Thank you... but no. I can't ruin your life for a long shot in the hopes that I *might* get my shit together." I pull away, and he releases me. My soul aches with the loss of his touch.

Then the idea of messing up his life because of my problems feels like a knife in my gut. I run out of the bunker, my mind spinning with Quade's offer.

Why would he do something like that for a loser nobody?

Even if he has a fleeting attraction to me, that wouldn't make a male abandon the entire life he's built. Maybe his wolf just can't stand to watch a potential pack member get carted off to the asylum.

However, the idea of growing closer to Quade tempts me.

I can't possibly be Quade's fated mate, but I wish he were my match instead of the one I have.

As I rush through the mostly empty quad to my dorm building, a tiny flower faerie flies into my path. She hovers right in front of my face, making me come to a complete stop. Her behavior is odd. From what everyone told me, the faeries pretty much ignore the students unless we harm their flowers.

Instantly, I glance behind me and down at my feet to check that I didn't damage something in my race to hide from my feelings.

"Hello." As pleasantly as possible, considering my mood, I ask, "Can I help you with something?"

The little being shakes her head no. Her blonde tresses flutter around her heart-shaped face as her wings beat at a blurring speed. "No."

I blink and wonder what's going on. "Then why did you stop me?"

"You feel like the Queen. And I was wondering if you knew her."

"The Queen?" I ask. "The Fae Queen? Why would I know her? I'm a nobody."

"That isn't true." She grins. "If you were a nobody, you would have no body."

Oh, little flower faeries...

"Do *you* know the Queen?" I ask to figure out what she wants from me.

"I met her many, many seasons ago. She has pretty magic... like you do."

"I have pretty magic?" I look down at my hands and see nothing.

"Sparkles—like crystals, caught in the sun."

Sparkles? Arden's nickname for me was more accurate than I realized.

The faerie flies close to my face and whispers. "Be careful. They will want all that pretty magic. But you need it to help." She zips off at a blinding speed before I can ask her what she means by helping or who wants my magic.

I fall asleep, staring at the ceiling, feeling through my mate bond that Rourke is *with* someone right now. It makes my whole body ache—with some sick connected need *and* in rejection that I'm not with him.

I can't go on like this.

Not long after I fall asleep, I feel myself shift into a lucid dream, similar to what Landis creates during his sexual-energy feedings. He hasn't visited me since I knocked him out of my dreamscape. I'm not sure if I want him to visit me right now—I feel so mixed up with Quade's strange offer and sensing Rourke's exploits. Although the memory of the earth-shattering orgasm Landis gave me is enough to make my core heat and my clit throb for attention.

"Shayla?" he calls from the shadows at the edge of my consciousness.

"Yes, Landis," I say and feel my body become frozen in place with his power.

His shadowform floats closer, but he doesn't try to touch me.

I whine, "Why can't I see you as you are... your physical body?"

"It's not how it works for me, I'm afraid. Does that bother you too much?"

"No... Well, yes. But just because I like the way you look in person. I want to gaze into your beautiful eyes and kiss your smile." Out of habit, I try to reach out to him. But I can't, paralyzed by his power. "Will it always be like this? Unable to touch you back? Unable to truly see you?"

"Fuck," he curses and draws away. "I'm sorry. You deserve more than I can give you." In a flash, he's gone, and the paralysis eases to nothing.

"Come back!" I yell into the shadows.

Then I feel a presence closing in. An incubus power... but it doesn't feel like Landis. Whoever it is, he isn't gentle.

I throw up my psychic walls, realizing my dreamscape is being compromised. The frozen feeling returns.

Fuck.

But this invader isn't entirely inside my mind... *yet.*

I don't know how long we psychically push and shove.

Energy gathers and gathers as it goes on.

Wind swirls around me—burning like ice.

Is that my magic or my attacker?

Landis says that my power feels like a hurricane. Maybe I can push this invader out, just like I did Landis.

But that was an accident.

How do I do it on purpose?

I remember my studies. Innate magic follows thought. *Imagination*.

I imagine my magic as a grenade. I will detonate, blasting this asshole right out of my stupid life.

Swirling, swirling. I feel him repeatedly slamming against my wall.

And then.

Boom.

28

BONDS & CURSES

BRANDEN

"On your knees," I order.

Rourke spins around and glares at me. "No. I'm not in the mood for games today." He paces the length of our secret hideout—an apartment under the dorms that only we know about. A place where we can regroup, get our... *aggressions* out, indulge in our sexual appetites without prying eyes and be ourselves with each other—completely.

"You haven't been in the mood since... *her*." Irritated, I flop on the couch and take a swig from my glass of wine.

This forgotten space is meant to be a teacher's apartment—immaculately decorated, all to ourselves. Not even the administration remembers it exists. Of course, all the brownie fae who clean the academy know, but we bribe them with treats, so they keep quiet and tidy the place.

"What's your problem *now*?" I snap. This whole thing with Shayla has us twisted up.

Fated mates.

Of course, he had to find her *and* knot her.

Fucking dumbass. If Rourke had used his brain for a second, he would have paused and wondered why he was *so* drawn to her. Now, we're *all* in this mess.

He wasn't cautious enough. He didn't take the time to see if he could sense her magic before he banged her. Too bad I didn't get close enough to detect that hidden magic simmering under her tantalizing skin.

Rourke saw what he wanted and took it. That has always been his problem, but that's a dragon for you—impulsive, passionate, and too hot for their own good.

I know that's how he got me in his bed.

But Rourke messed up twice that night—first, by beginning the mate bond and then by rejecting it. I can deduce he's more messed up by the rejection than she is. But I sense the incomplete bond hurts both of their souls. I know the reasons he rejected her. Loyalty—for me… and for his family. However, if I were with them that night, I would have told him to accept his fate. And then, maybe Shayla would have welcomed me into their lives… and into their bed. Now, we may never know.

"Any more creeps following her?" Rourke asks.

"I've been keeping an eye on her the best I can, and no, none that I've seen." I sigh. This isn't the first time he's asked. I know the mate bond pulls on him, but he's becoming obsessed. "It seems to have been a singular incident."

"But they meant to grab *her*. I've been thinking about it… they even had juice ready. Whoever was after her knew that she wouldn't drink alcohol. She was probably the only one there that night who didn't indulge. How many people know that she doesn't drink?"

"Her best friend, Myra, would know."

"Dammit." Rourke pulls on his beautiful golden hair. "Do you think whoever has her friend is extracting information about Shayla?"

"It isn't out of the realm of possibilities." I sit up and lean forward, my elbows landing on my knees. "Have you considered... that the secret society your father is entangled with might be behind this whole mess?"

"You think he would risk a curse, potentially ruining our family line, just to get rid of Shayla?"

"Honestly, it gives *me* shivers to think what your father is capable of—and that's saying a lot."

His fiery eyes flash at me, burrowing into my soul. "I don't know what to do. We both know I can't have her as my mate. She's..."

"Trash?" I offer, mostly to get a reaction out of him.

"That isn't what I meant." He kneels at my feet, and we're eye to eye as he settles himself between my knees. "I know not everyone can be born into wealth and power."

"Yeah, some of us have to be *adopted* into it," I say with a grimace.

My adoptive parents constantly remind me of their generosity in bringing me into their wealth. Their love? That's a whole other matter.

His hands come up to caress my face. "You know your background never bothered me."

"But you won't claim me. You don't dare let anyone know you're intimately involved with adopted trash—at least not without a coven mate circle to mask what we are to each other."

"Maybe I should just claim you and use that as my excuse to sever my bond with Shayla," he threatens.

I almost believe him. Almost. But he's still too caught up in appearances. He still wants his father's approval, although he'll never get it. And because I stupidly give a damn about him, I keep up appearances, too.

"Don't say things you don't mean. It's unkind," I warn, with a biting edge to my voice.

Rourke is treading the dangerous territory of old arguments and my raw pain. We have had to hide what we are to each other from his father for the last five years because I don't have the proper lineage. And also because his father wants Rourke to produce an heir with a house of impeccable status.

My birth family had dark secrets. And my adopted family may have status and money, but they, too, have their skeletons. I'm one of *many* children they adopted—all acquired for our powers. We were groomed to be their weapons. Rourke's father knows this and sees me as an acceptable bodyguard for his progeny, but nothing more.

"Maybe we should run away?" Rourke grins at me wickedly, bringing me back to the moment. "Like Shayla planned to."

"Yeah, and look how well that worked out for her." I pull at his wrists to make him break this intense contact, but instead, his mouth descends onto mine.

"Fuck." He growls against my lips. "I need you."

I don't respond in words. I can't. I don't want to admit, even to myself, how much I need him. But a happy future for us seems to slip further away every day.

Unless Shayla can be our answer. It's too soon to let Rourke in on that plan. He would somehow sabotage it. Besides, I need to know on my own if my idea has merit before I suggest such a thing. He's too emotionally charged to see the potential clearly.

Rourke hates he fell for her that night—not just the bond, but his heart—so he lies to himself and to me about how he feels. I suppose he has to lie—not to me, but to his family. I know he cares for her since he hasn't even attempted to be with another female since that night. And I don't think losing his interest in other women is from fear of the curse.

As for me? The broken mage is intriguing. And she isn't easy on my cock, either. I know why Rourke couldn't resist her, but he won't hear me confess that—not yet.

Rourke often *needs* women so that he can be the dom in the sexual dynamic. I get it. I enjoy sinking my cock into him and dominating him more than being his receiver. Besides, I cannot give him the softness he sometimes craves. I *cannot* play a submissive. So we have an agreement… we can be with others, as long as they are females.

Even though he often submits to me, he cannot give me that feminine energy either. He just doesn't have it. And there's a huge difference.

Yet, I rarely need to wander. I have only been with a few females. I usually take the opportunity to feed on their blood as well. While Rourke was busy screwing up our future with Shayla, I was having a tasty little snack.

Shayla has that softer energy we crave, yet she's tougher than I first gave her credit for. She just might be perfect for us. Only time will tell. Of course, if she can't deal with sharing her mate, I might have to take drastic measures. He was mine first.

When he senses that my mind has drifted, Rourke bites my bottom lip. *Fucker*. He's going to pay for that.

I unzip my slacks and pull out my hard dick. "Shut the fuck up and *show* me how much you need me."

His scent of arousal floods the air—smoke and cloves. He licks his lips and yanks my pants down to my ankles in one fell swoop.

I will admit that's fucking hot.

Rourke shoves at my chest, and I land with my back on the couch.

He takes a swipe of my thick cock with his exceptionally long tongue. His eyes roll back because my pre-cum is an aphrodisiac. He begins to stroke my length with one hand. With the other, he sucks his two fingers briefly and then slips them into my ass.

"*Fuck*," I moan as he works his way up to my prostate.

His mouth engulfs my shaft, sliding slowly, too slowly. He knows I hate that—and love it. "Don't play with me, or I'll tie you down," I threaten.

Finally, frustration gets the better of me, and I grab the back of his head and thrust my length down his throat. He doesn't gag.

"Good dragon," I praise. "You can take your cock out now."

He pulls out his dick and begins to work his long, thick length in tandem with his mouth's efforts.

I fist his hair but let him set the pace.

I lick my lips, craving to taste him again soon.

But not now. He needs to make up for fucking up our lives. Besides, seeing the knot that he developed when he was with Shayla still irritates me.

And now, I'm thinking of the little mage. Damn her lavender eyes, haunting me again. Goddess, how many times have I imagined how her soft body would feel sandwiched between us? Rourke's cock buried deep, his knot locked inside her cunt. I would work myself into her tight ass, bringing them both to a blissful climax, undoing them completely.

That girl would likely be a perfect little brat for me to master. I would have so much fun punishing her sassy mouth and then praising her when she submitted to our needs. How would her flesh look wrapped in my rope, tangled just the way I needed her to be? Would she ever trust me enough to do that?

Oh, to have both Rourke and Shayla at my mercy, both crying out, begging for release until *I* allowed it.

Fuck. I want that. *Goddess dammit.* I want *her.*

I hold my cock deep down Rourke's throat, preventing him from breathing. When he tries to pull away, I begin to fuck his face. With all the pent-up energy I feel in him and myself, it doesn't take much for me to come down his throat.

Rourke groans, yanks on his own cock, and finds his bliss as I come.

Wiping his mouth, he grins at me. "How did I do, bloodsucker?"

"Be careful, brat. Or I will bend you over this couch and use your ass. Then forbid you to find your release."

Suddenly, Rourke's eyes go wide. "Something's wrong." He gets up quickly and shoves his now half-spent cock back into his pants. His knot still needs another milking.

I stand, yank up my pants, and zip myself up. "What is it?"

He's never had the gift of intuition before. But he hasn't been linked to a wild-card mage before, either.

"Shayla," he whispers. "How do I know that?"

"You're connected, even if it's weak."

"Yeah… She said that she felt it when we were *together*." Rourke looks ashamed for a brief moment before shaking it off.

"Is that what's happening to her now?" I ask, "Is she suffering because of what we just did?" I don't like the feelings that thought stirs in me.

"I don't think so." Rourke frowns. "It's like she's in danger."

We slip on our shoes and race out of the door.

"Is she in our dorm?" I ask as I follow him up the stairs.

"Feels like it," he says without any certainty. "But not. I can't explain it."

"Is she in pain?"

"Fuck!" he yells and races faster, as if he truly loved her—not just because of the mate bond. Maybe my plan to make us a mated coven will work—*if* she can tap into her power *and* accept that Rourke and I have our own relationship.

Within minutes, we crash through the door, but all seems quiet. All our doors are closed, including Shayla's.

Rourke doesn't give a damn about her closed door and smashes the damn thing off its hinges.

There's a flash of light, wind, and magic, blowing him completely across the room, over the couches, and slamming him against the far wall.

Holy shit.

Arden explodes out of his room, bare-chested and on high alert. "What the fuck was that?"

The druid sees Rourke on the floor and Shayla's broken

door. He charges at Rourke, assuming that this is all Rourke's fault.

Which to be fair, I can understand, but I can't have the giant hurt my dragon. I use my speed to block his path and grab his arms, preventing him from attacking.

"Out of my way!" Arden bellows.

"This isn't Rourke's doing. He was checking on her." I use my compulsion on him when he doesn't want to hear me. "You need to see if Shayla is okay. *Now!*"

"Fine. I'm checking on Shayla!" he shouts at me, and I let him go.

I glance at Landis' door. Why hasn't the bastard made an appearance? Does he have something to do with this?

I suspect he's fed on Shayla during her sleep, but I didn't take him as one to harm his food source.

Checking on Rourke, he waves me off. "I'm fine. What the hell happened?"

"I was hoping you could tell me," I say and look back to see Arden safely entering Shayla's room. She didn't blast *him* out.

With a bit of assistance from me, Rourke gets to his feet. We both follow Arden into Shayla's room.

She's on her bed and out cold. Energy, power, and chaotic magic still swirl in the small space. What the hell happened? Is it still happening?

The room is in shambles. Fortunately, the little mage doesn't have many possessions to toss about.

"No one else is in here," Rourke says after several sniffs of the air. "No one's *been* in here."

"Not that we can *see*," I remind him.

"Where the fuck is Landis?" The lights go on in Rourke's eyes. "Do you think…"

"I think we should find out," I mutter, leading the group to Landis' room.

But it isn't me or Rourke who rips Landis' door open. It's

Arden. The hulking druid grabs the smaller incubus up by the collar.

However, curiously, the incubus doesn't wake.

"Is he inside Shayla now?" Rourke sounds worried, not possessive.

Then, someone knocks on our outer door.

Apparently, people don't like a lot of crashing and shouting in the middle of the night. Who knew?

Since I'm the most sane and conscious of the bunch, I answer the door.

Of all people, it's Hollis.

He has a lot of balls.

I know. I've seen them when he's shifted naked. *Damn.*

I don't blame Shayla at all for being attracted to the shifter. If it weren't for my relationship and the ugly history between the Lewellyns and him, I might have fallen for the professor myself.

"I need to see her." Hollis pushes me aside. If I hadn't seen his desperation, I might have taken issue with that move. As it is, I need him to find out exactly what's happening with our troublemaker. He's likely the one to figure it out.

Rourke steps out of Landis' room and stands in Hollis' path. "Where the fuck are you going?"

"I'm the authority here," Hollis growls. "And your mate is in danger. Now, if you want to continue with the pretense that you give a shit about her, you'll move out of my way. Immediately."

"Rourke," I call, not using my compulsion per se, but definitely using my personal influence to make him back down. "She needs help. And he's an expert. An *instructor*."

"Fine," Rourke bites out and steps aside. But he follows so closely behind the wolf that I'm not sure if he'll attack. "Wait, how did you know something was going on?"

"My wards are around the school," Hollis says as he rushes to Shayla's side, crouching down to inspect her condition. "They were triggered and destroyed."

The news about the wards chills me. Hollis is supposed to be one of the best in the realms. Who has the power to rip them apart?

Hollis continues, "Then I received reports of an altercation of some sort in your room."

"Oh." Rourke's shoulders ease slightly, but he tenses again when Hollis curses after holding open Shayla's eyelids and looking into her eyes. "What?"

Hollis spins and stands in one motion, coming right up into Rourke's face. "Was this your doing?"

"This is getting old," Rourke snaps back.

"Quade?" Shayla moans softly. She struggles to open her eyes and sees all four of us in her room—Rourke, Arden, me, and her teacher. Then she sees the mess of her belongings thrown everywhere. "What are you all doing in here?"

"What happened to you?" Hollis asks.

"I... someone... tried to get into my mind," she says, rubbing her head.

"Landis?" Rourke growls.

"It was an incubus, but not him."

"How do you know?" Rourke demands.

"Because he's been in my mind before, remember?" she snarls at him.

"How do you know he isn't tricking you?" Rourke asks.

"Knock it off," Hollis barks out. "The outer perimeter wards were triggered. That would suggest that Landis had nothing to do with this."

"Then why is he unconscious?" Rourke shouts back in his face. "We couldn't wake him."

"That's odd. From what I know about cubi, even during a shadowwalk, we should be able to wake him unless something's wrong." Hollis looks at Shayla. "I'm going to check on him. Can you wait here for me to come back?"

"I'm coming with you," Shayla says. Stubborn thing that she is, she pushes herself up to a sitting position but sways.

Arden, the hero *best friend*—yeah, right, *my fangs*. He doesn't want just a friendship. He rushes over and picks her up. "I got you."

She leans against his naked chest, and Rourke bristles.

That dragon had better either claim her or sever their bond. Otherwise, he might go mad.

29

POSSE

SHAYLA

My head is pounding, and my magic pulses under my skin. I sense there's less magic in me now, probably because I've just used up so much, forcing the mind invader out of me and destroying my room.

Arden carries me past my bedroom door, correction—where my bedroom door used to be.

"Did I do that too?" I ask, my voice hushed in shock.

"I did," Rourke admits, and his tan skin pinkens at the cheeks.

"Why?" I wonder if I'm seeing a moment of beauty in our mate bond—protection, caring, and connection for just a flicker of a second.

"I felt that someone dared to attack what's mine." His face becomes a closed-off mask.

"So sweet, asshat," Quade mutters as he walks into Landis' room.

I stare blankly at Rourke. "Would it kill you to see me as an actual person for once?"

He turns away from me and paces the center of the common room.

I don't have time for the dragon's crap. I need to know what's going on with Landis.

My heart aches when I see my incubus. On his bed, he's sprawled out and dead to the world. "Is he...?"

"He's alive," Quade answers. "His eyes are moving, as if he's in REM sleep."

Suddenly, Landis folds in half to sit up and grabs Quade by the throat.

Quade slams his forearms down on Landis' arms, easily breaking the hold. It also breaks Landis out of his shadowtrance.

"Shayla!" Landis cries out before seeing me safely cradled in Arden's arms.

"I'm here," I say soothingly. "What happened to you?"

"An incubus-mage attacked you. I could feel his presence. When your magic knocked him away, I followed his trail."

"How?" Quade's forehead knits in confusion.

"I could just... *see* it. I think Shayla hurt him. It was like a cosmic wound, leaving a trail of power."

I cover my mouth. "I hurt someone?"

Arden squeezes me tighter. "It isn't your fault. You were only defending yourself."

I nod, wondering why I'm the target for some mysterious incubus. It makes sense Rourke's family would be behind the attack. Who else?

"Do you know where this incubus-mage is now?" Quade asks Landis.

"I can still feel him. He's north of here... in town. I don't know the town well enough to give you directions, but I could take you there."

To my surprise, it's Quade that says, "Let's go."

Arden tenses and pulls me away from the group, as if they were about to carry me off to my doom. "That's not a good idea. Shayla's not okay."

"I'm feeling better," I argue.

My druid frowns at me. "I *know* that you're not a hundred percent."

"But Qu—," I stop and correct myself. "Mr. Hollis thinks we should track this person down," I grumble.

"I didn't say you were going." Quade comes up to look me in the eye. "They want *you*. And I don't intend to deliver you to their doorstep."

"But—"

"No! Stay here," Quade alpha-commands me. For a moment, it stuns me silent, perhaps because he's never really used his dominance so intensely over me before. Ignoring my ire, he asks the group, "Who's coming with Landis and me?"

"I'll go," Branden says. "I'm quick. You could use my speed."

"I thought students weren't allowed to go into town," I protest, not liking the idea of them running into danger without me, especially on my behalf.

"Unless chaperoned by an instructor," Quade points to himself. "Instructor."

I bite my lip and try to find another point to argue. His gaze drops to my mouth.

"We need to go now, in case the attacker goes farther than Landis can sense him. If he escapes to another realm, we'll lose the trail." Quade glances back at Landis. "You ready?"

"Let me put some clothes on," he says, and I realize that I don't see boxers or sleep pants where the sheet has fallen down around his waist.

I look away before anyone notices that I like what I see of the incubus.

"I'm staying with Shayla," Arden says, eyeing Rourke suspiciously.

"If I wanted to hurt her, I wouldn't have tried to see who was attacking her!" Rourke steps up, and suddenly, I'm pinned between two large males who are not happy.

"Enough!" Quade shouts, his wolf rippling over his skin. "You can all measure your dicks later."

I hold back a chuckle, but the absurdity of my entire life hits me, and I burst out laughing.

Landis smirks as he comes out of his room, pulling on a jacket. "Is our naughty girl imagining that scene?"

"She isn't *ours*," Rourke says.

"Well, she isn't really *yours* yet either." Landis cocks a brow. "So unless you want to sink your teeth and claim her for keeps, I'll call her whatever the fuck I like. Including *mine*."

My body tingles with the power behind Landis' words. I don't want to be claimed, but I like that he's standing up for himself and what we might eventually develop between us.

Rourke crosses the room, and I'm afraid of what he might do. This is so ridiculous. I've never had guys into me, and now, two are fighting over me.

Arden backs away with me in his arms. I wonder if he senses more than I do in this standoff.

"Don't get in the middle of what Shayla and I have to deal with," Rourke threatens.

"I don't have to be in the middle. Unless that's how you like a threesome."

"Fucking hell!" I yell. "I think I should have something to say about this!"

All five sets of eyes turn to look at me. They wait for me to say something.

Shit.

I regain my composure after I recover from all their intense attention. "Like Mr. Hollis said, you can have fun measuring your dicks *later*. Right now, we need to find who attacked me."

Quade gives me a lingering look, then throws Arden and

Rourke a steely glare before racing out the door and down the hall. Landis and Branden hurry off to follow him.

Which leaves my druid and dragon as my babysitters.

"You can put me down," I say to Arden.

Instead, he sits down on the couch with me on his lap. Unapologetically, he holds me close while Rourke glowers and sits down across from us.

"For someone who doesn't want anything to do with me, you act very possessively," I comment, irritated.

The dragon's hands clench at his sides. I can see the wheels spinning. I just have no clue which direction they'll go once he lets loose.

"I know..." He growls. "It's a dragon thing."

"I'm betting it's a mate thing too," Arden adds unhelpfully.

Rourke nods solemnly. "Yeah, well, it fucking sucks."

"Oh, please, tell me all about it. I have *no* clue how much it sucks," I say sarcastically and shift to face Rourke head-on.

"We'll get it taken care of," he says harshly.

"One way or another?" I frown, the insinuation clear that he wishes I'd disappear... permanently.

Rourke huffs, goes to his room, and slams the door.

Arden grins. "Well, that's one way to slay a dragon."

30

DRUID BONDS

SHAYLA

"*D*o you want to stay out here?" Arden asks as he holds me on the couch. "Or would you rather be in your room?"

I stare at Rourke's door and whisper, "I feel like he's going to storm out here and yell at me again."

I attempt to stand and wobble on my feet.

Arden's right behind me, making sure I don't stumble, like the protective teddy bear he is. I sigh when we get to my room with the door torn off. "Well, this isn't awesome."

We stand at the threshold and stare at all my stuff scattered about.

Arden sucks in a breath. "What the—" He points to my most cherished memento from my childhood. "Is that *the* sparkle pen from when we were kids? You kept it all this time?"

I blush. "Uh, yeah. It reminded me of a happy moment. Stupid, huh?"

"Not at all." Arden hugs me from behind. "Hey, come with

me." He guides me toward his room. At the threshold, he pauses. "Well, uh, sorry, only come inside if you feel comfortable being alone with me."

"Of course I do." I smile up at him.

"It's just… you've been through something horrible tonight."

"I feel safest when I'm with you," I confess in barely a whisper.

He's always ensuring I'm safe and taken care of. I suspect he does it more than I realize—which is already a lot. I've been eating better this last month than I have throughout my entire life. And Kat revealed to me that the school doesn't really have a "care package" for its new students. Knowing how prideful I can be, I'm certain it's Arden who has secretly helped me out like the good guy he is.

As we enter his room, I look at the bed and then at Arden's broad shoulders. "Uh… Are we going to fit?"

"Friends can snuggle up close, right?" he asks.

Friends…

"Yeah, of course," I say like it's no big thing. I remind myself that it's not much different from when we sit on the couch.

But it's *his bed*, and it does feel different… at least for me.

"Get in," he says.

I crawl onto the bed and clamber over his blankets to the side that's flush against the wall.

The big, beautiful druid closes the door and slowly walks over to me with his glorious upper half on full display.

My eyes travel up and down his rippling abs and chest as he crawls in beside me. His massive muscular body settles at my side, and my core heats up.

He props his head up on his arm and studies my face. "You okay?"

I turn and mirror him, resting my head on my bent arm. "I think so."

His left hand moves up my side, and I feel his electric healing touch.

"You don't have to waste your magic on me," I say. "I'm okay."

"It's never wasted on you," he says softly.

"That's sweet. I'm not saying I mind being comforted, but it's just..." My eyes fill with tears. "I never had this growing up —just being held. It makes me feel as if..." I can't finish the thought, and I cover my face.

"Am I making you feel bad?"

I hear worry and sadness in his voice. My eyes dart back to look at him. I blink the tears away to see his face, and they fall onto his bed in the narrow space between us. "No. The opposite. Feeling good feels so unfamiliar. To feel like someone lo—" I correct myself, "... someone cares about me a little bit."

"I care about you a *lot*. I always have." Arden's large thumb brushes the tears from my cheek. The small gesture makes my heart ache because I can't have him. I want to close the small distance and taste his luscious mouth filled with his sweet words. But the idea of ruining our friendship holds me back.

His green eyes seem luminescent in the dark room. "Shayla, I never could shake you from my mind all these years. I couldn't believe it when I saw you again. The only reason I never reached out before was that I thought you wouldn't have remembered me. Plus, I was going through my own shit because my parents died. I didn't want to burden you when I knew you had the world's worst mom."

"I didn't think you would remember me either." I frown, then shrug off my wondering what would have happened if we hadn't lost contact. "Are you saying my mother will never be up for Mom of the Year?" I chuckle wryly, trying to bring levity to this intense exchange. Isn't that what I do? Either I act defensively, or I deflect?

He doesn't play along with my deflection. Instead, he just gazes at me.

I stare back into his forest green eyes and get lost in the woods. I can practically smell the pines and crisp air. He makes me want to dance in his arms, bask in his beauty, and heal in his embrace. I *can't* lose him.

He gives me hope.

"Thank you," I whisper, my voice barely audible.

"For what?" he asks.

"Everything. Just admit it. I know you gave me those boxes the first couple of days."

"Fucking Landis," he growls.

I laugh, and my hand naturally lands on his smooth chest, over his heart. "He didn't tell me. It just makes sense. You're so kind to me and thoughtful. You always were. It's why I kept the pen you gave me."

"There's no other way to be when it comes to you."

"Maybe for your kind heart. But we both know that isn't true for everyone. I suppose at least one good thing came out of this mess with Rourke. I found you again." I grin playfully, "Sorry our reunion has been so drama-free," I tease. "I wish I could offer you a bit more excitement."

Arden studies my face, and for a moment, he looks as though he might kiss me. "We should get some rest."

His hand skims over the dip at my waist. Why does it feel like he wants to inch under my skimpy sleep shirt?

I pray that he will.

He cages me in, against the wall in the small bed. Lying next to him, gazing into his eyes, and feeling the heat of his body, my heart pounds with his warm touch.

His large frame feels like it blocks out the realms. And I want to find refuge with him for longer than my life will allow.

"I'm not tired," I say. My hand moves from Arden's chest to his shoulder. My thumb traces the druid tattoo, following it up to his neck.

That could still be taken as an innocent touch between friends, right?

Arden's eyes flutter closed. "*Shay...*"

"Yes?"

"You should stop," he whispers.

"I'm sorry." I yank my hand away as if I've been burned. And that's exactly how it feels, but the sting is in my heart.

Arden's faster than I realize. He grabs my hand and places it back over his heart. He looks into my eyes, seeing the hurt of his rejection. I know we can't have something between us. But I thought it was safe to touch him since he touches me so much—those little caresses during breakfast and dinner, or while he heals me, holding me in his lap and stroking my body.

Dammit. Arden's gotten under my skin.

It will break me when I have to leave him. Maybe they'll drug me when I'm thrown in the asylum, and I'll forget all about my druid. Hopefully, they'll put me out of my misery quickly. Because losing him will ruin me.

"Shayla?" he asks, perhaps sensing my affection for him clearly for the first time.

"I didn't mean to..." I breathe out.

"Mean to what?"

"I know you only see me as a friend. I got all mixed up since it feels so right being close to you—when you touch me. I didn't mean to make you uncomfort—"

His hand clasps the back of my head, and his mouth claims mine. His lips are delicious and full. I sink into him like a soft feather pillow, but his beard reminds me of his rough masculinity.

His tongue probes the seam of my mouth, and I allow him entry. His kiss becomes more urgent, commanding.

Arden owns me, heart and soul, with this one kiss.

My body responds by pressing my hips closer, then I throw my leg over his hip. My arm curls around his waist and my fingers dent his back, desperately pulling him closer even though there's no space left between us.

His hardened member rubs against my belly, and I want to feel him inside me.

He breaks away from our kiss and holds my chin, searching my eyes for something.

I fear he'll change his mind.

"We shouldn't," he groans.

Fuck.

"Why not?" I ask. If it's because he'll regret it, then I'll try to understand.

"You're mated to a possessive dragon," Arden hisses. "I don't mind sharing a place in your heart with the others, but he won't like it." He clenches his eyes shut, as if he could wish it away.

Sorry, buddy, I've tried that… wishing didn't work.

"He doesn't want me," I remind him. *Goddess*, what does he mean by sharing me with others? Does he mean he's willing to be in a mated coven with Landis and Rourke?

I focus back on what is happening now, not an impossible future. "I know Rourke's *with* someone else." I pause when I realize I'm being selfish, pushing for this. "I don't even know what will happen to me. I'm sorry I can't promise you more than this moment. But we can be with each other, right now, *if* you want me."

"You're right. *You are mine.*" He kisses me with ten years of repressed passion. My body comes alive like nothing I've experienced before—even with my fated mate. Maybe I feel this way because we have a past. We have a true friendship. I *feel* his love for me.

I gasp for breath as he nibbles and licks his way down my neck, consuming my every thought.

His large hand slides up my nightshirt, capturing my ample breast entirely.

Fuck. I'm melting for him.

His hands are truly magic incarnate, buzzing with affection

and desire. Cupping my entire tit, he pinches my nipple. I cry out in need.

His mouth reclaims mine to swallow down my moans.

With swiftness and agility that I wouldn't expect from his massive size, he spins us until I'm on top of him, straddling him. My legs hang off the sides of his torso, and my core molds itself perfectly to his thick, hard cock, with only our thin sleep shorts separating us. He's half-sitting with his back against the headboard of his bed.

In a flash, my top is gone and flying across the room.

Strangely, I'm not embarrassed to be exposed like this to him. I thought it would be awkward if we hooked up, but it feels... *perfect*.

His eyes eat up the sight of my full breasts, heaving with my ragged breath. With reverence, his hands slowly move from my waist and over my ribcage until they cover each breast. He leans forward, takes my left pebbled nipple into his mouth, and rolls it with his tongue. I rock against his cock, easing some of the throbbing tension building between my legs.

His hands slip back down to my hips. He uses his strength to grind me against his length.

He continues to suck my nipple and watches the blissful reaction on my face as he hits all the right spots with his entire girth and length.

Goddess, I'm going to come just from this.

"I'm not going to enter you tonight," he grunts. "The first time I take you, I'm going to dive into your cunt with my back against the earth. Then I can use my magic to shatter your world."

Holy blue balls. I almost climax with that thought.

"Cunt?" I breathe out, surprised by his language.

"I'm taking the word back from its derogatory usage. It comes from the Goddess Cunti, and you, my love, are a goddess."

My love? Goddess?

He captures my other nipple and sucks hard. His hand slips between us and under the hem of my flimsy night shorts, finding my clit slick with desire.

"Arden!" I call out, bite my lip, and come undone.

I rock against him, riding his body. A groan that sounds almost inhuman rips itself from my throat.

After what feels like an eternity in ecstasy, I collapse forward and kiss him once more.

Lifting myself up, I move my hand down his beautifully sculpted chest, then over his delicious abs. When I reach his waistband, he stops me. "You don't have to do anything for me."

I lock eyes with him. "Did you come yet?"

"No, but—"

Arden's door bursts open.

Rourke stands at its threshold, so livid that he's rippling with a shift. His eyes glow with fire. He sees both of us topless, and I'm straddling the druid with my hand reaching for Arden's cock. "What the fuck?" he growls.

"Yeah! What the fuck?" I repeat.

The dragon blinks at me, confused. "What?"

"I'm not your possession!" I snap. "You fuck whoever you want, so I get to be with someone who actually gives a shit about me."

"You are my mate!" He rushes forward and pulls me off Arden.

I believe the only reason Arden doesn't hold on to me is so that I won't get torn in half.

"Then do it!" I scream. "Mark me! And be done with it."

Rourke grabs the hair at the nape of my neck and angles my head. I wonder if I've provoked him enough for him to lose his senses.

My mate bond magic begs for this completion.

But *I* don't.

I shove at his chest, and it seems to snap him out of his

fevered haze. He lets me go like I'm some filth stuck on his hand.

"Fine. We take who we want," he says, but he doesn't look happy about it. "But if I *do* decide to claim you, you'll have to stop trying to trap all the rich cock you can."

I glare at him. "Is that *really* how you see me?"

Rourke looks at my discarded shirt, my exposed breasts, and Arden, looming protectively behind me. "Look at yourself. You've got something going on with Landis and Hollis, too. So I'm just calling it as I see it."

I'm just so tired of this crap. Tears well in my eyes. "What I have with Arden isn't a trap. Or a fling." My insecurity gets the best of me, and I glance back at Arden, "Is it a fling for you?"

He captures me from behind and envelops me completely in an embrace, covering my breasts from Rourke's view. He gazes down at me lovingly. "You have always been mine. Long before you met him."

"Bullshit," Rourke growls.

"Oh?" My eyes lock with the dragon's. "Are you *mine*? Are *you* going to stop fucking other people?"

His jaw quivers in irritation. He doesn't like that I can sense his indiscretions.

Without acknowledging our standoff, he storms out.

My shoulders slump. My mate bond feels like a knife in my stomach. Why does it hurt to fight with him?

Arden holds me tighter. "I'm sorry it hurts so much."

I spin and hug Arden, melting into my best friend and, hopefully, my future love. "I have to break Rourke's hold on me."

31

THE HUNT

LANDIS

I'm running through the campus grounds with Branden and Mr. Hollis. Well, this isn't where I envisioned my night ending up. I intended to pleasure Shayla again, and hopefully, not get blasted clear of her dreams this time.

But her attack has changed everything. An incubus mage is after her. It's my worst fear coming true.

From now on, my entire focus will be to protect her. Prove to her I can be more than a monster—like *he* is. Only after I convince myself I won't harm her, will I allow myself to physically sink into her sweetness and make her moan my name over and over.

On the way through the quad, we see the flower faerie, Lali.

Hollis calls to the little one and asks her to tell Ms. Boyd about our midnight 'field trip' to town. No doubt, Hollis chose the healer to give a heads-up because one of us might get hurt. But I'm glad he told someone because if something happens to

Hollis, at least Branden and I won't be expelled for being off campus.

As we continue our race toward the town on the other side of our school walls, I ask Branden, "Why did *you* volunteer?"

I sense at least *one* of his secrets, but it's not one for me to tell. I suspect he has many darker secrets locked away. But if he's going to be entwined with Shayla through his relationship with Rourke, I need to discover all his hidden skeletons. I must protect my shadowmate.

My shadowmate? Could she really be my true mate match?

It's the stuff of cubi legend—our desperate hope to be more than just energetic leeches. There hasn't been a case of a true shadowmate for over a century.

Sure, I'm obsessed with Shayla, but cubi can get like that. I want to give Shayla something I've never offered anyone else. Would I be able to control myself if I did?

"Someone's attacking my best friend's mate," Branden answers my question as we head to the back of the campus, where the town's edge nears the school's walls.

"Yeah, but she's a mate who both of you want to make *disappear*," I say with a curled lip of disgust.

"You *assume* that's what I want." Branden's tone suggests that he wants to keep her… maybe for himself.

I sense Hollis' energy flare and then tighten.

"Forgive the pun, but I'll bite. What *do* you want from her?" I ask the vamp. There's no reason for beating around the bush here. Branden will give me his version of a straight answer, or he won't.

"I want what's best for Rourke. If being mated with a potentially powerful mage like Shayla benefits him, then I'll make sure he has her."

"You think she'll be an asset," I grumble. "You see her as a tool, nothing more."

"And dragons, historically, have taken more than one mate,"

Branden says. "Rourke could match with another to have a socially acceptable female for public functions."

"So you'll have Shayla only to use for her powers and then get a polished wifey for the fancy dinner parties," I sneer.

"*I* will have nothing," Branden reminds me, his resentment clear. It confirms what my incubus senses sussed out when I met him two years ago.

"But if Shayla and Rourke create a mating coven, then *you* could be part of that," I throw out casually.

Hollis and Branden both look at me sharply. I honestly can't tell if they hate or love the idea. Or both.

I could get along with all of them in a coven, but I don't see everyone else getting over their shit.

"Mating covens aren't done anymore," Hollis says dismissively and rushes to unlock the gates. "Let's focus on finding this asshole," the professor orders.

A tingle goes up my spine. I wouldn't mind taking sexy playtime commands in a mating coven if Hollis were issuing them.

But this isn't the time for fantasies. I shove down my lust and nod in agreement. I need to focus.

Closing my eyes, I lock onto the energy of Shayla's attacker once again. "To the right, about three blocks deep and four over?"

Once Hollis relocks the gates and reestablishes the wards over the school, we race in the direction I mentioned.

"I can feel the bastard moving farther away from me," I grit out as we run.

We're almost at the place where I originally pinpointed Shay's attacker.

Hollis asks, "Do we need to change direction?"

Then suddenly, my prey vanishes from my senses completely.

"He's disappeared." I race toward the building in front of me—where I had just sensed the incubus mage moments before. Maybe we can find a clue to the attacker's identity hidden there. "My guess would be that he just went through a portal."

When I arrive at the attacker's last location, it's a large mage meeting hall. Or at least that's what it appears to be from the outside.

"My senses are picking up strange energies," I say, losing myself in a shadowtrance.

"I'll run the perimeter," Branden offers. Within a few moments, he's back, barely winded. "Nothing seems out of place from the outside."

"Then let's see what's happening on the inside." Hollis charges forward to the main entrance.

After a knock, we wait.

Hollis tries the door. Locked. No surprise. But a protection ward zaps his hand, and he curses.

"Let me try." I have the innate incubus ability to unlock doors. The damned ward shocks me too. I should've known an incubus mage would prevent another cubi from entering.

"Give me a second." Hollis waves us back. He holds his hands out and senses for the locking spell over the building. His attention narrows onto a spot off to the right. He chants a spell, and the complex web over the door glows faintly.

Using his knowledge and skill, Hollis picks a psychic thread and pulls. With my mage perception, I see the spell collapse. *He's good.*

The physical mechanism is still locked. Hollis rams the solid slab of wood with his shoulder, almost knocking the wind out of himself.

Branden helps him with his second attempt, and the door rips free, falling to the floor with a loud thud.

Darkness greets us.

Once again, I feel a strange malaise.

"Something's wrong," I warn them. "Be careful."

They race ahead without heeding my caution. Or maybe

they do, and this *is* them being cautious. Who knows with these guys?

Hollis sniffs the air. "This way."

Branden and I follow him down a corridor. At the end, we find an iron door. Confronted with the toxic metal, our fae genes make us all shiver with revulsion.

"What the fuck?" Branden hisses. "Why is this in the fae realm?"

"Let me shadowwalk around it, see if it is worth trying to break through," I offer and sit down.

Both of them watch me, which I truly despise, but we need to get to the bottom of this mystery.

After a couple of deep breaths, I fall into a trance, hoping to circumvent the iron door by having my shadowself pass up through the ceiling and back down.

However, when my shadow rises, I feel thin iron threads crisscrossing throughout the ceiling. The cables are in the walls as well. The incubus mage must have anticipated someone's astral form might try to break into this room. This realization makes me more determined to see what's on the other side.

I push forward, and the iron slices my shadowself. I think about giving up, but then I remember Shayla and the threat against her. I shove my shadow through, disregarding the searing agony.

Once past it, I reform back into a whole, but I'm wounded, damaged.

When I descend into the next room, I wish I hadn't.

Ten bodies are strapped to beds. Their energies are so depleted that I'm not sure they're alive.

I move closer, and I see their chests slowly rising and falling.

Five males and five females are lined up for some sort of experiment—or torture. Perhaps it's a bit of both. Whatever this is, there's no magic coursing through the victim's veins.

Looking at their faces, I recognize a couple of them from school. They're supernaturals.

I can't believe what I'm seeing. I have to get help.

Quickly, I search for a way to return without damaging myself more with the iron grid. I sense no easier way back to my body. I don't know if I would survive it a second time.

I hear Hollis yell, "Something's wrong! His soul's fading!"

"Move out of the way!" Branden shouts.

I sense him running toward me. He crashes against the door. I hear his bones crack. The door falls.

Branden grunts in agony—both from the impact and the iron door that burns him.

He scurries off the fallen door and collapses on the floor just inside the room of horrors.

Hollis pauses to see if Branden is all right, but the vamp's skin is already starting to heal.

I wish I could heal that fast. Although his bones will take longer, I suspect.

The professor runs to the closest female. "Shit!" There's something more to his tone than what I expected.

My shadowself slips back into my body, and I wheeze, "What?"

"I'm pretty sure this is Myra… Shayla's friend."

Branden picks himself up off the ground, limps over, looks at the girl, and nods. "It's her. And she's alive."

"Barely." Hollis looks at us. "I don't *scent* any magic in her at all. Do you?"

Both Branden and I shake our heads.

Hollis hurries around the room and checks on the others. "It's our missing students. They're all drained."

Using my mage abilities, I agree with his assessment, "I only feel a flutter of magic—or perhaps that's just what's left of their souls, keeping them alive."

Hollis scans the room, thinking. He turns to me. "Will you be all right here for a couple of minutes? I'm going to report this to the enforcers. It's only a few blocks away."

"Go." I say to ease his nerves, "Whoever is responsible for

this has left this place. They must have ran off when they felt us coming."

"I can't sense anyone else either," Branden confirms.

Hollis runs off, and I fall back to rest against the wall. There isn't anything I can do to help these poor souls.

Branden wanders over to Shayla's friend and stares down at her. "Do you think they'll make it?"

I'm taken aback. The vamp rarely speaks. To hear him sound worried over someone other than Rourke is bizarre. Maybe there's a conscience in there after all.

"I don't know how they're alive now." I frown, thinking about the implications for these individuals and the big picture. "What happens when a supe is completely drained of all that makes them supes?"

"I suppose we'll find out," he says softly.

"Do you think this has to do with the magic vanishing?" I ask.

His gaze snaps to mine, and I regret drawing his attention to me.

"How much do you know about that?" His voice is devoid of emotion, giving me nothing to sense how much he might know.

"Nothing much, but I've felt magic dwindling for years."

Branden nods but offers nothing more.

What if he knows a lot more about this than he's letting on?

Rourke's family practically runs the Magic Council. Plus, if anyone other than my own father could torture other supes like this, it would be the Lewellyns.

What will Shayla do when she hears about Myra?

This will devastate Shayla. I fear that her magic just might destroy the school. And if what I sense about her is true, she could do it.

32

THE RECKONING

SHAYLA

The dawning light of early morning filters into Arden's bedroom. I snuggle deeper into his hold. He's the very big spoon to my little one, with his morning appendage pressing against my ass. I wiggle into him, still freaking out a little bit that we kissed, and he made me orgasm from a dry hump. For whatever reason, it's hotter than it should be that I got off like that.

His arm drapes itself over me and cups my breast like I'm his favorite stuffed animal. I kind of love it. I've never been someone's comfort before.

It always seemed like a huge responsibility to be someone's anchor—and it feels like I've accepted that role with Arden now —to be each other's anchor. He's my teddy bear, too.

Arden senses I'm awake and kneads my tit. I grind my ass against his cock. He groans and tilts his hips to press into me more.

Then we hear someone entering the main room.

"They must be back," I whisper.

He gives my neck a nuzzle and a kiss, then pulls away so I can get up. He hands me my top, and I slip it on before he opens the door.

I shiver, sensing my world is about to fall apart.

Arden takes my hand and gives it a reassuring squeeze. Some of the tension slips away, but not all of it.

I see Branden and Quade first, heading over to the couches. Both look tired but okay.

My eyes snag on Landis, shuffling behind them. His aura is of a man who has been torn to pieces, but I can't see any physical damage.

"Landis!" I break away from Arden and rush to my incubus. I wrap my arms around his waist, careful not to make skin-to-skin contact as per his wishes. I search his smoky eyes, which are now a pale dull gray. "What's wrong?"

"Iron… sliced up my shadow," he breathes out.

"Are you going to be okay?" I ask.

"I hope so." He attempts a devil-may-care smile, but he doesn't pull it off.

I hold him tighter to me. "I'll help you."

Landis clears his throat and pulls back enough to look at me. "You can't, *remember*?" He looks at me pointedly and then at Rourke, now sitting on the couch with his arms folded over his chest and pouting.

I shake my head. "The dragon and I have an understanding. Until he actually claims me, we both can be with whomever we please."

Landis sighs gratefully and leans his forehead toward mine, staring deep into my eyes. "Then… we'll talk later." His voice turns weary. "But first, we have to tell you what happened."

"Did you find the person who attacked me?" I look at Quade and Branden.

It's an odd picture… Quade, Branden, and then Rourke are on the couch together.

Arden pats the seat next to him. And I join him. Landis sits on my other side.

My nerves begin to itch, and I hug myself, waiting for what feels like terrible news.

The silence stretches out too long, and finally, I look at Quade. "Please, just tell me."

My usually confident professor looks unsure and glances at Branden and Landis. He clears his throat and says, "Landis was able to trace the magical signature all the way to your attacker's location. But when we arrived, he was already gone. He fled through a portal."

"Can we track him through the portal?"

"No." Quade shakes his head. "It wasn't a fixed portal. It was a temporary one and carefully created so no one could track him, which means your attacker is a powerful mage or has one working with him."

"Were there any clues of his identity left behind?" Arden asks before I can wrap my head around the fact that a powerful mage wants to attack me.

"Not exactly. But we did find… *something*." Quade rubs his face, delaying whatever news has him in knots.

Cold dread washes over my body. "What?"

"We found the missing students. Their magic was drained."

"Myra?" I grip my own legs in fear. "Did you find Myra?" My nails dig into my flesh as I try to hold on to my sanity.

"We did."

"Is she okay?" I jump up, about to run and see her.

"She's… alive," Quade whispers.

"But?" I ask.

Branden cuts in when Quade doesn't answer. His voice has an unexpected tone of sympathy. "She might not be the same… *if* she pulls through."

"She's going to die?" Energy swirls around me. Pain and guilt cut me to pieces. "It's my fault. I should have looked for her. I should've found her before…"

Then rage churns within me.

I could have saved her from this fate. If only I had run off to find her. But Rourke and his family prevented me by threatening to lock me away.

"This is all *your* fault," I growl at the dragon.

His eyes widen with something that looks like fear.

"How's it my fault?" He leans back as if I were about to launch myself at him.

"You and this stupid mate thing—keeping me here. I could have helped her!"

"This isn't his fault. Or yours," Quade says in a calming voice. "Trained professional mages were looking for the missing people, and they couldn't find them. If it weren't for this mage attacking you, *no one* would have discovered your friend."

"Your magic hurt this guy," Landis adds. "*You* stopped him."

"My magic…" I mumble to myself. "Yes, I can use my magic now."

I harden my resolve, and my voice becomes steely. "*I* will stop this mage from hurting anyone else!"

My whole body feels tingly. On fire, yet, I'm freezing. An entire ocean crashes around, locked inside me. Winds swirl around me and, with it, bits of earth and sand.

And shadows that feel like unformed life wrap around my body and tighten their hold.

"Shayla?" they all call me in unison.

I look down to see that my hands are on fire.

NO! I'm like my mother!

Panic surges through me. This is my worst nightmare coming true. It's the reason why I've suppressed my magic.

"Oh, Goddess!" I scream and try to flick the fire from my fingers. "How do I make it stop?"

Rourke steps forward.

Branden grabs his shoulder. "Don't. She doesn't trust you," the vamp warns.

Rourke jerks his shoulder away from Branden's hold. "I know that," he hisses. But despite that, he turns to face me. "Shayla, you need to breathe," he says, his voice gentle. "I know about fire. So... I can help you." Slowly, he moves closer. "Just breathe. I know you're upset. And you should be. Not at us, but at the person or persons who hurt your friend. And if you keep channeling this rage into your magic, *you are* going to hurt your friends." He inclines his head to the rest of the males in the room. "You don't want to hurt Arden, Landis, or Hollis, right?"

He's right. I don't. They didn't hurt Myra or me. Rourke's smart to leave out his own name.

I shake my head no.

"Okay, now imagine your flame becoming smaller until it's just the size of a candle," Rourke guides me. "Just like turning down the flame on a stove."

Quade speaks up, "Yes, just like that. And now... the air is only a soft breeze."

"And every grain of sand can fall back to its place," Arden adds.

"Now, the water pounding in your veins is settling," Branden whispers.

He can feel the waters churning within me?

Only the shadows remain. They're wrapped around my body, holding me so tightly in their grip that it's almost hard to breathe.

Landis approaches—with a smile on his face. "Hello, my shadowkin. These are yours. Let them relax. I'll teach you how to use your shadows another day. Let them return to the ether."

The shadows dissolve. I fall, realizing the shadows are the only things keeping me standing.

Rourke catches me. Within moments, I'm in Arden's arms on the couch. The others stand in a circle around me. My eyes flutter shut as exhaustion hits me.

I hear them talk about me when they think I've passed out.

"Rourke?" Quade calls to his nemesis. "We need to know...

for your mate's sake. Does your father have anything to do with the missing students? And Shayla's attack?"

Rourke actually sounds concerned when he says, "I honestly don't know."

However, through our weak mate bond, I sense he's holding something back. He has a secret. Whatever is really going on, I intend to find out.

"Fuck. What are we going to do?" Landis asks.

"We can't tell *anyone* what she can do," Quade says. "Not yet."

"What *can* she do? I've never seen that kind of magic before. Or not combined like that." Branden sounds like he's in shock. Maybe impressed. Maybe even scared.

"I don't know what she is." Quade curses. "But if her mother is only a low-level fire mage, then what the hell is her father?"

"I'm guessing he has to be crazy powerful... dangerous," Landis says.

I think back to the horrible memory Landis witnessed when he entered my mind. My mother said my father promised their child would be powerful.

But if that's true, why did he abandon me? Does he even know I exist? Is he still alive? Or is he watching from a distance to see if I finally come into my powers?

"What about the end-of-term trials?" Arden whispers. "Everyone will see how powerful she is. And if she doesn't get a handle on it—"

"We'll cross that bridge when we have to," Branden cuts him off. "Hollis is right. If we let anyone know what she did just now, she'll be a bigger target than she already is."

"But someone already knows or suspects her gift," Landis argues. "That's why she's a target already. Right?"

If they're all afraid of what I am, maybe I *should* be locked up. What if I can't control myself next time? What damage could I do?

I still feel my power swirling inside me. So much power... I feel like a bomb ready to go off.

Oh, Goddess, what *am* I?

My blood ices over.

What if the mage hunting me hurts one of my friends? Or one of the other students?

What if *I* hurt Arden, Landis, or Quade?

I don't think I could forgive myself if I hurt Branden or Rourke—even if they might be my enemies.

If this incubus mage is after my magic, he might hurt the males in this room if they get in his way. Kat told me that all five of them are considered to be one of the most powerful among their kind. My attacker might want to capture and drain them for their magic too.

With that thought, a violent pain rips through my heart...

I can't lose any one of them.

But since I can access my powers now, maybe *I* can stop the attacks—even if doing so means sacrificing myself so that no one else gets hurt.

TO BE CONTINUED...
find out what happens next in
Shadowcraft Academy: Jinxed

If you enjoyed this book, please consider leaving a review. Reviews mean everything to indie authors and to me!

THANK YOU FOR READING!

Check out some of my other stories below:

Fae Hearted (Completed Series)
Shadowcraft Universe Origins story:
A human servant with a secret.
A tempting deal with an Elven prince.
Three elves willing to break all the rules for her...

Bewitching Her Monsters (completed series)
Would you like to read more in the Shadowcraft Universe?
Check out my new series about a funny, curvy, grown-ass
woman character and all her sexy "monstrous" males.

Chained Fates: Shadow Myths Book 1:
Four Demon Warriors. The last Serafim. One dark cell.
I find myself imprisoned with four gorgeous males
from a violent warrior species.
Will they take me with them if we can escape?
Will they give me what I crave—their touch?

Rebel Fates: Shadow Myths Book 2
The Egyptian gods were aliens, and their people still exist...

I'm done with Earth. The moon base has to be better.
Famous last words…
I'm not out of trouble yet...

The Karma Duet!
My Instant Karma
by Raven Vale has a MF HEA, but...
PLOT TWIST!
My Karmic Destiny
by Yve Vale means not having to choose,
and the FMC ends up with all 3 guys!

ALSO BY YVE VALE

SHADOWCRAFT ACADEMY:

(Dark Paranormal Academy Trilogy + Bonus Novella)

Hexed ~ Jinxed ~ Cursed ~ Blessed

BEWITCHING MONSTERS:

(Grown-Ass Woman & Monsters Trilogy)

Bewitching Her Monsters

Charming Her Monsters

Enchanting Her Monsters

Possessing Her Monsters

FAE HEARTED:

(Fantasy / Shadowcraft Universe Origins Prequel)

Between Realms

Tangled Secrets

Chaos Tempted

Bonds Eternal

SHADOW MYTHS:

(Science Fantasy Standalones)

Chained Fates ~ Rebel Fates

GODS ARE HIRING:

My Karmic Destiny

A Why Choose / RH continuation of

My Instant Karma by Raven Vale

ALSO WRITING AS...

WRITING AS RAVEN VALE

GODS ARE HIRING:

M/F Supernatural/Paranormal Romance Standalones

My Instant Karma

Cupid's Last Arrow

WRITING AS JADE VALE

CAGE BROTHERS:

M/F Dark Billionaire Contemporary Standalones

Cole's Resolution

For more book details, visit:

ValeRomances.com

ACKNOWLEDGEMENTS

A special thank you goes out to my husband for supporting me. Thank you for being my continuity editor and catching any rogue plot points.

Thanks to all my author and reader friends for their great advice, support, and friendship.

Also, I appreciate all of my wonderful fans! I love reading the beautiful reviews you leave or when you reach out to talk about my books. They are gifts to my heart and soul.

And my deepest gratitude goes out to all of you who have encouraged me in my life.

ABOUT THE AUTHOR

Yve Vale writes Why Choose: PNR, Paranormal, Monster, Fantasy, and Alien romance.

She loves spicy romance, fated mates, and redeemable supernatural bad boys who end up as cinnamon roll alphas for their woman.

She is a lover and a fighter. This is why her books feature a fair amount of action, both in romantic endeavors and in battle.

Stalk me here: https://ValeRomances.com